WICKED
BITE

JEANIENE FROST

WICKED BITE

A Night Rebel Novel

AVONBOOKS

An Imprint of HarperCollins*Publishers*

This is a work of fiction. Names, characters, places, and incidents are products of the author's imagination or are used fictitiously and are not to be construed as real. Any resemblance to actual events, locales, organizations, or persons, living or dead, is entirely coincidental.

WICKED BITE. Copyright © 2020 by Jeaniene Frost. All rights reserved. Printed in the United States of America. No part of this book may be used or reproduced in any manner whatsoever without written permission except in the case of brief quotations embodied in critical articles and reviews. For information, address HarperCollins Publishers, 195 Broadway, New York, NY 10007.

First Avon Books mass market printing: February 2020
First Avon Books hardcover printing: January 2020

Print Edition ISBN: 978-0-06-291308-1
Digital Edition ISBN: 978-0-06-269564-2

Avon, Avon & logo, and Avon Books & logo are registered trademarks of HarperCollins Publishers in the United States of America and other countries.
HarperCollins is a registered trademark of HarperCollins Publishers in the United States of America and other countries.

FIRST EDITION

20 21 22 23 24   LSC   10 9 8 7 6 5 4 3 2 1

To Gypsy and Loki, and every other pet
that's brought immeasurable joy to someone's life.
The world is a much brighter place with all of you.

Acknowledgments

If it seems like my Acknowledgments page keeps thanking the same people over and over, it's because the same group helps haul me over the finish line with every book. How could I NOT keep thanking them for that? And don't expect me to change who I thank first, either. Abraham Lincoln once said, "I have been driven many times upon my knees by the overwhelming conviction that I had nowhere else to go." When I've had nowhere else to go, and even when I've been too angry or arrogant to show up, You still haven't left me, Lord. "Thank you" is so inadequate by comparison.

As usual, enormous thanks also go to my fabulous editor, Erika Tsang; my wonderful agent, Nancy Yost; the amazing Pamela Jaffee, Caroline Perny, Kayleigh Webb, Nicole Fischer, and the rest of the hard-working team at Avon Books. Thanks also to dear friends Ilona Andrews and Melissa Marr, who offered encouragement and invaluable early critiques. Endless thanks and love to my husband, Matthew, my sisters Jinger and Jeanne, my father Bill, my many nieces and nephews, my great-Aunt Dottie, and every other family member who's had to hear "I can't because I'm on a deadline!" too many times to count.

Last, but definitely not least, thank you, readers! I've said it before and I'll say it again: without you, I'm just telling stories to myself. With you, those stories, characters, and worlds become so much more. They truly take on a life of their own with every reader who opens the pages. Author Charlaine Harris once said, "Here's to books, the cheapest vacation you can buy." I couldn't agree more. That's why I'm so honored to share my books with you, readers. I hope you enjoy the mini "vacation" you take with them.

WICKED
BITE

Ian

Why am I waiting for the bride of Dracula to grace me with her presence when I should be out looking for my runaway wife?"

Ian watched as his best mate, Crispin, glanced around to make sure Vlad hadn't been close enough to overhear him. Ian didn't care. Vlad owed him for . . . something. Ian couldn't remember what since it was tied to his mostly missing previous month, but he knew it was significant. Sod his host's temper tantrum if he overhead Ian calling him by his most-hated nickname of Dracula.

"The fact that you can't remember the real reason behind your new . . . attached state is why we're here," Crispin said. "Vlad's wife knows a secret you were hiding from the rest of us. If it's the cause of your partial memory loss, we need to find it out before we proceed."

Attached state. Ian's lips curled. Crispin still couldn't bring himself to say "marriage." Every fiber of Ian's being should reject that word, too. Instead, he was driven by a near-crazed need to find Veritas, also known as the little vixen he'd wedded.

True, he couldn't remember *why* he'd married Veritas. That part hadn't survived whatever process had torn most of his memories of the past several weeks from his mind. But he had a vivid recollection of their binding ceremony, even if the notion of him marrying anyone, let alone a Law Guardian, was laughable. Crispin had certainly believed Veritas's denials about their matrimonial state when she dumped Ian with Crispin a few days ago, then left with only a vague warning about an angry demon.

Ian didn't remember that part, either. He'd been unconscious, and with a vampire's near-instantaneous healing ability, that shouldn't be possible. Whatever had stolen his memories had also left him—briefly—as vulnerable as a human, and the only person who knew how both had happened had fled.

Sometimes, Ian was so angry over that, he could scarcely focus on anything else. But the rest of the time, his need to find Veritas had nothing to do with anger and everything to do with the more powerful feeling burning through him.

"Ian." He looked up to see a raven-haired woman in the doorway, her scowling spouse right behind her. "Sorry to keep you waiting," Leila continued before glancing behind her at Vlad. "We were late because we were fighting."

"Over me?" Ian let a sly smile lift his mouth. He would have taunted Vlad anyway—it was his nature—but for some reason, he had a stronger-than-normal urge to annoy his host. "Don't tell me I forgot something *else* significant about the past few weeks?"

Vlad's growl at the innuendo caused Leila to shoot her husband a look. "Your famous temper is why you're waiting outside during this conversation," she told Vlad. "I can't trust you not to get your flame on otherwise, even if Ian is just being Ian. And really." Now Leila's attention was back on him. "Can't you resist being sleazy for *five* minutes?"

Ian gave her his most innocent grin. "Me? Innocent as a lamb, I am."

"Yeah, if that lamb also had a werewolf curse," Leila murmured. Then pity filled her gaze.

Ian stiffened, though his grin remained in place. Whatever secret Leila knew about him, it was bad.

"You need to go, too, Bones," Leila said, calling Crispin by his vampire name instead of the one he'd been born with. "What I have to say is for Ian alone."

Crispin's features drew together until he duplicated Vlad's scowl. "I hardly see why that's necessary."

Vlad's sharp laugh sliced the air. "If I couldn't convince her to change her mind, you think *you* have a chance?"

Crispin looked as if he did. Before he could open his mouth, Ian pushed him toward the door. "Don't start a row, mate. Don't know what you're fussing about. I can tell you what she says afterward."

"You didn't before." Crispin's voice was tight. "You refused despite that refusal endangering your life."

Phantom pains stabbed the back of Ian's head. He managed not to flinch. He'd shared much of what he remembered about the past month with Crispin, but not this.

"Things have changed," Ian replied. What Crispin didn't know, he couldn't fret about. "Go on. The faster you leave, the faster we'll have answers."

Crispin looked at Leila. Her expression hardened into a perfect mask of "you *don't* stand a chance." He sighed in defeat, then followed Vlad as the Impaler, who, after a final glance at his wife, also left the room.

"Let's tour the dungeons," Ian heard Vlad say. "I have a sudden urge to stab something with a hot poker."

Leila shut the doors, cutting off whatever Crispin's response was. Ian waited until he was sure Crispin and Vlad were far enough away, then said "Spill," to the lovely brunette.

"What's the last thing you remember from the time you spent helping me and Vlad?" Leila asked him.

"Driving away while wanting to kill your husband," Ian replied, shrugging. "Don't know why. I can't remember much of the month after that, either, except for the slivers shoved into my mind a few days ago from a creature I'm fairly certain was the Grim Reaper. But those memories mostly consist of the woman who married me, then fled."

And ignored his repeated calls and texts in the three nights and four days since. Why? Another clear memory he had was of Veritas shouting, "Don't go!" at him with the same blindingly intense emotion he felt for her. Yet she'd abandoned him when he'd been at his weakest, and he had no idea why.

"If you have more to add, be quick about it," Ian went on. "You've already cost me two days' looking for her by insisting this meeting be in person."

"This isn't the kind of news you relay by text or over the phone," Leila said softly.

"Does it have to do with Dagon?" When Leila's eyes widened, Ian grunted. "Crispin told me Veritas warned him that a demon named Dagon was after me. Happen to know what I did to brass him off?"

Leila looked away. "No. But Dagon really hated you, and you avoided him with a warding spell until you thought Mencheres had been murdered—"

"Murdered? By whom?"

Leila edged away from the new harshness in his tone. Then a sparking line of white extended from her right hand; a reminder of the voltage running all through her body. The lights in the room also briefly dimmed as she pulled power from them, too. She was readying herself in case he attacked.

Must be very bad news, indeed.

"A group of necromancers had the power to kill me," she replied in a steady voice. "They told Vlad they would unless he killed Mencheres for them. Vlad faked Mencheres's death to buy time to find them, but you were there when Vlad made the supposed execution video, and you didn't know the person Vlad killed was only glamoured to look like Mencheres. So, when you saw what you thought was Mencheres's body, you . . . you cut off your protective ward to summon Dagon. He came, and you sold your soul in exchange for Mencheres's life." At that, her voice cracked. "I saw it, but I couldn't stop you. I'm so sorry, Ian. So very, very sorry . . ."

She kept speaking, reiterating apologies, regrets, and other platitudes he paid no attention to. He was too stunned by *sold your soul*. He would've sworn she was lying, except his vampire sire, Mencheres, was one of the few people in the world he *would* have sold his soul to save. And had, if Leila were to be believed.

This must be why his blood tasted wrong. He hadn't told Crispin this, either, but since he'd woken up in that whorehouse four days ago, his blood had been altered. He'd hoped there was another reason aside from being branded by a demon who now owned his soul. Apparently not.

After everything he'd overcome in his life, he'd been taken down by a simple trick involving a glamour spell? Gales of harsh laughter broke from him. Leila backed away, her electric whip growing until it coiled at her feet.

"No need," he finally managed to say. "I've never harmed someone for merely being the bearer of bad news."

"And Vlad?" she asked in a cautious tone.

Another burst of bitter laughter left him before he controlled himself. Oh, he *would* like to kill Vlad, but he couldn't. His own fault was glaringly clear. "I should've sensed the glamour Vlad used on the poor bloke he killed. I also should have verified that Mencheres was dead before bargaining away my soul. I didn't do either, so that's on me, not Vlad."

Leila's whip disappeared back into her hand. Then she sprang forward, taking his hands. "Once again, I am so sorry."

Ian jerked away from her pity. Leila gasped, then her eyes narrowed and she tried to run her right hand over every inch of his skin that wasn't covered by his clothes.

"Stop that." What sort of pity-pawing was this?

"It's gone," Leila said with shock. She got in a few more swipes before he held her wrists in front of her. She only rubbed his hands with her fingers, repeating "It's gone."

"What's gone?" Her sanity, clearly.

"Everything! Take off your pants. I need to see if that's still there, too."

Ian rolled his eyes. "It is, and while I would've found it hilarious to cuckold Dracula under his own roof a short time ago, I'm not interested now—"

"Neither am I," Leila interrupted. "But I *am* interested in seeing if you still have Dagon's demon brand on your groin since nothing else on your skin is the same."

Ian loosened his grip on her wrists. "Explain."

"You remember that I pull psychic impressions from people when I touch them with my right hand?" At his impatient nod, she went on. "When I touched you months ago, I saw your worst sin, same as when I touch anyone for the first time. Your skin was also littered with emotional imprints from other people, but now, they're all gone." She tapped him with her right hand for emphasis. "Makes you wonder what else might be gone, right?"

Could he have somehow gotten out of the soul deal? Ian let her go and unzipped his trousers. Leila knelt down, whisking the hem of his shirt out of her way. At the same moment, the drawing room doors opened, revealing Vlad and Crispin.

Ian began to laugh. "For once, I can honestly say this isn't what it looks like."

"I imagine it's not," Vlad replied coolly. "Were you examining his cock because you suddenly decided you were in the market for erotic piercings, darling? If so, I would have modeled some for you. I'm a much better subject."

Ian snorted his disagreement while Leila sputtered, "I was looking for *demon brands*, not that!"

"Yes, so could someone either look under my cock or hand me a mirror?" Ian interjected. "I'm flexible, but even I can't bend that far."

Leila backed away, flustered. Crispin strode over, frowning as he bent down. "No brand of any kind," he said after a moment.

"I'm telling you, it *was* there," Leila insisted. "I saw Dagon put it on Ian when he sealed their soul bargain!"

Crispin rose to shoot a horrified look at Ian. "You bargained your soul away to a demon? *Why?*"

"What you'd expect—more power," Ian said, giving Leila a warning glance. He couldn't have word of his real reason reaching Men-cheres. His sire didn't deserve that pain.

"But now the brand's gone," Leila said. "So is the original mem-ory of Ian's worst sin and a bunch of other stuff. I need to check the rest of him to see what else is missing. Take off all your clothes, Ian."

Ian drew his shirt off and stepped away from his crumpled trou-sers. Then he couldn't help himself—he winked at Vlad over Leila's shoulder as she began to run her right hand over his naked body. Vlad glared at him, but not a hint of fire or smoke escaped him. Must be secure in their relationship.

Leila was brisk yet thorough. When she was done, she said, "Not only is the demon brand gone, there's no psychic evidence that it was ever there. In fact, your whole body reads as new."

"I'm more than two hundred and fifty years old," Ian reminded her.

"Your skin isn't," Leila said bluntly. "It's so new, there are only essence imprints from four people on it. You left one, Bones, when you were very worried about him. Cat left a worried one, too, and the essence trails by Veritas are practically screaming with worry and regret. Lastly, some terrifying creature left one on your head, but aside from that, you're a blank slate, and unless you were re-cently skinned or you somehow regrew a whole new body, I have no idea why."

Those phantom pains stabbed him in the head again. For a ter-rifying moment, he felt swallowed by darkness. Then his vision returned and he saw Crispin glance away as if he knew something he didn't want to admit.

"Mate," Ian drew out. "Have something you want to add about the story you fed me concerning how I spent my last month?"

"I might have left a few pieces out," Crispin began.

Ian was gripping Crispin by his collar before Leila could finish gasping. "Holy crap, you can *teleport*!"

"What?" Ian bit out.

"She said it was safer if you didn't know," Crispin said, hedging.

Crispin had been hiding the reason why Veritas had left him? "Know *what*?"

Now Crispin's gaze didn't waver. "Four days ago, Veritas called me and Cat to retrieve your mostly withered body from an abandoned amusement park. You were surrounded by dozens of demon corpses. Don't know how either of you survived such an attack, but Veritas said that your marriage was a sham, your memory was gone, and more powerful demons would be after her. She made us promise to feed you lies about your whereabouts this past month, saying you would only be safe if you stayed far away from her."

She'd left him to protect him? And Crispin, who *definitely* should have known better, had let Veritas face that danger alone while stalling Ian's attempts to find her? He'd roast Crispin's arse and shove the burnt pieces down his throat! But first . . .

Ian pushed Crispin away, then turned to Leila. "Your psychic abilities include finding people in the present through essence trails, do they not?"

She sighed. "Yes. Come here."

Leila placed her right hand on Ian's cheek. The voltage she emitted made his jaw ache, but he didn't flinch. After several minutes, Leila dropped her hand. "I can feel Veritas, but I can't see her at all."

Of course not. With demons after her, Veritas had cloaked herself from every tracing spell imaginable. He hadn't married a fool.

He teleported out of there without another word, leaving Crispin and the rest of them behind. Sod his mate's attempt to protect him. Sod Veritas's fear for his safety, too. He wasn't about to lose her by playing it safe.

Don't go! her pained shout rang again in his mind.

"Don't fret," Ian muttered. "I'm coming."

Chapter 1

Three weeks later

$\mathcal{I}$ dropped out of the dark Egyptian sky, landing near a Jeep that stood out like a neon sign against the sea of sand around it. Unlike the famous section of the Valley of the Kings, this stretch on the western edge wasn't popular with archeologists, tourists, or anyone except criminals.

Lucky for me, my job was hunting criminals.

No one was inside the Jeep, but it was overloaded with what appeared to be ancient Egyptian funerary artifacts. I walked around to the back and saw a small stone slab half pulled back from a hole in the ground. Ah, a hidden tomb. Two distinct voices came from it as well as lots of odd swishing sounds.

Grave robbers. I hated grave robbers.

I pulled out a sharp silver knife and a double-pronged bident made of demon bone. Now, I was armed to fight two out of the three supernatural species that existed. Right before I jumped into the hole, I lit my gaze up with vampire green.

Two men looked up at me in surprise. At first glance, they were normal Middle Eastern men, but then their eyes turned glowing red. Demons. And the ground around them slithered in every direction.

Snakes. I hated those even more than grave robbers.

I landed on the nearest demon, knocking him down while ramming both ends of my bone weapon through his eyes. His eyes burst into flames as death cut his scream short. I yanked the bident out and immediately flew up, leaving the other demon to smack into the wall instead of me. Before I could stab his eyes out, too, he teleported away.

He reappeared on my right, fist flying. I ducked under the punch, then pain exploded in my head from a blow to my left. Damn demons and their ability to teleport.

"You'll pay for murdering Malfeous," he snarled before flinging several cobras at me.

Dick!

I fought my urge to shake them off me. Their bites wouldn't kill me, but he could. I kept both weapons at the ready, spinning in quick circles so he couldn't sneak up on me again. He reappeared in front of me, swinging one of the tomb's ancient axes. I threw myself backward, but not in time. My throat burned and blood splashed his face from the deep slice the ax made. When I hit the ground, the impact made new pain erupt in the back of my head.

Good. More pain meant the ax hadn't cleaved all the way through or I wouldn't feel anything. Being dead was painless, or so all the ghosts I knew had claimed.

The demon grinned and licked my blood. Then shock replaced his sneer at its taste. "What—?"

I hurled my silver knife into his open mouth, pinning his head to the wall. Then I flew at him, shoving the bone bident into his eyes until I felt the tips hit the wall.

His eyes exploded, smoke and blood pouring out. The sulfur scent choked me, but I shoved the bident in harder. Relief overtook battle exhilaration as he began to shrink into the skeletal state of true death.

I yanked my weapons out and whirled, ready in case any other demons teleported in. After fifteen minutes, I tucked the silver knife into my belt. That wouldn't kill demons. Only bone of their own brethren would, and now, I had plenty more to make new weapons with.

I tore the arms off the two demons, throwing them out of the hole above me. Then, I began to explore the tomb. Time and dust had faded the paintings and hieroglyphs on the walls, but I saw the falcon-headed god Horus in one scene and the green-skinned god Osiris in another. There were more paintings showing scenes from the life of the deceased. There should have been various personal effects, statues, treasures and other ceremonial items, too, but the tomb's inner hall had been stripped. That explained the overloaded Jeep.

The seals on the doors of the inner chamber were broken, too. I went inside, angry but not surprised that both artfully painted coffins containing the mummy had been breached. Only the clay jars containing the mummy's internal organs were left. Then I smelled something unexpected. Fresh blood.

I nudged a mass of cobras aside to reveal the body of a young woman opposite the sarcophagus. Her skin was the same golden bronze as mine and she had long black hair that covered her face. When I brushed it away, I swore.

I'd been tracking her since I'd hacked into all the recent medical records posted online using a program that a hacker friend of mine had created. I was searching for a very specific type of psychosis: people who claimed they came from another time and who had no modern records to prove otherwise.

I winced as I looked at her body. Large gashes covered her torso, but the wounds weren't sloppy. They were precise, avoiding vital organs or arteries in order to deny her a quick death. Beneath the blood, I saw markings inked onto her body. I rolled her over, revealing more markings hidden beneath her. As soon as I did, dark magic crawled across my skin with the unsettling sensation of dozens of spiders.

A nearby cobra suddenly reared up and struck me in the face. Annoyed, I flung it aside, only to have another one bite my leg. Enough! I grabbed as many as I could and flew out of the tomb.

Once outside, I let them go. It took several more trips before I was through, but I was glad to get rid of them. They must have been brought in to add to the poor woman's terror. Fear was a powerful ingredient in dark magic, and someone had performed a horrific ritual on the slain woman.

I went back to her body, using my clothes to clean her blood off the symbols. I recognized a few, but I didn't know the others, and I knew a lot of magic. I took out my mobile and snapped pictures of them. Then, I bent down next to her, closed my eyes, and released the hold I had on my deepest senses.

The magic used to perform the ritual hit me first, choking me with a sickeningly familiar taste. *Dagon.* The smell of her blood, fear, and the sulfur stink from all the demons had been too strong for me to scent my worst enemy before, but I could taste Dagon's magic now, and it was all I could do not to vomit.

I swallowed hard and pushed past it, searching to see if she had other magic traces within her. Death had left almost nothing behind, but then Dagon's magic soured my senses again, though far fainter this time.

She'd had some of Dagon's power deep within her. I knew only one way that could have happened. She'd been telling the truth to the mental-health facility she'd escaped from. She *wasn't* from this current time. She was from long before it.

Maybe that's why she'd been spotted running into this dismal part of the desert. It was a wasteland now, but a few millennia ago, it had been part of a prosperous city, and when people were frightened, they tended to run home.

I sat back with a frustrated sigh. Had Dagon murdered her because she was one of the newly resurrected people who had been freed when the souls Dagon hoarded inside himself had been released? Dagon *was* spiteful, but there was one thing demons valued even more than payback: power.

I traced the markings again. A lot of power had been siphoned from this woman with her gruesome death. From the look and scent of her body, I'd only missed saving her by hours. Earlier this evening, Dagon might have been right where I now knelt, weakened, unsuspecting and oh-so killable, if I'd only been a little faster getting here . . .

But Dagon had gotten away. The other demons with him almost had, too. If I hadn't had a birds-eye view of the Jeep while flying over the desert tonight, I never would have found her, and I'd been tasked with finding all of the newly resurrected souls . . . except the one I most wanted.

Pain rolled through me, familiar and relentless. It burned until I looked at the slain woman with the darkest kind of envy. She was out of reach of the pain I couldn't escape from. It made me actually glad I was now as mortal as any other vampire. It meant this awful ache would end when a lucky stab through my heart with silver finally killed me.

But before that day came, I had a vow to fulfill.

I hadn't been able to save this woman, but I wouldn't leave her where she'd been murdered. I picked her up and flew her out of the tomb. Then I dug a new grave using my hands since I'd brought weapons with me, not a shovel. Still, with the soft sand and my supernatural strength, it didn't take long.

Once she was properly buried, I said a prayer asking the gods to show her mercy. Then I stared at her makeshift grave, that aching part of me wondering if I'd soon be like her: dead and rotting in an unmarked grave somewhere.

If so, I hoped my last thoughts were of Ian. I wanted to remember his cocky grin, his quick wit, his bone-deep loyalty and his ferocious courage. Most of all, I wanted to relive what I'd felt when I was in his arms. I'd never before felt so completely exposed yet wholly accepted. Cherished. Maybe even loved, if we'd had more time . . .

With a hard swipe, I dashed away the tears that snuck down my cheeks. I couldn't let myself dwell on Ian. If I did, I'd run back to him no matter that my presence would draw all the demons after me right to his side. I'd already gotten Ian killed once. I wouldn't let that happen again.

Yes, I might end up dead and in an unmarked grave before this was over, but there were benefits to being over four-and-a-half-thousand years old. If I didn't explode the way I normally did when I was killed, I was still so old that my body would probably turn straight to dust. No rotting in a grave for me.

As the modern saying went, I just had to look on the bright side.

Chapter 2

I spent the night in the desert on the off chance that Dagon might come back to the tomb. He couldn't teleport anymore. My father, the former Warden of the Gateway to the Netherworld, had removed that ability from him, so Dagon would have to walk up or drive up like everyone else.

He did neither. In the end, I drove the Jeep far away from the tomb and left an anonymous call about it to the Egyptian Ministry of Antiquities. They'd make sure the relics were properly cared for. Dawn ensured that no demons would be around since they couldn't tolerate the sun, and I went back to my hotel.

I opened my door and was immediately mobbed by a flying gray bundle. I caught Silver, hugging the Simargl to my chest. He made happy yipping sounds despite being a supernatural creation instead of a canine. Still, Silver resembled a gray Samoyed, if you didn't look close enough to realize he was covered in downy feathers instead of fur. And, of course, there was the very un-doglike aspect of his wings.

"I missed you, too," I told Silver, giving him another hug before setting him on the floor. Silver looked expectantly behind me at the closed door, his wings wiggling with hope.

"No," I told him, fighting the new crack in my voice. Seeing Silver still waiting for Ian to come through the door was another kick to my heart.

"No," I said again, more firmly this time. Silver's wings drooped as he walked away, giving the door a last glance before he resigned himself to it staying closed.

"Hungry?" I asked to distract him.

It worked. He followed me, wings wiggling happily again. I ordered room service as I took off my ripped, bloody clothes and wadded them into a plastic bag. I'd throw them away where they wouldn't be found later. For now, I put on a robe and waited. Silver wasn't the only one who was hungry.

Twenty minutes later, Silver was devouring his plate of sautéed vegetables and I was wiping a stray drop of blood from my mouth. The room service attendant had no memory of feeding me, of course. He'd only remember that I was a good tipper.

I was on my way to the shower when my mobile chimed, indicating a new text. I ignored it, anxious to get the stench of death, blood, and dark magic off me. My phone chimed a few more times. I continued to the bathroom. I had taken a leave of absence from my job as Law Guardian, so it couldn't be work related, and most of my closest friends were dead. If I were looking on the bright side of being a currently-on-leave workaholic who'd outlived nearly everyone I cared about, I'd say that meant I could get back to whoever was texting me when I was damn good and ready.

I showered, taking my time. After that, I dropped my glamour, losing the appearance of a blue-eyed, petite blonde I normally wore. When I looked into the mirror, I now saw my real image of a taller, curvaceous woman in her mid-twenties with silver eyes and long, almost-white hair streaked through with gold and blue. I dried my hair, put on a robe, and went back into the other room. I'd log in a few more hours of online research trying to find the next resurrected soul before I allowed myself to sleep. This was my life now. It might be emotionally empty, but at least it was productive.

Silver was on the bed, his gaze following me with drowsy expectation. He was waiting for me to cuddle him before he fell asleep. Cuddling Silver would be the highlight of my day, but first, I picked up my mobile.

Nine unread texts. My stomach clenched. Only Ian left that many in a row, though I never read them. My father assured me that all of Ian's memories of me had been wiped from his mind, so I surmised that Ian kept calling and texting because someone had told him we were married.

He needn't worry. I was getting the few people who'd witnessed the ceremony to "forget" it and thus nullify it. Until then, I didn't need to torture myself by listening to Ian's voicemails or reading his texts, though I'd accidentally caught, "I'm warning you," from him yesterday before I hit delete.

He had nothing to threaten me with. Ian couldn't hurt me more than he already had if he made it his life's goal to try. Seeing his dead body had ripped my heart out. Weeks later, I was still trying to put myself back together.

But these texts weren't from Ian. Serious charges have been filed against the council because of you, read the first one, from Xun Guan, my oldest friend and a fellow Law Guardian. Come in at once. The next one was from Felix, another Law Guardian. You must appear before the council immediately to answer charges involving you.

What? I scrolled to the next one, from Thonos, the council's official executioner. Your presence is required. The man who claims to be your husband has refused to leave until the charges he's brought against the council regarding you have been addressed.

"He what?" I shrieked.

That scared Silver so much, he flew up and hit the ceiling. I was too shocked to comfort him. I scrolled through the remaining messages, their pertinent parts burning into my brain.

Ian is accusing the council of forced spousal abandonment . . .

Claims the council is keeping you away from him in violation of our laws and your will . . .

Refuses to leave until you present yourself to confirm or deny these charges . . .

"You arrogant, reckless maniac!" I raged, hurling my mobile across the room. It shattered and I cursed myself next. Now, I had to use someone else's phone to call and beg the council not to kill Ian before he did something to merit a death sentence, if he hadn't already.

"How could you go to the *council?*" I continued to fume as I threw my clothes on. "Bones told you our marriage was a fake! And you never cared about the law. Why would you do this?"

I'm warning you.

Ian's partial text flashed across my mind. So much for thinking he had nothing to threaten me with! But how could I have guessed that he'd sue the highest ruling court of vampires? Here I was, running all over the world fulfilling the vow I'd made to bring Ian back from the dead, and he was daring the Grim Reaper to come back for seconds!

Now, I had to go to the council, talk them out of whatever retribution they were planning, then abandon Ian all over again. It would hurt less to tear my guts out and stomp on them.

But I had no choice. I couldn't leave Ian at the council's mercy. I also couldn't ignore a direct summons from the council. If I did, I might as well resign as Law Guardian on the spot.

I ground my teeth until my jaw crunched. Ian wanted a meeting, probably to have me formally renounce our marriage so there'd be no doubt in anyone's mind that he was a free man?

Fine. He'd get his meeting, and I hoped I could convince the council to let him live long enough to regret it.

Chapter 3

The rugged limestone peak of Mount Lycabettus jutted above Athens, Greece, like an imperious stone giant. I remember when people said that this spot was created when the goddess Athena accidentally dropped a mountain after receiving bad news. Later, it was said that this was the home of fearsome wolves, hence its play on the word *lycos*—Greek for wolves. Both legends had it wrong. As was often the case, the truth was much stranger.

Mount Lycabettus was the official location for the ruling council of vampires. Oh, the council had other, lesser courts across the continents, but this was where all eleven members of the council presided when court was in session, and they only all came together when the charges were truly severe.

Like, for instance, the entire council being sued by a vampire known more for snubbing the laws than following them.

I began my climb up the worn stone steps that led to the modernized amphitheater at the top. The cable car wasn't running tonight since none of Mount Lycabettus's famed attractions were open. The surrounding city of Athens might be as boisterous as ever, but the silence on the mount was almost eerie. Normally, this was a bustling tourist attraction, with its rich history and unparalleled views of Athens. Now, it was as quiet as the grave.

No demon should be stupid enough to attack the vampire's highest court while it was in session. Still, I scanned my surroundings with every upward step. Had news of this lawsuit reached Dagon?

It might have. Vampires were as prone to gossip as any species. If Dagon *had* heard of tonight's events and decided to risk an ambush, I was without weapons to fight him since defendants could hardly arrive armed at court—

Wait, what was that? I tensed when I heard it again. Ian's voice, his British accent as smooth as ever. Hearing him was its own form of assault, making me stop so I could take a moment to collect myself. *You can do this. Come on!*

I resumed my climb, my pace brisk. I was almost at the top of the mount when I stopped again because I heard something even more unlikely than an approaching horde of demons. Great gods above the earth and below it, was that the council *laughing*?

". . . then I landed next to him, dropped the warlord at his feet and said, 'Is this the sod you're looking for?'" Ian was saying, followed by fresh bursts of laughter.

Somehow, Ian had he gotten the normally dour council to sound like a bunch of merry drunks at a comedy club! I'd underestimated his charm, and I shouldn't have. Even back when we first met and I was only using Ian as bait to draw out Dagon, he'd charmed me, too.

And now, I had to act as if I cared nothing for him.

I entered the amphitheater, my gaze drawn to Ian as if pulled by an invisible force. The last time I'd seen him, his hair had turned white from his death and his face had been more bones than features. Now, his hair was back to its lustrous, deep auburn shade and his profile showed his flawless alabaster skin, a hint of his high cheekbones, the line of his chiseled jaw, and part of his dark, winglike brow.

As if sensing my stare, he turned toward me. I looked away so I didn't have to meet his eyes. Still, my brief glimpse branded itself onto my brain.

He'd dressed for the occasion, wearing an ebony suit that draped over his body so perfectly, it had to be handmade. He had a white shirt underneath it, the complicated silk knot at the neck held together with a jewel that winked crimson when he turned. Seeing him so whole, so gorgeous, so *alive* made my throat burn, my chest tighten, and my eyes sting.

Horrified, I realized I was about to cry. I'd done everything I could to prepare myself, and one look had razed me.

I dug my nails into my palms until I felt blood. The slight pain wasn't much, but I clung to it. I would *not* humiliate myself by crying in front of Ian and the entire council! I'd picked my navy skirt suit because it was elegant yet somber; the right balance for court. Now, its dark color concealed the blood I'd drawn, and the perfume I wore to hide the scent of my emotions covered its faint scent.

When Ian drawled, "My runaway bride, here at last," I dug my nails in harder, then took in a breath to steady myself.

Big mistake. His cognac-and-caramel scent invited me to breathe it in until he filled me, and being so near to him meant his aura brushed mine as if his power were stroking me.

Somebody, kill me now.

To distract myself further, I took in the surroundings I'd ignored before. The seats of the amphitheater surrounded the stage and reflected the moon's pale, silvery rays back at us as if they were additional lights. Those seats were empty since the only people sitting were in eleven large thrones at the center of the circular stage. Hekima, one of only four women on the council, nodded at me. Her salt-and-pepper hair was in its usual severe bun, but her brown eyes were warm. Out of all the council members, I liked her the most.

I smiled at Hekima before giving a more formal nod to Haldam, the official spokesperson for the council. Then I inclined my head at the remaining nine council members before turning my attention to the other people on the stage.

Mencheres, Ian's sire, was here. His long black hair hung down over his shoulders like silk scarves, and his obsidian gaze was accusing when it met mine. *Don't blame me, blame Bones for this!* I wanted to retort. I'd told Bones to protect Ian and ensure that he kept a low profile. Simple instructions, but with this lawsuit, Ian had practically painted a target on his back before firing himself from a canon during a demon fireworks display.

At least Mencheres loved Ian. That meant I could count on him. Ian would just kill his way out of here if the council called for his death, but I had friends here that I didn't want to see harmed. Mencheres's formidable powers plus my own abilities meant I could get Ian away without any bloodshed.

I looked away from Mencheres to Xun Guan, my longtime friend and former lover. Her expression became hooded as she glanced from me to Ian. I responded with a slight shake of my head. *No*, that shake told her. *I'm not changing my stance about denying my marriage.*

Xuan Guan tilted her chin. *Message received*, that slight gesture said. Then she turned away, showing only her lovely profile and her jet-black, high-swept hair.

I moved on to Thonos, the council's official executioner. His unruly black hair was pulled back in a knot, so Thonos must not have gotten the news that man-buns were out. I nodded at him, then flicked my gaze to Julius, Priscilla, Gan, and Vachir. My sense of foreboding returned. The council had been laughing, but things could turn deadly fast. They'd certainly prepared for it, having six of their strongest Law Guardians here.

"Honorable judges," I said, greeting the council. "I present myself as requested."

Their mirth disappeared. "Veritas," Haldam said, stroking the long white beard that matched the snowy hair trailing down his back. "You have been apprised of the charges against us. Before we proceed, we need to first establish if this man"—he nodded at Ian, as if I needed reminding who he meant—"is truly your husband?"

I chose my words carefully. "No, though he has reason to believe that he is—"

"Such as remembering the ceremony?" Ian interjected.

My gaze swung to Ian as if he'd yanked on it. *Gods, his eyes*, staring into mine with an intensity that belied the carefree yet cocky slant to his mouth. Yes, there *was* recognition in them. Somehow, Ian remembered me, and not just as the coldhearted bitch he'd thought I was before we'd partnered up to take down Dagon months ago!

I was about to fling myself into his arms when I realized how much was missing. Ian might know me more than he had before everything had started between us, but not as much as the last time we'd been together. I'd never forget the way he'd looked at me during what should have been the final moments of his life. Now, everything that had been in his gaze then was gone.

My hope vanished. Nothing had changed. I was still a demon target, and he wasn't the same Ian who'd died in my arms.

"Your memory is a delusion born of too much Red Dragon combined with an enemy's spell," I said, dismissing him without another look. "For a short time, I, too, believed that I'd bound myself to him in marriage while under the effects of the same drug and spell," I continued, returning my attention to the council. "Fortunately, that belief proved to be false."

"Bollocks," Ian said silkily.

I didn't swing around to look at him again, but it was close. What in the seven hells was he doing? I was handing him his freedom while also giving him a plausible excuse for his reckless lawsuit. All he had to do was shut up and take it!

"We *were* under the effects of a spell," I repeated, my tone sharpening. "One that was cast on us as we finished dispatching the last of the Red Dragon dealers in New York several weeks ago. That's why we believed ourselves to be married, and why we repeated that mistaken belief to Xun Guan and her trainees."

"Then why was I with you in the first place?" Ian asked in that damnably caressing tone.

My teeth ground before I forced my jaw to relax. "You took me to inform me of a possible Red Dragon dealer. By the time I confirmed your suspicions, we were attacked, necessitating you to act as my backup despite you being a civilian."

"I arrived too late to assist," Xun Guan interjected. "When I

came upon Veritas and this civilian, she had already killed the Red
Dragon dealer and the source, as well as several of the dealer's as-
sociates."

"But not after being forced to drink large quantities of Red
Dragon in order to get to them," I added. "That, combined with
the spell I later found out had been cast on us, resulted in our com-
promised mental states and false memory of being married. Due
to my advanced strength and age, my memory of the true events
returned over the next several days. His memories," I shrugged as
if unconcerned, "clearly still have not."

"Ian," Mencheres said. "Perhaps you should consider this clari-
fied version of events?"

Ian ignored his sire. "A question for you, honorable judges." His
tone was carefree, but I caught the edge that said he was deadly
serious. "Is there any precedent of a vampire marriage being an-
nulled if both parties were intoxicated or under other mind-altering
influence when they made their vows?"

"There has never been an accepted annulment process for a vampire marriage," Haldam replied, which was true despite it being
infuriatingly archaic and unfair.

"We don't need to concern ourselves with that because *we're
not married*," I all but growled.

He flashed me a grin that didn't fool me. His turquoise-colored
gaze was sharklike. "You have another definition for when two
vampires cut their palms and claim each other in front of witnesses,
one of whom is glaring at my back even now?"

"How do you remember that?" I burst out, noticing that Xun
Guan was indeed glaring at Ian.

"More pertinent is whether he speaks the truth," Haldam said,
to sounds of agreement from the rest of the council.

I went with the only response I could. "As I said, we were both
extremely intoxicated plus reeling from the effects of a spell. It's no
surprise that our memories differ."

Ian's hand swept toward Xun Guan. "She wasn't drunk or spelled.
Ask her if we bound ourselves together that night."

How do you remember that? I screamed silently this time. He couldn't remember everything. If he did, he wouldn't be trying to prove a marriage he'd wanted no part of when it had happened.

Haldam waved Xun Guan forward. She came, reluctance rounding out the straight lines of her posture. *Please,* I tried to convey during the brief glance we exchanged. *Please don't confirm what he just said!*

"Xun Guan." Haldam's commanding voice filled the amphitheater. "Did you witness a binding marriage ceremony between Veritas and this vampire? Or did you not?"

Xun Guan straightened to her usual, regal posture. My hopes plummeted. I might have gotten her to agree to "forget" what she'd seen as far as keeping silent in the face of my denials, but lying to the council? She wouldn't, not even if she believed I'd made a terrible mistake while very drunk and spelled, which is what I'd told her. Xun Guan loved me, but she loved the law more. She always had. It's why I'd never been able to share my secrets with her.

"Yes," Xun Guan said in strong, if strained, voice. "Yes, I did witness that, honorable judges."

The vampire world's most notorious bachelor had just succeeded in proving the validity of our marriage to the highest court in vampire society. Now nothing but one of our deaths could end it. Why had Ian, of *all* people, done that?

Chapter 4

*I*an's voice shattered the silence. "Now that that's sorted, I formally withdraw my lawsuit. Clearly my bride wasn't being unlawfully kept from me against her wishes by this council. Poor lamb just didn't remember the happy occasion."

That snapped me out of my stunned muteness. "This 'poor lamb' still doesn't owe you anything, marriage or no marriage."

"She is correct," Hekima said. "While our laws forbid divorce and also permit the slaying of any person a vampire spouse commits adultery with, they do not demand that spouses cohabitate or even speak to one another. If Veritas doesn't want you, you have no recourse before this court, young man."

"Agreed," Ian said, making me more suspicious. He was never agreeable unless it suited him. "And for wasting your time, you have my sincerest apologies." He punctuated that with a bow that managed to appear both graceful and contrite. "Since I've always considered words an insufficient form of amends, allow me to present an offering indicative of my remorse," he finished, then whistled.

Three vampires I'd never seen before hurried into the amphitheater. Each carried three large crates stacked on top of each other. They set the crates down in front of the council. Ian whisked the lid off the first crate before I could sputter out an apology. He was trying to bribe the council into forgetting about his slanderous lawsuit?

"Ian," I hissed through gritted teeth. "A word?"

"In a moment," he said, pulling back a layer of packaging to reveal glass-enclosed, aged parchments. "Now, then, history considers the destruction of the Alexandria library in forty-eight B.C. as one of the world's greatest losses of knowledge. Fortunately, as with many other things, history is incorrect. Not all the library was lost. Here is what remains."

At that, Haldam actually got off his throne to take a closer look. After several moments of carefully rifling through the first crate, he turned to the other council members.

"This appears to be genuine."

Haldam sounded so surprised, he didn't seem to notice that he'd reverted back to speaking in his native Latin. Now all the council members got off their thrones to cluster around the crates and examine their glass-encased documents.

"How did you come to possess this?" Hekima asked.

Ian gave her a brilliant smile. "Mark Anthony presented the remains of the library to Cleopatra as a gift. Their daughter, Patra, later acquired it. You'll remember Patra declared war on my sire, Mencheres, several years ago? After Patra was killed, her belongings were plundered by those who'd fought at Mencheres's side. I claimed this library as my part of the spoils."

I shook my head. Of course Ian wouldn't settle for Patra's gold, jewelry, or other everyday riches. He'd only want the rarest type of treasure as his prize. Now, he'd dazzled the council by gifting them with it. They would have taken offense at money, but the Alexandria library was priceless for its treasure trove of lost history. It was also rumored to contain many long-forgotten spells. In the council's never-ending quest to stomp out magic, they'd want those spells in their hands versus the hands of other vampires.

I had to give Ian credit—the council was so entranced by discovering what treasures the scrolls contained, they barely seemed to notice him anymore. I had to take advantage of their distraction before one of them snapped out of their wonder over the return of the famed lost library and sentenced Ian to decades in prison for suing them.

"Since I'm still on leave, honorable judges, I'll take my remaining time to straighten out this situation so it poses no further issue when I return to work," I said.

"See that you do," one of them murmured, too low for me to catch who. I did catch some of their glances as a few of them briefly looked up from the crates. They contained combinations of reproach, disdain, and other unflattering opinions.

They might be impressed by Ian's gift, but their opinion of him hadn't changed. Having our marriage confirmed didn't just complicate things for me personally; it would also throw up roadblocks professionally. I'd seen it with other female Guardians who'd married people the council didn't approve of, though male Guardians seemed exempt from this form of career censure. Humanity didn't have a monopoly on sexism.

That was a problem for a later day. My immediate problem flashed a devilish smile at me. "Shall we?" Ian said, holding out his arm. "Unless you'd prefer me to carry you over the threshold, my not-so-blushing bride?"

My glare promised vengeance, but we had to get out of there. Still, I ignored his arm as I brushed past him.

"Veritas." Xun Guan gave me a pained look when I reached her. "I am so sorry."

"It's not your fault." I said it briskly, but I meant it. I was responsible for this mess, not her.

She brushed my cheek. "If I could have spared you this—"

"You could have," Ian interrupted, reaching my side. "You chose not to. Knew you would. I might not remember much, but I remembered *that*."

I was trying to absorb *I might not remember much* when Xun Guan's dark brown eyes turned green and her hand dropped to her sword. Ian saw it and snorted. "We're at court where all duels require legal merit. You have none. Laws, eh?"

"Why are you antagonizing her?" I asked, low.

"Because of how she looks at you," he responded, his eyes never leaving Xun Guan's face. "Now that we have this moment, let me be frank, Xun Guan. If you act on what's in your gaze, I won't make the mistake of treating you like some poor, lovelorn lass. I'll treat you like the dangerous warrior you are and rip your head off the first chance I get. Quite clear?"

Her gaze was now blazing green and her knuckles whitened on the hilt of her sword. "It will be a pleasure to kill you when your time comes," she said in Mandarin.

"Back at you," Ian replied in the same language.

I pushed him out the door, hissing, "Haven't you caused enough trouble?" while thanking all the gods that Mencheres immediately filled the space behind us. Now Xun Guan wouldn't be tempted to follow Ian outside. Ian could beat her in a fight. Xun Guan didn't know that, but I did, and I refused to play a part in her death.

Thankfully, Xun Guan didn't follow us. My relief turned out to be short lived. As soon as we were outside of the amphitheater, Ian spun around. My hands were still in front of me since I'd been pushing him. He caught them, then hauled me close.

Time seemed to freeze. My grip on him instinctively tightened as I stared into his eyes, memories of the last time we'd been like this slamming into me.

I brushed my lips over his knuckles before releasing his hand. "Speaking of fighting, those demons screeching over their salt wounds aren't going to kill themselves. Stay here. I'll be back after I take care of them."

Ian smiled, half teasing and half enticing despite being barely conscious. "Give me a moment and I'll join you. Can't have you tiring yourself out. We have a celebration . . ."

That's all he'd gotten out before Dagon shoved that first bone knife through Ian's skull. Once again, I heard my own scream and felt a surge of sheer panic as Ian's eye began to smoke. *"Don't!"* I shouted at Dagon. *"Please, stop!"*

Dagon had no intention of stopping. He'd only delayed to draw out my pain. I ripped my hands away, saying "Don't touch me!" with all the vehemence of the grief I'd felt back then.

"Fine," Ian said, stepping back. "I won't touch you as long as you don't attempt to disappear on me again."

Panic of a new kind made me snap, "You heard the council. You can't *make* me stay with you."

"I can until you give me the answers you owe me," he replied, his gaze hardening. "You wouldn't do it by text, so now you'll do it face to face."

"I have questions, too," Mencheres said coolly.

Take a number and get in line! I thought. Ian seemed to agree. "Mine take precedence, Mencheres, but neither of us is asking her anything here. Too many ears."

I seized on that. "You're right, we need to leave and I have places to be. Text me. This time, I *swear* I'll reply—"

His laughter cut me off. "You have a better chance of convincing me to stake myself, and I'm not even joking."

But I can't be around you! I wanted to scream. *It's killing me, and if I don't leave you soon, it will* really *kill you!*

I forced those emotions back, wishing I could draw on my other nature to erase them entirely. But if I let that half take control, I'd be unfeeling, yes, to the point of being a mass-murdering sociopath. That would hardly do.

No, I'd have to see this through. "Fine. I'll go with you, but first, I have to stop by my room to retrieve something."

"I'll have one of my men pick it up," Ian said, nodding at the three vampires who silently followed us.

"No." I was so emphatic, his brows went up. "Only I can get this, and that's nonnegotiable."

He shrugged. "As you wish, but then I'm coming, too."

"As am I," Mencheres said.

"Of course you are," I muttered. "Helicopter mom."

Ian laughed. Mencheres gave me a dark look that I ignored as I put some much-needed distance between me and Ian on our descent down the mount. Even still, I could feel Ian's aura enveloping me like a hidden embrace while the weight from his gaze settled into my back as if it were a supernatural anchor.

It hurt so much being near Ian when he wasn't fully *Ian*. He might look, sound, and act similar, but this Ian hadn't shared his secrets with me while also getting me to share my deepest secrets with him. This Ian hadn't faced Dagon with me, and this Ian hadn't sacrificed himself for me in what should have been his final act because he'd—almost—fallen in love with me.

No, this Ian's interest in me boiled down to bruised pride and a determination to obtain knowledge that would put him in more danger than he was already in. If Ian knew that the demon he'd only heard of in passing had *killed* him . . . he'd never rest until he settled that score. And Ian couldn't beat Dagon. I wasn't even sure I could unless I accessed power that might turn me into something worse than Dagon.

That's why I had to get away from Ian as fast as I could, and I already had a way to do that. For now, I'd let Ian believe he'd won. Men were so much easier to manipulate when they thought they had the upper hand.

Besides, this night might have turned out spectacularly bad for me, but it was about to get a lot better for someone else.

Chapter 5

$\int$ ilver mobbed me in his usual way when I came through the door of the villa I'd rented. When he saw Ian behind me, the Simargl's feathers nearly burst off his body from joy.

"Don't worry, he's friendly," I said when Silver dove at Ian, yipping uncontrollably.

Mencheres was nonplussed to see a winged, doglike creature flying around Ian. Ian didn't appear surprised. He pet Silver during the Simargl's wild aerial circles, then caught him and hugged him when Silver launched himself at Ian's chest.

"Who's a good little lad?" Ian asked, then chuckled when feathers flew as Silver's wings beat frantically in response.

"You remember him?" I asked in a neutral tone.

He gave me a sardonic look. "I remember killing several vampires to rescue him. Didn't know why until this moment. He's the source of the Red Dragon from that night, isn't he?"

"What else do you remember?" It flew out before I could stop myself. Just as quickly, I regretted it.

Ian's gaze gleamed. "Wouldn't you like to know? But it's my turn to ask questions, and I don't fancy asking them here. We've probably been followed by one of the council's many pawns."

"Probably," I agreed, saying a few quick words over Silver. By the time I was finished, his downy feathers now looked like fur, his wings were nowhere to be seen, and he had a new tail where there had only been a smooth rump before. The dog collar he already wore completed his "normal pet" disguise.

Ian watched, a slight smirk curling his mouth. Did he remember that I was only speaking the spell for Mencheres's benefit since I didn't need to say anything in order to practice magic? Or was that one of the memories he no longer had?

It didn't matter. Time to go. "I know a private place where we can talk," I said, heading toward the door. "Come."

Ian blocked my way, moving faster than I thought him capable of. "Déjà vu," he said in amusement. "Not the first time you've spoken to me the same way you'd command your pet, is it? Did you have better results back then? If so, you're about to be disappointed."

I closed my eyes. Now Ian wasn't the only one experiencing déjà vu, though mine came with a stab of pain. Still, he was right. Snapping out commands might give me some much-needed emotional distance, but it wouldn't work with him. It never had.

"Fine. I'd like you to accompany me to a place I know where we can talk," I amended. Anything to get across the threshold.

"No." Ian's easygoing tone was at odds with the new hardness in his gaze. "You lost your right to pick the spot when you forced me to sue the council to make you stop ignoring me."

"I didn't know you'd remembered anything," I began.

"If you'd read *one* text or listened to *one* voicemail, you would have!"

His snarl caught me by surprise. Then it made me angry. True, ignoring him might not have been brave or noble, but I'd earned a little selfish cowardice after sacrificing over four thousand years of vengeance to bring him back to life!

"Who do you think you're speaking to?" I demanded.

Ian dropped to his knees. At first I thought he was mocking me, then I was alarmed by the way he grabbed his head. That wasn't mockery. It was agony.

Mencheres shoved me aside to kneel next to Ian. Blood trickled from Ian's nose, ears, and eyes. Panic froze me. The last time I'd seen Ian bleed from his eyes, he'd died.

"What's wrong?" I rasped, trying not to scream with fear.

Mencheres didn't glance up. "Do you even care?"

Only his devotion to Ian kept me from ripping all the water out of him right then. "Yes," I said, forcing my panic back so I could kneel next to Ian, too. "I care far more than our short time together accounts for," I admitted.

"When are emotions ever ruled by something as trivial as time?" Mencheres muttered. Then his dark gaze lasered on mine. "From what Bones told me, a creature did this to Ian."

"A creature?" Whatever it was, I would kill it.

"Bones called it the angel of death," Mencheres said, stunning me. Now I knew who the "creature" was. "Ian said it was the Grim Reaper. Whatever it was, it told Ian that it could restore part of Ian's memories, but those memories could break his mind. Nevertheless, Ian insisted."

"No," I whispered while Ian clutched his head and more blood poured from him. My Netherworld-warden father had removed Ian's memories to limit the trauma he and the other resurrected souls had experienced while trapped inside Dagon . . . and to keep them from knowing the extent of the power they'd consumed while devouring their way out of the demon. So why would my father give Ian back some of those memories? More important, why hadn't he *told* me?

Ian stopped clutching his head with the same suddenness that he'd dropped to the floor. He was on his feet before I could speak, flicking the blood from his face and frowning at the crimson stains on his white shirt.

"Don't know why I bother wearing anything other than black." Then his brow arched as he took in me and Mencheres, still on the floor. "Not dallying there long, are you?"

"Dallying?" I repeated. "Do you have any idea what just happened to you?"

He shrugged. "Vampire version of a nasty migraine. Nothing to fuss about."

"Nothing to fuss about?" Now Mencheres was the one incredulously repeating Ian. "This is very serious, Ian!"

He rolled his eyes. "Since when did a little blood give a pair of multimillennia-old vampires the vapors? Really, I'm starting to be embarrassed for the both of you."

"Enough." Mencheres's voice was harsh. "I can stand no more of your mockery."

"Then don't stand it," Ian said with equal harshness. "I told you not to appear before the council with me today. You came anyway. I also told you not to follow me and Veritas here, but here you are. Enough, yourself, Mencheres. Let me be."

"Not until I discover if she played a part in you bargaining your soul," Mencheres replied in a blistering tone.

Aw, fuck, I thought, just as Mencheres's power lashed out to immobilize me. That same power caught Ian in its invisible vise, freezing his hands in what looked to be mid tactile spell. Even Silver was trapped by Mencheres's telekinesis.

I glared at Mencheres. He glared back, now so dispassionate it was unnerving. "I will free your mouth if you promise not to speak a word of a spell against me. Blink once for yes."

I blinked once. That punishing pressure relaxed from my mouth. "You overstep, Mencheres," I said with cold fury.

"You have no idea how far I am prepared to 'overstep' if it means saving Ian's soul," was his equally icy reply.

"I'd be a lot angrier at you if I didn't feel the same way about him." Then I paused. Why had I told Mencheres that? Especially with Ian close enough to hear it?

Mencheres came nearer. "Did you play any part in Ian bargaining away his soul to a demon?"

"No." Who had told Mencheres about that? Ian? I couldn't ask him. It was clear Mencheres hadn't released *his* mouth. It was frozen in a tight-lipped line as Ian glared at his sire.

Mencheres was now right behind me. "Do you know *why* Ian struck that deal with Dagon?"

"Yes," I replied, then would have slapped myself if I could have moved my arms. I'd sworn never to tell Mencheres this! So why had I just admitted knowing it?

"Then tell me the reason," Mencheres all but purred into my ear.

I had to slam my jaws together to keep from replying. Even then, grunts I had no control over came out between my clenched teeth. That's when I realized what he'd done. At some point, Mencheres had cast a truth spell on me. *Good one, old friend!*

Still, I wasn't about to break my vow. *You should've been more specific about the promise you forced from me,* I thought grimly. *I don't need to speak a spell to free myself.*

I let my hidden power free. Time froze in the room. Mencheres's hold over me snapped as it immobilized him in the moment. Freed from his grip, I walked to the door, calling out for Silver.

The Simargl flew over to me just as Ian took a step forward, stopped as if he was stunned that he could move, then took another step, this time in my direction.

I was also stunned. "*How* are you now immune to time freezing?" As soon as I asked it, I knew. Ian must have absorbed this immunity from Dagon. What other abilities did Ian now have?

He flashed a quick grin at me. "Must be the demon brands. They do have their perks before the bill comes due."

He still thought Dagon owned his soul? I'd clear that up later. Right now, I had to get away from him. I grabbed Silver, opened the door and stepped over the villa's threshold.

Ian was in front of me in the next instant, shocking me again. Had he . . . had he just teleported?

"What's this?" he snarled when he reached for me, but couldn't get past the threshold.

"Insurance," I replied in an even tone. "I spelled the villa. Anyone can enter, but no one aside from me and Silver can leave until after dawn."

He gave me a look of such frustration, I almost smiled. Now he knew how I'd felt the past twenty-four hours. "That's why you in-sisted on coming back here," he said through gritted teeth.

"Yes. I even have my bags already stowed in my car," I added in a mocking tone. If I were lucky, I'd make Ian so angry, he'd never want to see me again. "This villa's privately owned, so demons can't enter unless invited, but do yourself a favor when the spell lifts. Leave the country and then *lay low*. You've already put your-self in danger by broadcasting your whereabouts with this lawsuit. Don't make it easier on the demons looking for you with more splashy public appearances."

Something gleamed in his eyes. An expectant light that belied his trapped circumstances. "We're not nearly finished with each other, my clever, calculating wife."

I flinched at the "w" word. His mouth curled when he saw it. Then I forced myself to smile back as if I hadn't a care in the world. "As I said, the spell that'll keep you inside the villa abates at dawn, but the time-freezing spell will drop soon after I leave. I'm sure Mencheres will enjoy having your undivided attention for the next several hours."

"Clever, calculating, *and* cruel." Ian's voice dropped to an insinu-ating purr. "No wonder I married you."

Damn him! I couldn't stand to be reminded that I had the legal status of something denied to me in every way that counted—a place in his life. To cover that, I gave another fake smile.

"Good-bye, Ian."

"For now," he said in a tone that reminded me of velvet-lined whips. "But not for long."

Chapter 6

He's bluffing.

I repeated that over and over during my drive to Mycenae. As luck would have it, one of my leads on another possible resurrected soul was only about two hours away. I drove straight there since I'd already lost over a day dealing with the disastrous court hearing. Silver would just have to wait in the car while I found out if this was a real sighting or another false lead. Either way, once I was finished, I intended to follow my own advice and get the hell out of Greece.

I hoped Ian did, too, as soon as the spell lifted. He couldn't be so reckless as to stay and keep looking for me, could he? My stomach clenched. *Yes.* Ian was fearless and he didn't remember how powerful Dagon was. Or how vindictive.

I had to make sure that he left. I drove one-handed while I dug through my purse for my mobile. Then I called the number I'd programmed in several weeks ago. Instead of the male British voice I expected, a woman with an American accent answered.

"Bones's phone. You've got Cat because he's busy."

"Hi, Cat," I said with false cheerfulness. She wasn't my intended victim, but Ian had me so wired up on frustration and fear, she'd do. "Are you or Bones near Greece?"

"Veritas? What's wrong?" Cat asked, sounding wary now.

"What's wrong?" It burst out of me loud enough to make Silver jump. "You and Bones promised to keep Ian safe, but less than *one month* after I leave him with you, he's angering the highest court in vampire society while practically GPS-ing his location to Dagon since *everyone* knows where the council meets when they're in session!"

"Now, look—" Cat began.

"I still don't know if it was Ian's stunning bribe or the council's shock that someone had the balls to sue them that kept them from sentencing him to death!" I continued to rage. "Either way, I've got Ian safely confined in a villa with Mencheres until dawn, but he needs to get out of Greece as soon as the spell lifts. Obviously, I can't trust Ian to stay out of danger on his own, so I ask again, are you or Bones near Greece?"

"Are you done?" Cat asked in a sharp tone.

"Yes, and I'm waiting for your reply."

"Oh, I didn't mean are you done talking," she said, now sounding dangerously cheerful. "I meant, are you done losing your shit? Because if you think *you're* fed up after dealing with Ian for one night, try dealing with him for the past few weeks. Bones and I have chased him all over the fucking world trying to get him to listen to reason, and thanks for telling us that Ian can now teleport, by the way! I've had better luck chasing a ghost, and I mean that *literally*."

"Ian can teleport?" I'd so hoped what I'd seen at the villa had just been him moving very fast . . .

"Yeah, and last week, Ian let us know he was sick of us trying to baby-sit him by leaving a few spells behind for us. One of the spells turned me mute for two days, and another melted Bones's fangs off! I didn't even know that was *possible*—"

This was backfiring fast. "Uh, I'm very sorry—"

"—but his fangs were *gone!* Ian's lucky they grew back or I'd be hunting him down, all right, and that demon would have nothing on what I'd do to Ian once I caught him."

"Perhaps calling you wasn't such a good idea," I muttered.

"You bet it wasn't," she flared. Then her tone softened. "Look, I get that you're scared for him. I don't want Ian to get hurt, either. But he's made it clear he won't be controlled by Bones, by me, or anyone else. I give it two minutes after your spell's up before he's gotten away from Mencheres, too. So, if you want Ian out of Greece, you'll have to get him out yourself. You're the one he's obsessed with anyway."

"I can't." Despite my effort to maintain control, my voice cracked at the last word. "It's not safe," I finished in a stronger tone.

Cat sighed. "I know you said demons were after you, but that's not going to stop Ian. He's not the run-and-hide type. He's the stay-and-fight type. Believe me, we tried to get him to change, and we failed."

I almost flung my mobile through the windshield, because she was right. Dammit, she was right! Ian had never backed down from a fight, no matter the danger. Now what was I supposed to do?

As if I'd asked that out loud, Cat said, "If I were you, I'd concentrate on killing whoever is threatening Ian. I know that's damn near impossible, but I still think you'll have a better chance against a bunch of pissed-off demons than you will at getting Ian to suddenly stay inside and take up knitting."

She was probably right again, but I had an oath to fulfill. Still, this was one more reason to want Dagon dead, and I didn't have to *abandon* my oath to search for the other resurrected souls in order to kill Dagon. I could multitask.

"My apologies for my misdirected ire before," I said.

Cat grunted. "Don't worry. Love makes us all crazy—"

I hung up so fast, I didn't hear the rest of her reply. Was what I felt for Ian that obvious? Silver whined, laying his head on the console between our seats. He always sensed when I needed comforting, and yes, I needed it badly right now.

Still, I had a job to do. That's why I pet his head only once before turning my attention back to the road.

The day before yesterday, a man had been arrested for causing a disturbance at the famed Lion Gate in the ancient city of Mycenae. Nothing unusual there, except cell-phone video showed the man shouting in a sixth-century B.C.E. Greek dialect. Add the man's off-camera escape from no fewer than five security officers, and this was a lead I would have investigated right away if I hadn't had to rush off to court.

If this was another resurrected soul and Ian's lawsuit meant that Dagon beat me to him again, I'd be so *pissed*.

I sped up. Over the next hour, city lights were replaced by the faint glow from the stars. By the time I reached Mycenae, modern buildings were nowhere in sight. There was only the rolling hills of Argos and the ruins of the former great citadel.

"Mycenae rich in gold," Homer had written in his famed poem about the fall of Troy at the hands of the Greeks. The riches of Mycenae were long gone, but hints of the citadel's former glory remained, such as part of the fortress's wall on the highest hill; the tall stone entryway to the rumored burial site of King Agamemnon, or the aforementioned Lion Gate, where two leonine stone carvings marked the entrance to the city.

During the day, this area was dotted with tourists. At half past four in the morning, it was empty. Or it should have been. When I parked in the lot reserved for tour buses, I heard a faint cut-off scream.

I'd dressed for court, not for battle, so I didn't have any weapons on me. I grabbed a satchel I'd packed some demon bone knives and silver knives in, then flew toward the sound, leaving Silver behind in the car. As I flew, I prayed to any gods that might be listening. *Please don't let me be too late, please don't let me be too late . . .*

The citadel was now silent. I detected no movement among the pale stone ruins, either. I dipped lower, losing my visual advantage to utilize another sense. Yes, there. By the entrance to the underground cistern. I smelled blood.

I landed and then crouched low to enter the tunnel where the ancient city's former water supply had been stored. It was dry now, which was unfortunate. I could've pulled the energy the water contained to increase my strength, but the only liquid I now sensed in the cistern was blood. The scent was almost choking as I descended the rough, uneven steps of the steeply sloped tunnel. But no scent of demon. Just blood and the sickly smell of terror.

Then a soft, anguished noise came from farther ahead. I aban-

doned caution and flew the rest of the way. I knew that sound.
Someone was dying in agony.

After two turns, the end of the narrow tunnel came into view. A
white-haired, dusky-skinned man with unlined features raised his
head from the ripped-open belly of another man, whose eyes were
glazing over in death.

My impact knocked the gore from the murderer's mouth.

Our tight quarters meant my momentum slammed us both into
the wall. The white-haired man cursed me in preclassical Greek as
he tried to bite me with a mouth now stretched to impossibly large
dimensions. I leapt back, avoiding his snapping jaws.

Not a demon or a vampire. Ghoul, to use the modern word. They
normally ate the dead, but from the state of the four bodies strewn
like rubbish in the tunnel, these victims had been eaten alive. And
I'd arrived too late to save any of them.

"Murderer," I spat in the same preclassical Greek dialect.

"Dead walker," he replied in a hiss.

An ancient slur against vampires. Another hint that he was not
from this era. "The world has no shortage of dead for your kind to
feast on. You ate these people alive. Why?"

He smiled, showing that he still had chunks of viscera in his
teeth. My stomach heaved. "The dead do not make beautiful music
with their screams."

Some of the souls that were released are very dark, my father had
warned me about the people Dagon had trapped inside himself. No
shit. This ghoul was cruel enough to be Dagon's best friend, if he
was one of the resurrected ones.

I had to find out.

"Did you wake up and find that the world had vastly changed
since the last time you saw it?" I asked as I avoided his next attempt
to grab me. With the tight confines of the tunnel, I had to bash into
the walls to do it. The ghoul grinned, enjoying the sight of me in pain.

"Everything I know is gone." Confusion and rage thrummed
through his tone. "Now, metal horses bring strange-tongued in-
vaders to gawk at my city's bones, so I feast on theirs!"

He was one of the people I was looking for, all right, and he'd chosen to squander his second chance at life by eating innocent tourists. I couldn't kill him fast enough, but I'd packed my satchel only with knives, and I needed a sword for ghouls. My car had a sword in it. Could I get it and return before the ghoul fled?

Ghouls couldn't fly. I had a chance.

"Don't go anywhere," I said, and flew out of the tunnel.

Silver was growling when I got back to the car. He probably smelled the blood from my close contact with the flesh eater. I didn't have time to reassure him. I grabbed the sword, slammed the door, and flew back toward the cistern.

The ghoul was emerging from the tunnel. His sneer changed into a frown when he saw my sword. That was something he recognized, despite missing the past several thousand years. Swords predated even me.

"For the crime of murdering innocents, I sentence you to death," I said, and flew at him.

Before I reached him, two large forms slammed into me from either side. Bones crunched and my head rang as I was smashed between them. The impact left me so dazed, it took me a few seconds to fly away. Those seconds cost me deep, agony-inducing tears into my shoulders and almost allowed the ghoul to pin me to the ground. I flew away just in time. Then, from the safety of my higher vantage point, I finally saw what had hit me.

"Oh, come on!" I said with a groan.

Two huge pale-gray lions paced near the ghoul beneath me. That would have been shocking enough as lions had long ago disappeared from Greece, but these lions were made out of stone. I could taste the magic that turned ordinary rock into the prowling, deadly cats, and it was so foul, I wanted to gag.

The oldest souls will be slowest to regenerate, my father had said. *But when they do, the power they consumed from Dagon's essence will make them formidable . . .*

No shit again. How was I supposed to defend myself against creatures made of magic-infused stone?

$\mathcal{I}$ suppose asking you to reconsider the lions and fight fair is out of the question?" I said, more to give myself a chance to think than any belief that it would sway the ghoul.

"Fight fair?" he repeated, as if he'd never heard of the concept.

"Didn't think so." I sighed, eyeing the lions.

My sword wasn't much defense against solid stone, and stone also didn't contain water that I could rip out to incapacitate the lions. Granted, most spells ceased when they ran their course or the person casting them died, but in order to kill the ghoul, I had to be on the ground where he—and the lions—were.

If only I could freeze time to slay the ghoul! But I'd just used that power, so it would take days before I could utilize it again. No, I had to do this the hard way. I rocketed myself at the ghoul, trying to catch him off guard. He ran faster than I expected to the shelter of the cistern's entrance. I pulled up at the last second to avoid bashing into the rock wall, then lunged at the ghoul again.

The lions tore into my back before I could reach him.

I whirled, sparks flying from my sword from how hard it clanged against their stone bodies. It didn't penetrate, but their teeth did. Those long stone teeth might be blunter than a lion's real fangs, but they ripped into me as if they were the predators their magic-infused bodies mimicked.

Something smashed against my head, causing me to see stars. I half staggered, half flew away, avoiding the ghoul's next blow. He chased me, but not far enough. He was too smart to leave the protection of the cistern's entrance for long.

If I couldn't get him away from the cistern to ambush him from above, then I had to make that location work for me.

Pain won't kill you, I reminded myself as I stared at the remarkably flexible stone lions below. *Only decapitation or silver through the heart will. So, time to be a chew toy.*

I pretended to charge the ghoul again. He retreated into the tunnel, and the lions jumped me as soon as my feet hit the ground. This time, I let them drag me between them for a short distance before I fought back and got away. My ruse cost me two hunks from my legs and a gaping hole in my side before the wounds healed with vampiric swiftness, but the ghoul was now at the entrance of the tunnel instead of inside it.

I charged him and the lions mauled me again. This time, I dropped my sword as if I could no longer hold it while fighting off the great beasts. The ghoul said he liked to hear his victims scream before he killed them . . .

My gamble worked. The ghoul ignored my fallen weapon and edged toward me instead. I kept staggering back as the lions drove me toward the entrance of the cistern where the ghoul was. When I reached it, I darted past him, then pretended to trip on the steps. The lions fell on me at once. Their weight was crushing, but between the slant of the staircase and the great stone beasts, I was now invisible to the ghoul.

I pushed past the pain to channel all my magic into creating an unbreakable barrier over my body. The lions' roars sounded like rocks smashing together as their fangs met resistance instead of ripping through more flesh and bone. But this spell wouldn't last. Magic against magic was unstable.

Come on, murderer. Come and get me . . .

The ghoul commanded the lions to let him pass. They did, and he squeezed by them to enter the narrow tunnel where I was sprawled. I waited until he was close enough for me to clearly see his smile. Then I smiled back—and leapt at his head.

I held on with all my might, ignoring his screams and the brutal pounding he gave my unprotected torso. The lions roared again, coming to his defense. I flung the ghoul and myself backward, the steep stone steps adding more punishing blows as we tumbled down into the stygian darkness. All the while, I held on to the ghoul's head, using every bone-crunching jolt of our fall as added momentum while I lodged my arm under his chin and twisted.

His head had come off by the time we reached the first landing.

For a few moments, I was so exhausted that I sat with it in my lap. Then, I threw it aside, hearing it bounce its way down the rest of the steep staircase. The lions had collapsed as soon as the ghoul's head came off. Now, they were a collection of scattered stones on the steps instead of the solid, lethal creatures they'd been moments before.

I stepped over those stones as I climbed back up the steps. I was almost at the tunnel's entrance when I saw a man crouched about twenty meters away. He had a long, tubelike object balanced on his shoulder that was pointed right at me—

Oh, *shit!*

I retreated into the tunnel, then was hurtled backward from the tremendous explosion.

EVERYTHING. HURT.

I opened my eyes, then shut them when they immediately filled with gravel. I tried to wipe that away, but my arms were pinned. So were my legs. I couldn't even wiggle.

Panic rose. I fought it back while trying to remember what had happened. That's right, the man outside the tunnel had pointed some kind of rocket launcher or other military-grade weapon at me. I'd flown back into the tunnel to avoid getting shot, but from the taste of blood and gravel in my mouth, the tunnel had collapsed on top of me.

If I had any room to *move*, I could use my formidable strength to begin digging out of this. But my arms and legs were pinned beneath multiple heavy rocks. How long would it be until people started clearing away the stones? Mycenae wasn't the most popular tourist destination in Greece. Worse, the cistern was hardly the most famous aspect of the ruins.

What if no one bothered to clear away the rocks for weeks? Or longer?

And what if the man who'd blown up the tunnel decided to make sure I didn't survive? Enough flame accelerant poured on top of the rocks would eventually reach me. Then all it would take was a match to turn my prison into a stone-lined inferno . . .

Don't panic! I thought, feeling it rise again. *You can't move, but that does* not *mean you're helpless.*

I concentrated on the magic inside me, bringing it forth while trying to ignore the continuous pain from the heavy stones. When I had enough, I sent that magic out to coat the stones around me. After that, I whispered a spell to form a perimeter around those stones. I was light-headed by the time I finished, but the magic was now as ready as a cocked gun.

I pulled the trigger. The stones around me exploded so thoroughly, they disintegrated into sand. The ones of top of those didn't collapse into the empty cavern that now formed around me, either. The perimeter I'd made held them up.

I got up slowly, wincing at the many shards my body expelled as I healed. My ears still rang from the explosion, but soon they healed, too. It would take everything I had, but I could repeat this process all the way to the surface. Thankfully, it wasn't too far . . . What was that?

I listened harder, catching faint fragments from an argument several meters above me.

". . . felt that explosion? I told you, she's not fucking dead," a male voice snarled.

". . . still can't stay. Sun's coming up!" Different male voice.

It was? I'd been unconscious for over an hour, then. My head must have been badly crushed by the initial cave-in.

". . . we go back without her . . . dead anyway," the first man said.

"Then *you* stay and burn!"

Only one species burned in sunlight. Demons. I gave my stony prison a grimly appreciative look. All those rocks crushing me had also saved me. Without any empty space around me, the demons had had nothing to teleport into.

Now they did. I searched through the centimeters of crushed gravel on the ground for my weapon's satchel. At some point, it had been ripped from my neck. But I didn't find it, and magic didn't work on demons.

I put the rock wall to my back and readied myself to attack. I'd fought demons weaponless before. All I had to do was use their own bones to stab their eyes out—

A tall man teleported in, his back to me. I hurled myself at him, only to pull back my fists when I recognized his frame and the shoulder-length auburn hair that swung as he whirled to face me. My momentum still made me crash into him, though, and he laughed as he caught me.

"Running into my arms? You *really* don't like it down here."

Another rock must have crushed my head and caused me to hallucinate. That was the only logical explanation for *Ian* being the person whose arms were around me now.

"How are you down here?" I said in disbelief.

In reply, his arms tightened. A nauseating blur later, we were at the entrance of the tunnel instead of trapped inside it. Cat hadn't been exaggerating about Ian's teleporting skills. No wonder she and Bones hadn't been able to keep or catch him.

"No great mystery as to where you were," he replied. "Those sods," a nod at the nearby bodies of two men with smoldering eye sockets, "were arguing about which of them would risk the rising sun to teleport down there and kill you. I stabbed their eyes out before they realized a vampire had teleported into their midst instead of one of their own kind. Almost too easy—"

"But how did you know I was in *Mycenae?*" I interrupted.

His turquoise gaze gleamed with emerald. "Think I didn't know you'd flee the first chance you got? Didn't expect the villa spell, but by then my tracker was already in place."

I still felt like this couldn't be real, but I began searching my jacket pockets for the tracker anyway.

He only winked. "If we were playing hot and cold, you'd be icy right now."

"Then where is it?" I asked, still reeling.

"Don't you have better things to fret about? Like, for instance, how two demons managed to ambush you so impressively?"

I already had a theory about that. "Dagon's after the people I'm tracking. He must have seen the same video I did, that led me to this place. So, he sent two of his demons here to stake it out in case I showed up."

Dagon must not want to face me himself yet. He must still be too weak, but that wouldn't last. Someone as determined as Dagon would find ways to scrounge every bit of power he could. He obviously still held a grudge. Those demons hadn't *accidentally* been carrying a weapon powerful enough to take down a tank when they came across me.

Ian grunted. "Right wanker this Dagon is."

"You have no idea," I muttered, a stab of memory causing me to push away from him.

"Careful," Ian said when my preoccupation made me ignore the loose ground at my feet. I almost tripped, but I caught myself, then looked at the pile of rocks where the ancient wall used to form the cistern's entrance.

These ruins had survived for several thousand years, but they weren't the only priceless loss today. Four murdered people were still buried beneath this pile of rubble. Four innocent lives I might have saved if I'd been faster, smarter, stealthier . . . just *more*!

Now, all I could give them was the dignity of being found. I'd place an anonymous call to the Greek authorities later about them. It felt so inadequate, but aside from killing their murderer, I could do no more to help them.

To cover my lingering frustration and guilt over that, I kicked one of the demon corpses nearby. "That's what you get for shooting at me with an anti-tank weapon," I muttered. "Gods, I hate demons!"

"And I don't fancy coppers, present company excluded," Ian replied. "Place will be crawling with them soon since one of the detonations set off the museum's alarm."

Yes, I'd also heard the mechanical wail from the only modern building located within the ruins. Before I could reply, Ian vanished. He reappeared almost immediately, Silver tucked under one arm and my purse slung over his shoulder.

Then, he grabbed me and everything blurred again. When it stopped, a stunned glance revealed rows of tall stone columns from the Athenian goddess's temple gleaming in the early light of dawn.

"Here we are," Ian said, as if teleporting us over a hundred kilometers away, to the Parthenon, was nothing exceptional. Silver didn't seem nonplussed by the swift, drastic change of location. When Ian let go of him, the Simargl scampered off to explore his new surroundings.

Then Ian smiled at me, enticing and oh-so dangerous to my still vulnerable heart. "Alone at last."

$\mathcal{I}$ backed out of his grasp. His smirk mocked the distance I put between us. Anger stifled the part of me that had been far too focused on how good his arms had felt around me.

"Don't let your impressive new abilities go to your head," I said in my coldest tone. I couldn't let Ian know how he affected me. He'd only use it against me. "I might not be able to outrun you now that you can teleport, but there are many other ways I can still escape you."

"All involving my intense pain, no doubt." He sounded amused. "Tempting as that may be, you won't need such measures. Earlier, you agreed to talk with me where the council couldn't overhear us and Mencheres couldn't interrupt us. This meets both those requirements."

I'd only said that to get across the villa's threshold to spring my trap! I hadn't truly intended to talk to him. It was pointless. I couldn't tell him the truth, and he was too damn clever for me to get away with lying to him.

My need to stall caused me to do what I never allowed myself to do: fall back into memories of what the Parthenon had looked like when it was new, its columns whole and gleaming under the bright Grecian sun instead of highlighted by artificial lights in its ruined state.

Then I rewound to centuries before that and the smaller, far less impressive temple that pre-dated it. I rewound to several millenniums before that, when this mount was empty and the city was nothing more than some sparsely populated wooden huts.

When I blinked, the sight of the Parthenon's long-standing ruins caused all my years to crash back into me. As I struggled between *then* and *now*, my sire's oft-repeated warning rang in my head. *You must never allow yourself to be consumed by the ancient past. Countless aged among our kind have lost themselves to madness that way. Always focus on the present. Speak the modern language. Wear modern clothing. Think with modern thoughts. That is the only way you'll survive, Veritas . . .*

I'd heeded Tenoch's advice in all ways but one. I couldn't let my many tortures and executions stay buried in the sands of what was now modern-day Iraq. Instead, I'd sworn that one day, Dagon would pay for all the people he'd tortured and murdered, myself included. More than four thousand years later, I was still dealing with the repercussions of that promise.

Now, so was Ian.

"There's nothing crueler than time," I murmured. "It stretches when you're in pain, flies away if you're happy, and crushes you when you remember all the years that are now gone."

Ian seemed surprised by the change of subject. Then, his gaze became hooded. "True. And every so often, time can also be stolen from you. It was from me, and I won't stop until I've recovered every bit of it."

I let out a short laugh. "Then those 'migraines' you're so dismissive of will be the least of your problems. You don't want to know everything you've forgotten, but I will tell you this—Dagon has no claim on your soul any longer. It's yours again."

His brows rose. "Demon deals are unbreakable unless the demon dies. Are you saying that Dagon is dead?"

"I *wish*," I said with feeling. Then I retreated into my icy Law Guardian persona. "Dagon's deal with you has been nullified. The details are unimportant. What is important is that you're free, so take your freedom and go."

His gaze gleamed with green highlights. "There are many words I'd use to describe marriage. 'Free' isn't one of them."

"Whose fault is that?" I snapped, before composing myself again. "I have no intention of asserting my rights over you. I'm sure you feel the same way about me. That makes our marriage nothing more than an unfortunate technicality."

He tapped his chin. "Not sure I agree. I wanted to rip Xun Guan's head off over how she incessantly eye-humped you. The more the merrier, I usually say with lovers, but I seem to be jealous and possessive over you."

I covered my shock at that with more chilly deflection. "What makes you think we were lovers?"

His grin was everything that made Ian unforgettable. "Oh, I have many of *those* memories." Then his voice deepened. "Though sometimes, I wonder if they're real."

"Why?" I shouldn't have asked. Why had I? Maybe Mencheres's truth spell on me from earlier hadn't worn off yet.

He came nearer, brushing my arms with the lightest of strokes, which still caused shivers to race over me. "Because nothing that good could possibly be real," he murmured, and bent his head.

I turned away before his mouth touched mine. Then I pushed him back. Doing both took all of my strength.

"Your memories are wrong," I said, proving Mencheres's spell was no longer affecting me as that was a lie. So was what I said next. "During our brief alliance, yes, we had sex to break up the monotony of laying out our trap for Dagon, but it was nothing exceptional. Once we'd both gotten what we wanted from Dagon, we were glad to part ways with each other."

Ian's brows had risen at the start of my heartless rendition. By the end of it, they were almost in his hairline. Then he burst out laughing.

"What's so amusing?" I asked in my chilliest voice.

"You," he said, still chuckling. "Knew you must fancy me to convince Crispin to lie his arse off to protect me from a demon I can't remember, but I didn't realize *this*."

"Realize what?"

He gave me a sunny smile. "You're madly in love with me."

"What?"

He waved away my gasp. "Nothing to be ashamed of. You're in the company of multitudes, though none of *them* got me to the proverbial alter the way you did. Have I mentioned how impressive that was? Blimey, talk about making the impossible a reality."

Outrage had me sputtering. "You are such an ass—"

"Can't blame it on the Red Dragon, either," he went on as if I hadn't spoken. "I've been high on that several times, yet never woken up with a wife before. Means I must have wanted to marry you, too, shocking though the thought may be."

"Your arrogance is *astounding*—"

"Then again, I do know you're mine," he continued, eyes gleaming now. "Did I tell you I sometimes feel things before they happen? Ah, I can see from your expression that I did. Imagine my surprise when I felt that you were mine the first time I saw you. Felt it again with every memory I had of you. Felt it when you were lying your arse off to the council about me, too, and I *really* felt it when I walked into your hotel room and breathed in your true scent." He came close, letting me see him inhale again. "Knocked me right off my feet," he murmured. "'Course, that also could have been the new memory it elicited, but either way, I know you're mine. And so do you."

"Bullshit," I said with all the emotion I was denying.

Ian only smiled. "Keep pretending, then. I don't need you to admit what you feel in order for you to help me recover what I've lost. You can show me."

I regained enough control to ask, "How will I *show* you?"

"Being near you has already inspired one new memory. I expect more will come the longer we're together." His gaze turned knowing. "Did you realize that? Is that the other reason you've tried so hard to avoid me?"

"No." But now that I *did* know, it would be.

If Ian remembered everything, he'd never let me pay the price for his resurrection alone. His sense of honor would demand that he hunt down the other souls along with me, danger be damned. I had to get away from him before that happened. But now that he could teleport, how could I escape?

Of course. Ian *was* formidable, but he did have one rather large weakness.

I came toward him and dropped my glamour. My skirt suit was already ripped from the ghoul fight and being buried alive, so my real curves almost overflowed the torn fabric, now too tight. His gaze raked me from the top of my streaked, silvery hair all the way to my feet, and his nostrils flared when he caught my real scent.

"There you are," he said in a throaty voice.

"Here I am," I agreed softly.

Then I put my arms around him, steeling myself not to get lost in the feel of him. He pulled me close, his body flush against mine. Every nerve ending I had caught fire. So much for me maintaining control. Still, I couldn't stop now. I tilted my head back and parted my lips, an invitation for him to kiss me.

His eyes glowed emerald as he took me up on it.

Chapter 9

*H*is mouth slanted over mine. My nails dug into his shoulders as his tongue invaded with sensual flicks that made me ache, burn, and then ache again. I wound my hands into his hair to pull him closer. He reached up and squeezed them as if daring me to grip him tighter. I needed him distracted, so with a moan, I yanked on his hair hard enough to crush his mouth into mine.

His response lifted me off my feet. I matched each deep, possessive stroke of his tongue while gripping his hair as if his arms weren't the real things keeping me aloft. I should be focused on enacting my spell, but his taste, his touch, the feel of his body . . . oh, I'd needed this. I'd needed it more than blood.

He pulled my thigh up so the bulge in his pants sensually ground against my center. Sensations burst within me and I let out a choked gasp. His kiss swallowed it as he did it again. Inner nerve endings shredded with such sharp ecstasy, I almost came.

I could no longer remember why I'd started this. All I knew was his scent, his taste, how tightly he held me, and the sound he made when I rubbed against him. His hands tightened on my hips and a coppery tang suddenly flavored our kiss. One of us had scored our tongues against a fang. When Ian stiffened in surprise at the taste, I knew it had been me. Dammit! I couldn't explain why my blood wasn't normal without dragging him deeper into the mess I was trying to keep him away from. Guess I had to finish that spell after all—

He grabbed his head and his whole body sagged. Fear shot

through me as I caught him before he hit the ground. What was happening? I hadn't hit him a spell yet!

I understood when blood began trickling from his eyes. He'd been hit with a new memory. I'd wanted to knock him out with a spell so I could leave, but I hadn't intended to incapacitate him *this* way. More blood came from his ears, and panic cleared away my desire. Would this new memory destroy his mind? My father had warned Ian that that could happen, and . . . why were my hands still stuck to his head?

I tried to pull them free and couldn't. What? I tried harder. I couldn't even yank any of his hair out. How could that be . . . ?

"You spelled me." I groaned, remembering him squeezing my hands. Ian hadn't been encouraging me to release my inhibitions. He'd been working tactile magic on me. I'd intended to distract him with desire in order to hit him with a spell, and the sly bastard had beaten me to it!

A feminine laugh jerked my head up. The filmy body of a ghost in Puritan dress floated over me, her impish grin at odds with the severity of her drab, overmodest garb.

"He played you like a flute," Leah said, still laughing. "What spell do you think he used on you?"

"Sampson's Strength, probably. It's unbreakable." Why hadn't I paid attention to what he was doing with his hands? I knew tactile magic was his strong suit. Now, I couldn't even help him while his mind might be shattering from a new memory!

Leah gave the blood trickling from Ian's eyes and nose an unconcerned glance. "Don't be alarmed—this has happened before. It doesn't seem to have any lasting ill effects on him."

I was relieved, but still stressed enough to be snappy. "You could have mentioned that before, *and* you could have mentioned that Ian remembered me."

Leah gave me a jaded look. "You told me never to leave his side. How could I tell you anything without leaving his side? It's been challenging enough following him after he teleports, and as you know, the dead don't have cell phones."

"Couldn't you send *another* ghost to deliver the message?"

She shrugged. "One ghost he might dismiss as nothing, if he glimpsed me. But two ghosts, with one of those ghosts telling the other to pass along a message about him?"

"You're right," I said with a sigh. "I only asked you to protect Ian if need be. I didn't ask you to spy for me."

Leah had been the perfect guard. Ghosts were largely ignored by vampires since they tended to be mindless energy snippets that merely repeated the same activity. But Leah's uniqueness didn't end at her sentience. She had also weaponized her ability to induce terrifying hallucinations.

Ian was tough, smart, and skilled, but if he were jumped by a large-enough group of demons, he'd need an edge. Leah was that edge. Now, she'd done such a good job of shadowing him, she'd witnessed me getting trapped by him. No wonder she was laughing. I might laugh, too, if I wasn't worried about Ian while also cursing myself for getting so caught up in his kiss, I hadn't noticed the magical handcuffs he'd clapped on me.

Leah gave me a speculative look. "He's not going to give up on his quest for answers, you know."

I shook my magically bound hands at her. "Starting to get that impression, thanks."

She laughed again. "I can see why you like him. He's always doing the unexpected, isn't he?"

"Tell me about it," I said dryly. "I—"

I stopped speaking when Leah abruptly vanished. Moments later, Ian sat up, shook his head as if clearing it, and wiped the blood from his face. Then he grinned as he saw my hands still stuck to his head.

"Ah, that spell worked on you."

"You tricked me."

I tried to summon up my anger over it, but it had vanished. That's how great my relief was that whatever memory he'd recovered hadn't broken his mind.

He wagged a finger at me. "*You* tried to trick me first. Or am I supposed to believe you were struck with a sudden urge to kiss me that had nothing to do with an attempt to hit me with a knockout spell?"

Arrogant ass. "Maybe I did want to kiss you."

His grin disappeared, replaced with an expression so intense, I had to look away. "Then prove it. Kiss me again."

I was suddenly aware of how my legs were pressed against his and his mouth was only inches above mine. Worse, I could still taste him on my lips, smell his scent clinging to my body, and feel every flex of his muscles. I closed my eyes, trying to focus on anything except the near overwhelming urge I had to relinquish my control until we broke many of the long-standing ruins around us with our passion.

"Let me go, Ian." The words were more than a request. They were practically a prayer.

My hands fell from his head as he broke the spell on me. At once, I was up and moving away, but he was faster.

"You know running from me won't work. Besides, you owe me a date."

That stunned me into stopping. "What?"

"A date," he repeated, an impish smile curling his mouth. "A platonic one, though I can't imagine how you got me to agree to *that*. Still, a promise is a promise, and you promised to let me show you a good time if we both survived."

I stared at him. A new memory had almost split open his head, and he was talking about a *date*? "You can't be serious."

His eyes gleamed a richer shade of turquoise. "Never been more so. Still, if you're not the type to honor your word—"

"I always honor my word," I interrupted, then stopped when I caught a glimpse of Leah over Ian's shoulder. She was doubled over with laughter. *Trapped you again!* she mouthed at me.

She was right, but Ian wouldn't keep trapping me if I didn't want to be caught. That was the simple, brutal truth.

And how could I leave him alone, anyway? He'd shown an absolute lack of interest in staying out of danger. Maybe agreeing to go on a date would get him to leave Greece, at least. Still, I couldn't give in too easily. He'd smell a trap.

"Come on, Ian, I'm almost embarrassed for you," I said. "You used to have thousands of people lining up to be with you. Now, you're reduced to calling in an old promise for a date?"

He smirked as he came nearer. "That would be much more insulting if the scent of your desire wasn't still covering me."

"I kissed you to distract you," I countered. "You just dropped from a memory before I could cast a spell on you."

"Oh, you cast a spell on me, make no mistake." All at once, his voice was a deep, sensual rasp. "One that's more powerful because no magic was involved. I might not remember all of our time together, but I'm calling in your promise of a date because of what I *do* remember."

I had to fight to keep my body from reacting to the new, rich timbre in his voice. He sounded that way in bed, and it made me feel dangerously weak.

"What *do* you remember?" I asked, my voice throatier than I intended it to be.

He leaned down, bringing his mouth next to my ear so that his words were a warm caress. "That's for you to find out only if you accompany me on a date tonight."

I should refuse. I should, but . . . again, I couldn't trust him to stay out of trouble on his own. At least if I was with Ian, I could mitigate the amount of danger he could put himself in. If that didn't work, I could always hit him on the head hard enough to knock him out, then imprison him in a suitably escape-proof dungeon. Vlad had one of those. I'm sure he'd save a space in it for Ian . . .

"One date," I said.

His smile was a satin-lined trap closing around me. "You won't regret it."

I doubted that. I just didn't know if I'd regret it sooner rather than later.

Chapter 10

I an had already booked us on a flight to Paris. That's how confident he'd been that I'd agree to this date. He hadn't remembered to include Silver, but Ian mesmerized the flight attendant into adding Silver as my "emotional support" animal.

Then, he left me alone after checking the three of us into the Hotel Plaza Athenee. Our suite had two bedrooms, giving me privacy while ensuring that Ian and I were still under the same roof. He didn't need such measures. I wasn't going to sneak away. I'd decided on a new strategy for tonight.

It was afternoon—demon-free time—so I went shopping on the avenue Montaigne. Paris's picturesque, tree-lined street was famous for its high-fashion stores. I bought my outfit from the most pretentious one, got a bite to eat from a store clerk, then went back to the hotel and spent a solid hour getting ready.

When I was done, my hair was in wire-stiff curls, heavy makeup covered my face, perfume covered my natural scent, gaudy jewelry dripped from my neck and ears, and my dress was a ridiculously expensive creation that only looked good on vastly underweight women. Even in my usual slender-formed glamour, it wouldn't be flattering on me. In my true form, my curves bulged in all the wrong places, and its tight sheath meant I could only walk with mincing, delicate steps.

Ian had fallen for a warrior woman. I now looked like a spoiled fashion victim that would need assistance climbing into a cab. If I could conjure up a swoon at the presumed sight of danger, I would be the perfect repellant for him.

A knock sounded on my bedroom door promptly at seven. I opened it, hiding my smile as Ian's gaze swept over me in surprise. Then I let my smile bloom until it wreathed my mouth in the coyly expectant way some women do when they are waiting to be complimented while also pretending to be shy.

"I know it's not the latest trend, but I could *barely* find anything to wear," I said with the same vapid intonation as a particularly annoying reality TV star.

A sound came from him that could have been a laugh. Then he said, "Nonsense, you're ravishing," with such smoothness, I thought I had to be mistaken about the laugh.

He came inside, revealing a bouquet he'd concealed behind his back. A dozen red roses, except their petals were too thick to be natural and they glittered like finely cut crystals.

I touched one of the brilliant blooms. It felt cool and hard the way crystal would, but its petals bent beneath my finger as if it were a real flower. "What are these?"

"They're called Faerie Queen Crimsons."

I gave him a look over the top of the dazzling bouquet. "You're giving a Law Guardian illegal magic flowers?"

His smile reminded me of the crystalline roses: dangerously beautiful because once you saw it, nothing else could compare. "No, I'm giving *my wife* a gift I thought she'd enjoy."

I thrust the flowers back as if they suddenly burned me. "I'm not your real wife."

"A Law Guardian disagreeing with the highest court in vampire society?" He tsked. "What is the world coming to?"

"You could care less about the law," I snapped, my simpering date façade crumbling.

He grinned. "And you hate your hair, that dress, and those ridiculous tottering shoes, but here we are."

He came in and set the flowers on an end table. The roses stood upright as if their long stems were contained by an invisible vase.

When the overhead lights hit them, they glittered so brightly, a myriad of colors scattered across the room. They were beyond gorgeous, and so obviously magical that I'd never have gotten them for myself. I'd consider the risk too high and my happiness too . . . unimportant. As usual.

Did Ian remember that about me? I couldn't tell, but it was obvious I couldn't trick him with my vapid-date façade. He'd either seen right through it or he remembered the truth.

"These shoes *are* ridiculous," I agreed, kicking them off. Why did modern women torture themselves with such contraptions? "I also hate how stiff my hair is, the stench from this perfume, and this gods-awful dress I can barely move in. Fuck it, I'm showering and starting over."

Ian's laugh followed me as I went back into the bathroom. "I'll wait here."

A QUICK SHOWER, blow dry, and normal amount of makeup later, I put on a black silk pantsuit. It was chic enough for a date while also giving me pockets to store my weapons. After my near-escape from the Mycenae ruins, I'd never be without them on me again, especially at night when demons were free to roam.

Ian had on black pants, a black jacket, and a deep umber-colored shirt that should have clashed with his hair but didn't. Instead, his auburn hair and the shirt looked like different shades of an ever-deepening flame. I tried not to focus on that by wondering what he had planned. Paris's many landmarks, clubs, opera houses, and restaurants certainly gave him no shortage of options. But after thirty minutes, Ian pulled up to the last place I expected: an amusement park.

I stiffened. "Why are we here?"

"Someone with your long life-span has already eaten at all the finest restaurants, drunk all the best wine, seen all the museums, attended countless operas, and been to so many clubs, they all look the same," he replied. "But I wager you've never been to one of these simply for a fun evening out."

A strangled laugh escaped me. "You're right. The last theme park I went to was no fun *at all*."

He turned the car off. "This one will be."

I almost refused to go inside. Then I realized I couldn't ask for a better reminder of why I had to get away from Ian. Dagon had murdered Ian at an amusement park. He must not remember that, but I did.

"Can't wait," I said stiffly.

I maintained that stiffness through the first hour. Then my iciness began to thaw. This park couldn't be more different from the one we'd battled Dagon at. That had been a broken-down shell filled with the silence of long abandonment. This was an elaborate wonderland of rides, stores, and soaring attractions, like the fairy-tale castle that loomed over the main park.

Granted, at first all the excited squeals from the children reminded me of the demons' death cries from that day, but by the second hour, I was smiling at the screeches. When was the last time I'd been surrounded by screams of *joy*?

By the third hour, Ian had cajoled me into riding some of the park's many attractions. He enjoyed them with his usual abandon, but what surprised me was that I enjoyed them, too. For a few moments, acting like the children around me allowed me to let go of the constant stress, fear of failure, and sadness that had consumed me the past several weeks. How had Ian known that I needed this? I hadn't even known it myself.

By the fourth hour, I was grinning as I let the rollercoaster whip me around with the kind of force I only felt when locked in a death match. I even raised my arms and let the wind play with my hands as the cars hurtled us toward the bottom. When the ride came to a stop, I said, "Again!" with the same greedy glee I'd heard from countless children this evening.

Yes, I was thousands of years too old for this, but so what? I had the rest of my life to act my age.

Ian laughed, flashing his lit-up gaze at the attendant. "One more time for both of us."

"One more time" turned into three, until my head spun from the repeated g-forces and the simple joy of reveling in the moment. By the time fireworks broke out over the castle, signaling the park's closing, I was happier than I would have thought possible at the beginning of the night.

"This was nice," I said as I watched the sky explode with colors above us.

He laughed. "Normally, I'd take such faint praise as failure, but from you, it means tonight was a smashing success."

"Yes, your record of showing your dates a good time is still intact," I assured him.

"I do have a reputation to maintain," he said with a sly grin. Then that grin faded and his expression turned serious. "In truth, I wanted you to have a good memory to replace the wretched one of the two of us at that other theme park."

The blood in my veins turned to glass. Ian *remembered* that?

"Now, what were my last words?" he asked almost casually.

I was so shocked, I was stuttering. "W-what?"

"My last words before I died. What were they?"

I took several steps backward, then hit a metal gate. A quick glance revealed that Ian had picked a deserted place with no exits to spring this on me. I couldn't fly away from him, either. The brightly lit park had too many security cameras.

"I figured out why my body read as new to Leila," Ian went on in that deceptively causal tone. "It's why I have a demon's abilities without the demon brand, and why I no longer owe Dagon my soul. I died, yet here I stand. Care to tell me how?"

"Ian . . ." I couldn't tell him I'd saved him. I refused to saddle him with a debt he'd feel honor-bound to repay.

"I think I know," he said lightly. "Granted, my first glimpse of the Grim Reaper was so terrifying, it was easy to forget his real appearance, but his hair *is* quite distinctive." He paused to run a hand through mine. "So are his eyes, and your blood isn't vampire, demon, or ghoul. Knew you were more than a vampire, but I hadn't remembered what that 'more' was. I do now. You're half of whatever he is, so either you or he plucked me out of hell and brought me back."

Dammit, he knew too much! I had to tell him something.

"It wasn't hell." I met his gaze, steeling myself. "Dagon had been hoarding souls he made bargains with inside himself. We didn't know that until we killed him and he burned through one of them to resurrect himself. Then he killed you and swallowed your soul, so the darkness you remember is being trapped inside him. It's also how you absorbed some of his power. I had my father pull you out because you'd saved my life earlier that night, so I saved yours as repayment, making us even."

You owe me nothing, hung unspoken in the air between us. I wanted to stress it, but that would make him suspicious. No, I had to act nonchalant.

Ian stared at me, his gaze relentless. "I remember part of that story very differently. Dagon didn't take my life—I shoved that last bone blade through my eye myself."

The memory scalded me so deeply, I flung him away. Before I could blink, he grabbed me. Everything blurred, and when it stopped, we were in an empty section of the vast parking lot, the noise from the now faraway park fading in the distance.

"Why did I do it?" he continued. "I must have told you."

"I don't remember," I lied.

He stroked my cheek, his touch gentle despite his iron grip on my arms. "My last memory was the look on your face. There's no chance you forgot any of it."

There wasn't, even if I lived another four-and-a-half-thousand years. But I still couldn't tell him. It hurt too much . . .

Two people materialized behind Ian. For a split second, I thought I was having a PTSD attack with vivid hallucinations, because I recognized one of them and this *couldn't* be happening. Not again.

The boyishly handsome, blond-haired demon grinned much the same way he had when he'd shoved that bone knife into Ian's eye several weeks ago. Only this time, the knife in Dagon's hand was silver, and he was grinning as he aimed it at Ian's back.

Chapter 11

My other nature ripped free as if I'd never had the power to hold it back. My vision blackened, my emotions iced over, and my skin split from the power exploding out of me. I couldn't see Dagon fall to his knees, but I could feel it. I could hear him, too. He was screaming with what sounded like unbelievable pain.

How curious. I hadn't even started to rip him apart yet—and what did Ian think he was doing, pushing me aside?

"Get behind me," I heard Ian hiss. "A dozen more demons just teleported in here!"

I felt the bone knife Ian withdrew from his coat. Felt the water pulsating inside of him, its power calling to me. Then my vision cleared and I saw the new demons. They were behind Dagon, who was writhing on the ground in much the same way Ian did when a new memory overtook him.

Ah, yes, my father had ensured that Dagon couldn't be near Ian without crippling pain. The Warden must not have told Dagon that. How predictably evasive of him. Now, Dagon was helpless and he couldn't teleport away to save himself—

Ian flung his knife and speared Dagon through the eye. Ian reached for his next weapon, but I knocked it from his hand. Dagon was my kill, mine! Then I ripped the water out of Dagon, smiling as the bloody deluge coated the stunned demons around him. I yanked most of the water out of them, too, pulling it forward to hit Ian like a red wave. It coated Ian while barely drenching me because he still had me behind his back.

That would remind Ian that I could take care of myself.

I was about to freeze the bloody water into ice knives when Dagon rasped, "Get me out of here!" Then Dagon and the demon closest to him disappeared as that demon teleported them away.

"No!" my vampire nature screamed.

Her rage catapulted her back on top. The other demons tried to teleport away, but most of them were too desiccated to summon the necessary power. Ian began teleporting among them, ramming his knife through their eyes before they healed enough to vanish. Still, a few teleported away before Ian got to them.

"Let me back up," I said to my vampire half. "I can finish this." I just had to rip a little more water out of the other demons to ensure their doom—

"You let Dagon get away!" my vampire half screamed. "Now shut up and stay down!"

Ian paused in his slaughter to swing an amazed glance my way. "Do you need a moment alone with yourself so the two of you can sort this out?"

One of the remaining demons took advantage of Ian's distraction. He muttered a spell and a bright red beam formed, hurtling toward Ian. Ian teleported away, but the beam followed him like a heat-seeking missile. Ian held out his hands, fingers blurring as he conjured up a blocking spell.

My celestial half shot back on top, sending a frozen wall of bloody water to capture the beam. The beam blasted through it as if it wasn't there. Ian was still conjuring his blocking spell, but he was out of time. When that red beam slammed into him, my vampire half wrested back control.

I sucked in a breath that exploded out with relief when that beam bounced off Ian without causing any harm. Instead, it reversed course and aimed itself at the demon who'd cast it. He tried to run, but he was too weak from water loss. I pulled my bone bident from my jacket and hurled it at his face. One end missed his eye, but the other tip sank home.

I flew at him. Ian beat me, teleporting over and ramming that second tip home before I reached the demon. The demon's face exploded in a cloud of smoke and sulfur.

Leah suddenly zoomed past me. The remaining demons began screaming and tearing at themselves in horror over whatever hallucinations the ghost had forced into their minds. It allowed Ian and I to slaughter them with an ease that would have felt cruel if they hadn't come with Dagon to kill us.

When Ian was about to shove his knife through the last demon's eyes, I shouted, "Don't, I need one alive!"

He only stabbed one of the demon's eyes out, muttering, "Hurts, doesn't it? I certainly didn't forget *that*."

"I'll keep this area clear, but you shouldn't linger," Leah said before streaking toward the other end of the parking lot.

Ian glanced at her before his gaze swung back at me. "The spell that demon flung at me bounced right off me. How?"

"I put a deflection spell on you before I left you. Prevents any magic from touching you that doesn't come from me, but it only works once." And it had taken a *lot* of power to do that spell, but I left that part out.

Ian snorted. "You had a ghost babysitting me *and* affixed a deflection spell onto me? Blimey, you make Mencheres look like an amateur when it comes to overprotectiveness! He'll trip over himself welcoming you to the family when he hears of this."

"I'm not part of the family," I said, ignoring his challenging arch of the brow.

"Yes you are, and who was that blond sod you sent screaming to his knees before he got away?"

My shock lasted only a second. Of course Ian wouldn't recognize Dagon. The demon was the starting point for everything my father had ripped from Ian's memory.

"That was Dagon. If, ah, you didn't know who he was, why did you chuck your knife into his eye?"

Ian shrugged. "You attacked him first, so I surmised he was the one who most needed killing."

Dagon needed killing, all right, but it was my father's spell reacting to Ian's proximity that had sent Dagon screaming to his knees, not me. "You," I said to change the subject, shoving my bident under the demon's remaining eye. "Start talking. What was Dagon doing here tonight?"

"Kill . . . him," the demon said, his glance indicating Ian. Then he laughed, a dry, crackling sound. "You're not supposed to be here . . . halfling. We heard . . . you'd left him."

"Halfling. How marginally insulting," I said mockingly. "Don't tax yourself thinking up something better, though. You'll need all your wits to tell me everything Dagon is up to."

"Kill . . . him," the demon repeated, his one eye glaring at Ian.

My other nature hit the bars of her cage hard enough to make my vision briefly go black. I kept her down, but I was shaken. Was it always going to be like this? Fighting my other half when my stress levels were high?

"I could rip the last of your water out of you and choke you with it," I said in a dispassionate tone. I might not let my other nature get control again, but I could pretend I would. "Or, you could tell me what I want to know."

"Dagon is . . . weaker." The demon's voice cracked even more. Talking must be hard on his shriveled vocal cords. "Needs to slaughter . . . souls that got away . . . to take back power they stole from him. Why Dagon killed . . . the woman in Egypt . . . and others. But he really wants . . . him." Emphatic nod at Ian. "Used . . . the blood he'd collected from . . . an old amusement park . . . to cast spell to find him—"

I shoved the blade through his eye. It was that or let my other nature rocket back on top. Hearing how meticulously Dagon had plotted Ian's death shredded my control.

"That was premature," Ian remarked, yanking his blade from

the now dead demon's other eye. "He might have had more information."

"Maybe you don't realize it," I said between clenched teeth. "But I'm having a problem at the moment."

"Does that problem have eyes that shoot silver beams while darkness billows behind her like a cape?" He grinned. "Made me rock hard seeing it."

He was aroused by my supernaturally sociopathic other half? "Fuck. You," I bit out.

He nodded. "Solid plan."

He snatched me close, murmuring, "Don't," when I tried to shove him away. "Your other half never fights for control when you're in my arms, does she?"

Damn his selective memory! Yes, I felt too much when I was in Ian's arms. Those feelings might lock the bars on her cage, but oh, how they ripped at my heart now.

One crisis at a time.

With that in mind—and yes, some personal motivation—I wrapped my arms around Ian and kissed him with everything I'd been holding back before.

His grunt of surprise turned into a groan of pure lust. When I pulled away, his lip was bleeding. He grabbed my hair, stared into my eyes, then kissed me with such savage passion, my whole body vibrated from desire.

"Veritas!" I faintly heard. I pushed past the erotic fog enough to hear Leah say again, louder, "Veritas!"

"Sod off, ghost," Ian growled.

I dragged my mouth away to see Leah hovering over Ian's shoulder. "You are getting carried away," she said in a tone that reminded me she'd been a Puritan when she was alive. "I've already seen too much with the two of you."

I glanced at Ian . . . and Leah hadn't exaggerated. His umber shirt was in tatters from where I'd torn it in blind need to touch his skin. His jacket had fared better, but not by much, and one more rip at his waist would have his pants off. As it was, they appeared held up more by Ian's erection than by their remaining fabric. Add that to the blood covering him from the red wave I'd hit him with, and I'd seen people mauled by mountain lions that looked in better shape.

"Oh," I said, mildly embarrassed. On the plus side, I didn't feel my other nature at *all* anymore.

"Quite," Leah said in an acerbic tone. "I don't dare leave to give you privacy, either. I left for that reason earlier, which is why I wasn't there when the demons first attacked you. It's also unwise to continue your tryst in the exact same spot the demons found you at, don't you agree?"

I did, and if I'd been thinking with my brain instead of my lower parts, I would have realized that.

"She does have a point," Ian said. "Hold on."

I didn't have a chance to say anything else. Ian's arms tightened, then everything around us blurred again.

Chapter 12

When it stopped, we were back in our hotel room with Silver flying around in joy at our sudden appearance. I didn't take time to pet him, though. I left the room and went straight to the adjacent hotel room door. Ian, no surprise, followed me.

"What are you doing?"

"Blocking Dagon's blood trace on you." After a few sharp raps, the door opened, revealing a rumpled man in his fifties.

"What?" he began in French, then stared in horror at Ian.

Before he could scream, I hit him with the power in my gaze. "You're perfectly calm," I told him in French, pushing him aside to enter his room. "You're not concerned with anything we're doing."

Once inside, I grabbed one of the room's complimentary coffee cups and took out my silver knife.

"You feel no pain," I told him, making a small slice in his wrist while I held the coffee cup beneath it. When the cup was full, I sliced my finger on a fang and rubbed my blood over the slice in the man's wrist. It healed in seconds.

"Once we leave, you won't remember us or anything we did," I told him. "Now, go back to sleep."

He got back in bed. His eyes were already closed by the time Ian and I left.

"Dagon murdered that woman four nights ago, so he's had the power to track you ever since," I said once we were back in our room. "Your ability to teleport might have thrown him off initially, but why did he wait until tonight to attack you?"

Ian shrugged. "Likely because I spent half that time with the entire vampire council."

I stared at him. "You're right."

Dagon wanted Ian dead, but the demon was no fool. Murdering Ian while he was under the protection of the highest court in vampire society would be seen as an act of war. Vampires and demons might detest each other, but neither side wanted war. Ian's litigious stunt had probably saved his life.

He flashed a cheery grin. "More proof that married men live longer than single ones."

"How'd you get so good at teleporting?" I asked, ignoring that. Then I ran water into the sink until it was full. "You've only had this ability for what, three weeks?"

"Four," he replied, a brow arching when I looked back at him. "Had plenty of incentive to practice with Crispin and Cat hovering over me. How do you think I finally got rid of them? I'm finished with people telling me they know best about my own life."

That was directed at me, and I was torn. If I were Ian, I wouldn't put up with people withholding parts of my past, either. I grabbed his hand and held it over the sink. Then I dipped a finger into my hotel-neighbor's blood and started filling the blocking spell with power.

When I used up the power from the water in the sink, I sent my senses out and used the power from the water in the rest of the hotel. My other half reacted, of course. I owed my affinity with water to that part of me, not my vampire side.

When the spell was ready, I flash-froze some of the water into a sliver of ice. Then I raked that shard across Ian's palm. His blood darkened the water, and at the same time, the other man's blood in the cup began to boil.

I took my finger out of the boiling cup and drew a blocking symbol across Ian's forehead. As soon as I was done, the cup shattered, but no blood stained the tile. It had all flash-boiled away when the spell sealed itself into Ian's skin.

"There," I said in satisfaction. "Dagon can no longer use your blood to find you."

A slow smile curved Ian's mouth. "Have I ever told you you're irresistibly attractive when you use forbidden magic?"

"Yes," I said, then could have kicked myself. Now his gaze was filling up with green flame.

"Don't," I said when he reached for me.

The look in his eyes made me shiver. "You want me, and I want you more than anything I've wanted in my entire life."

I had to look away. If I didn't, I would take him up on every decadent promise in his gaze. "Yes, I want you. But desire is an emotion, not a decision, and I still say no."

The green flame left his gaze and his eyes hardened into turquoise gems. "Very well, I respect your decision. Now, respect mine and tell me everything you've been hiding from me."

"You do notice the blood leaking from your eyes, ears, and nose every time you get a new memory? That's a massive cerebral hemorrhage, so your own body is telling you to leave this alone. Didn't the Grim Reaper also warn you that pursuing your memories could destroy your mind?"

"He did," Ian said at once. "I told him I wanted my memories back regardless, and he, a creature who had no regard for me, still respected my decision. Why can't you?"

I'd tried avoidance, half-truths, outright lies, and fake personas. Nothing had worked. Might as well go with the truth.

"Because you're right! Yes, sex with you was amazing. Yes, I know why you killed yourself, and *yes*, I remember your last words. That's why I can't bear to talk about them. Back then, I felt things for you I hadn't allowed myself to feel in thousands of years. And I *did* respect your wishes. That's why, when you insisted on facing Dagon with me, I didn't stop you, and what happened? You fucking *died*."

I found myself heaving in breaths as if the sobs I'd been holding back were now beating against the confines of my body.

"People die, Veritas." Ian's voice was soft, yet no less emphatic. "It doesn't mean you were wrong to respect my wishes. It simply means no one is immortal."

"I used to be," I muttered.

"What?" he said sharply.

Damn whatever it was about Ian that always led me to spill my secrets! "Never mind. What's important is that if you remember everything, you could end up with the vampire version of brain death. You hide your brilliance to manipulate your enemies because they all make the mistake of underestimating you, so are you going to risk *all* that knowledge for a few details that have no bearing on your life now?"

"Yes."

I slammed my fists against my legs hard enough to crack the bones. Ian's gaze darkened with concern. I seized on that like a drowning person grabbing at a lifeline.

"Fine, you don't care about the danger to yourself? What about the danger to me?"

Now I had his full attention. "What danger?"

This was more than I wanted to reveal, but if it would stop him from finding out the rest, I'd let it rip.

"Know when I started having my split personality problem? After you died in front of me. I didn't even know my other nature *could* break free, but she did. Now"—I gave a frustrated swipe at myself—"if I'm not careful, she'll take permanent control. So, if you feel any gratitude for me bringing you back from the dead, don't endanger me by staying, *or* by pressing me for details that endanger you, because in case you haven't noticed, she bursts free whenever you're in danger."

He'd been listening with furrows dug into his features, but at the finale of what I thought was a good argument for him to get the hell out of there, his frown smoothed.

"Ah, I see the problem." His tone was so light, it was almost cheerful. "You're so strong, it's been ages since you've been knocked on your arse. You're also so brave, it must've been even longer than that since you've felt fear. I've had more recent experience with both, so let me remind you: when you're knocked down, you get back up, and when you're afraid, you press on regardless. As the saying goes, sometimes you have to kick the darkness until it bleeds daylight. Besides, fear can be a good thing. It reminds you not to take what you care about for granted."

"Take for granted?" I repeated in disbelief. "Did you listen to *anything* I said?"

"I listened to all of it, and both of us know that ignoring a problem won't make it go away. Also," he flashed a charming smile, "your blocking spell might stall Dagon now, but it won't stymie him forever. Do you truly want me out there with only a ghost to watch over me?"

He'd just put into words everything I'd been worried about. "You're using my fear to manipulate me. Whatever happened to pressing *past* my fears?"

His flash of teeth wasn't a smile. It was a warning. "Did you think I'd play fair? I won't, and since you're being truthful, I'll be equally frank: I don't care that demons are after you. I don't care that you have a warring nature of indeterminate supernatural origin, and I don't care that you're afraid of what you feel for me. I only care that you *do* feel it, and since you admitted that, I'll let you in on another secret."

Suddenly, he was gripping my shoulders, while his gaze was the real weight that kept me rooted where I stood.

"I might not remember my last words, but this whole time, I've remembered what I felt when I said them."

Chapter 13

The statement hit me like a full-body blow. His last words had been *could have loved you.* All this time since, I'd believed everything Ian had felt for me was lost along with his memories.

"How?" I asked in as calm a voice as I could manage.

A brow rose. "I woke up in that whorehouse with a pounding headache and a burning conviction that I was supposed to be somewhere else, *with* someone else. None of Crispin's lies dissuaded me. At one point, I said, 'Where is she?' Then your father showed up. Crispin nearly fainted, but I told Crispin he was only seeing what he feared on this side of the veil."

"How?" I burst out without any calmness this time. "The Warden told me he'd erased every part of your time with me!"

Ian's grip on my shoulders became caressing. "He told me he said that to ease your pain in case I felt nothing for you, but that when emotions ran deep, they could never fully be erased."

The words slammed into me, making me as raw and vulnerable as an exposed nerve. I'd spent my life detaching from people because my survival depended on no one getting close enough to find out my secrets. Now, I was feeling everything and I had no idea how to handle it.

"I'm going to need additional clarification," I found myself saying. Then I groaned. Over four thousand years of cold survival mentality had me sounding like an IRS agent questioning a taxpayer about a dubious deduction!

He snorted. "To *clarify*, I might not have known your name, how we came to be together or why you'd left me, but *you* were not erased. That's why I was willing to chase you to the point of proving our marriage to a council I despise. It's also why I'm not going anywhere now. I won't let a little danger stop me from fighting for what I want."

The choked sound I made was part laughter and part despair. "It's more than 'a little danger,' and you know it."

"My favorite kind, then," he said with a dark laugh.

"You assume I want to start things with you again." My voice was almost a whisper. "What if I don't?"

He smiled, sensual and absolutely ruthless. "If you could stop what you felt for me, you already would have, so don't waste your energy on a battle you *will* lose."

A strangled laugh escaped me. "If I didn't know how much you liked pain, I'd punch you in the face for such conceit."

His chuckle was drenched with wickedness. "Threats of violence? Now you're just trying to switch me on, aren't you?"

Heat swept over me. His hands were still on my shoulders, and his clothes were so tattered, one tug would have them on the floor. I wanted to do that so badly, my hands ached. But when Ian moved closer, I twisted away.

"We need ground rules first."

"No we don't." His voice was a growl. "Do anything you want to me. I promise to love all of it."

A thousand explicit thoughts raced through my mind, making me lose a step backing away. "Not that," I forced myself to say. "Ground rules for you getting your memories back."

His eyes blazed emerald. "Your turn to elaborate."

I took in a breath, regretting it when his scent filled me. It was heady with lust—another wrecking ball to my willpower.

"You want to reclaim your lost memories despite the risk. You're right; that is your choice to make, not mine. So, ask me anything, and I vow to tell you the truth. But then you agree to leave and stay hidden until I take care of Dagon."

His nostrils flared. Anger or anticipation, I couldn't tell. "That's your offer?"

"Yes."

"I counter." Now I knew what the flare was. Anger. "You tell me nothing, but I stay and help you take down Dagon, and we let fate decide what I do or do not remember."

I closed my eyes. "Ian . . ."

"Yes, I know. Danger, mayhem, and vicious demons await." Amusement threaded through his voice now. "The same awaits me if I leave you and Dagon finds me, so I ask again—which do you think I have a better chance of surviving? With or without you?"

Damn him for knowing exactly where to strike. Not that I'd made it difficult. No, I'd bared my most vulnerable spot, and like the ruthless fighter Ian was, he'd aimed right for it.

Well, I knew one of his weaknesses, too. "No sex," I said, opening my eyes. "You stay, you keep your cock to yourself."

He clasped his hands over the member as if sealing a solemn oath. "Very well. Until you request otherwise—and you *will*—consider this locked away."

"That's not all," I said, determination blanketing my more fragile emotions. "If my other nature assumes control, you teleport away, because she is dangerous."

His brows rose. "'She' is you, you know."

"No she's not, and don't assume she cares for you like I do, because she doesn't."

He parted his lips as if he were going to argue. Then he shrugged. "Very well."

This was too easy. Ian had to be up to something.

"I also have responsibilities that will require me to leave at a moment's notice, and no, you can't come. Agreed?"

"My compliments on your ego," he replied, grinning. "It's quite impressive if you thought I'd insist on being chained to your side every moment of the day."

"Fine," I said in frustration. "Now that that's settled, we need to leave. Dagon might not be able to track you through your blood any longer, but he'll still be searching for you, so we need to get far away, fast."

Ian stretched his arms while arching his back as if relieving a kink. The movement shifted his torn clothes, revealing his taut abdomen as well as lots of groin cleavage. I looked away, knowing none of this was accidental. When I looked back, a little smile teased his mouth.

No, not accidental at all.

"You might want to change," I said as if I hadn't been caught admiring the show. "Being half naked and coated in demon blood is bound to attract the wrong kind of notice."

"Mmm, yes. Also need to shower so I don't give Dagon the chance to track me through *his* people's blood, if he's clever enough to think of that—"

Ian stopped talking and tensed. At once, I looked around for danger. "What?"

"Blood is the most common way to trace someone." Ian spoke as if he were still working something out in his head. "Essence trails are next, if you know a powerful-enough psychic, but both can be blocked. What can't be blocked is power, and a demon's power is as unique to them as their blood."

"It could be," I said, mulling the possibilities now, too. "But power traces fade quickly. I know where some of Dagon's power was several nights ago, but I doubt the traces would be concentrated enough for us to use to make a locator spell, assuming I could figure out how to do one that could trace a demon by their power alone," I added.

"We have a more concentrated dose of his power right here."

I gave him a confused look. Then I understood.

Ian had absorbed a lot of Dagon's power when he clawed his way out of the demon. What if I could use what was in Ian's body to find Dagon? If so, then I could also use it to find the other resurrected souls, too! But . . .

What if Dagon was already tracing them that way? He was far more versed in dark magic than I was, and Dagon had a vested interest in murdering the other resurrected people to recoup the power they'd stolen from him. The demon had also said Dagon had killed the woman in Egypt "and others" for that same reason. How many others?

I'd made a vow to my father, but I couldn't keep that vow if Dagon murdered the people I was tasked to find. No, I had to find—and stop—Dagon first.

I gave Ian a level look. "I don't know how to do that kind of spell, but we're going to have to try anyway."

His grin was wolfish. "Know an advantage to being married to a law-breaking scoundrel who has friends in all the wrong places? I *do* know someone who should be able to do that spell."

Chapter 14

Two days later, Ian drove us to the town limits of Centralia, Pennsylvania. The area seemed innocuous enough, if abandoned and overgrown, but one sniff told me I wouldn't like whatever Ian had planned next.

"Why does this place reek of demons?"

Ian flashed an unconcerned grin. "Who else would have the power to do the type of spell we're after?"

"Me, once I figure out how, because no one in their right mind would use demons to trap another demon," I pointed out.

He gave me a tolerant look. "Not all demons are bad."

Technically true. Nechtan, a demonic imp I'd first befriended a couple thousand years ago, was a sweet creature who'd been abused by his crueler brethren. But Nechtan was the exception, not the rule.

"Even if you happen to know a non-evil demon here, this town reeks of several demons. Not one."

"A few live here," Ian agreed. "Some lower-level demons moved in after humans abandoned the place decades ago, when the coal tunnels beneath it caught fire and couldn't be put out. But most scorned living in and around a coal mine."

That, I believed. Demons liked to live large, which wasn't difficult for a species with supernatural abilities, eons of longevity, and absolutely no morals.

"Demons also have a secret safe house to shelter renegade demons, among others," Ian went on. "I know the proprietor of such an establishment. He's powerful enough to do our spell, but while I don't know where he is, I know a demon who should."

"What would push the *demon* culture's boundaries enough to make some go into hiding?" Then again, I probably didn't want to know. I had enough horrors to fill my nightmares as it was.

"Usually, it's as simple as being different," Ian replied, adding in a jaded tone. "You of all people should know how most species are prone to criminalizing *that*."

I did. Vampires usually slaughtered cross-species people like me as soon as our existence became known. Fearmongering had also led to magic being outlawed when long ago, enough vampires claimed that those with magic were plotting to enslave their non-magic brethren. They'd had no proof, but it didn't matter. Magic was declared illegal and all vampires caught practicing it were executed. From that brutal purge, the council, Law Guardians, and Enforcers had been born. I only joined their ranks to use the access my job gave me to secretly help the people abused by these laws. Did Ian remember that?

Even if he didn't, I'd agreed to let fate decide what he remembered, so all I said was, "Do you trust the demon you're coming here to see?"

"I trust that he'll regret it if he betrays me," he replied with casual lethalness. "He doesn't know the extent of my abilities. You can't reveal your abilities to him, either. That's why you're staying with the car while I go into town."

"Oh, sure," I said. "I was just thinking I needed to get my nails done."

My sarcasm only made him grin. "Sometimes, my personal business will cause me to leave at a moment's notice, and you can't expect to be chained to my hip *every* moment, can you?"

Ohhh, the vindictive shit! I'd make him pay for throwing up my own words to me. But first . . . "Enjoy all the personal time you want, *after* I go with you to meet this demon."

"Not going to happen, luv. One of this demon's abilities is seeing the source of people's magic. If you come, he'll spot your half-demigod nature before you can say hallo."

And word was already circulating about me. Tenoch warned me this would happen if anyone saw what I was and lived to talk about it. Dagon's survival was coming back to bite me in yet another way. But I still wasn't going to let Ian walk alone into a town full of demons just to stop one more person from learning my secret.

"I'll stay out of sight, then."

"Yes, by staying here," he replied in a steely tone. "If there's trouble I can't handle, I'll send up a magic flare. You'll be more than close enough to see it and come running."

He wasn't going to be dissuaded. Fine. I'd stop arguing. "Very well, then."

He gave me a jaunty smile as he got out of the car. "Should only take a few hours."

I watched him walk down a road with cracks big enough to allow brownish overgrowth to infiltrate the asphalt. Then he turned right at what had probably once been the main street of town. When he was out of sight, I continued to remain in the car . . . for another five minutes.

Then I got out and streaked after him. He must have lost his mind along with most of his memory if he thought I'd stay back the *whole* time.

EVEN WITH THE sulfur stench and the fainter smell of burning coal, Ian's scent was easy to follow. I stayed downwind so he didn't catch *my* scent, and I flew so my feet didn't make any of the crunching noises his did as he walked on the winter-dry foliage. After several minutes, Ian ducked into a cavelike structure. Must be the entrance to the mine.

I paused at my perch behind the roof of a former gas station. I needed camouflage before I proceeded. Good thing I knew exactly how to hide myself. I just needed a little help.

I cut my finger, using my blood to draw several symbols on the roof. Then, I filled them with the barest amount of power. I didn't want my magic sensed by the town's demons.

"I summon the spirit of Leah, daughter of Siobhan," I whispered at the symbols. "Leah, hear my call."

Moments later, the outline of a severely cut black-and-white dress appeared, then Leah herself bloomed into focus.

"I cannot fathom why he believed you'd stay in the car," were her first words. "Does he remember *nothing* about you?"

I stifled a laugh. "Ian's memory might be erratic, but his stubbornness is the same, which is why I need another favor."

She smiled with anticipation. "Concealment?"

"Please."

Leah held out her arms. I went into her embrace, feeling the chill of power instead of the corporeal form of a woman. But Leah's power was greater than flesh and bone. It was also ironic. Leah hadn't become a witch until after she'd been executed as one back when the American colonies were new.

Leah's power continued to cover me until I felt like I'd been plunged into icy water. Then I watched as my body turned filmy like hers before it vanished altogether. Once it did, Leah's form vanished, too. Thus drenched in her power, she was able to pick me up and whisk both of us into the mine.

At first, it looked the way I expected an abandoned mine to look, with crumbling support columns and pieces of equipment half buried in the stony ground. But the coal track running into the darkness was in pristine shape. Leah followed it, and minutes later, lights cast a golden glow in the distance and I heard laughter and music, of all things. At a sharp bend after a right-hand turn, the façade of a derelict mine vanished.

What I saw could have doubled as a jazz club. Cigar smoke hung in the air while a skilled quartet on a nearby stage played soulful music. Couches, chairs, and tables were spread out from a stone-carved bar in the main room, with two smaller wood-and-steel bars visible beyond the dance floor of a separate room. Floating orbs cast a cozy glow while allowing its darker corners to host danger or romance, depending on the occupant's mood. With its privacy, lack of humans, and stellar music, I might have become a regular if it wasn't also filled with demons.

At least a dozen of them were draped over the couches in the main room. Others shuffled together on the dance floor, and another baker's dozen sat on stools in front of the three bars. "A few" demons in town, my ass!

And Ian was sprawled on one of the couches as if he were just another demon enjoying the music instead of a vampire surrounded by enemies who could turn on him at any moment.

Chapter 15

A red-haired demon with a bad spray-tan, leather pants, and a leather bra went up to Ian. I tensed, but all she said was, "What's your pleasure, gorgeous?"

A waitress. No surprise that nothing was free among demons, even in a secret underground jazz club. Then the smile Ian gave the waitress made me glad I was still invisible. Otherwise, he'd see the holes I was glaring into him for the way he looked at the cleavage the curvy demon made sure was at eye-level for him.

"Depends on my mood," he responded in a luxuriant tone. "Some nights, I'm smooth brandy. Other nights, I'm single-malt bourbon. On occasion, I'm even fine wine, but tonight, I'm hard whisky, straight up."

Her gaze swept over him, taking in the muscled planes of his chest, as he'd unhooked a few buttons in his shirt since I'd last seen him. She even reached out to trace his chest as if seeing whether he felt as luscious as he looked. I knew he did, and from the seductive way she bit her lip, she thought so, too.

Slap her hand and tell her to fuck off! I seethed. Ian did neither. He only smiled wider.

I was going to kill him. I'd kill her, too, but I'd be gentle about it since she wasn't the one who'd constantly reminded me that we were married. That's why she'd barely feel it when I murdered her. But Ian? Oh, yes, he'd feel it.

"Hard whisky, no chaser, coming right up," she said in a bedroom-voice purr, then turned and went to the bar.

A black-haired demon with skin as pale as Ian's filled the space next to him on the couch. "Michael," Ian greeted him. "Long time, mate."

"Long time," the demon agreed. "I'm surprised to see you here, especially with the rumors I've heard."

Ian let out an indulgent laugh. "Which ones?"

Michael smiled, but no humor lit his red-tinged eyes. "The one where you and some Halfling murdered dozens of my kind."

That turned more than a few heads. I stiffened, but no one did anything more than look. Yet.

"A Halfling, how exotic." Ian sounded bored. "Tell me, how did I and this curious creature slaughter so many demons?"

The waitress returned with Ian's drink, pausing Michael's reply. Ian saluted her with his glass before pressing a hundred-dollar bill into her hand.

"Keep 'em coming, poppet."

She tucked the bill into her cleavage, then made a show of fluffing her breasts as if the cash had somehow managed to flatten them.

There goes your painless death!

"Details are sketchy," Michael said once she'd walked away. "Some say the Halfling is a demon-vampire hybrid. Some say she's a vampire-witch hybrid. Some wonder if the story is just bullshit meant to scare other demons into backing Dagon."

"Eh, Dagon," Ian said as if he remembered everything about the demon. "Always trying to mastermind something."

Michael's brows rose. "You're saying none of it is true?"

"Tell you what is true, I need to speak to Ashael," Ian replied, and raised his glass. "Ashael, this is Ian. A bag of jewels is yours if you come to me at once."

With that unusual toast, Ian downed his shot and waved for a new one, which his very attentive waitress handed him. Then he repeated the toast and drank again.

Not a toast, then. An alcohol-based summoning ritual. Ashael was either very powerful to hear Ian's call with such a weak conduit, or he was so attuned to booze that he should get an AA sponsor immediately.

Then again, Ashael could also be very clever. By giving people a weakened summoning ritual to use, Ashael could choose to ignore it, whereas the usual blood, specific symbols, and true-name ritual made a demon's appearance mandatory, not optional.

Michael grunted. "You're brave to summon Ashael. If he believes these rumors, he'll slaughter you on sight."

Powerful *and* clever, then. My teeth ground. *Stop calling him, Ian! You're already in over your head.*

"You're still on about that rubbish?" Ian scoffed. "Would've thought you were too old to believe in fairy tales."

"So, it isn't true?" Michael persisted.

Ian gave him a tolerant look. "Mate, if it were, would I be drinking all by myself in a place like this?"

Yes! I silently screamed. *Because you're trying to be the first vampire to kill another vampire from sheer stress alone!* Gods, there were days when I missed my former, blissful apathy. Caring about someone this much was exhausting.

Michael shrugged, but none of the intentness left his gaze. "I suppose we'll find out."

The other demons started drifting closer to Ian's table. Worse, it sounded like more demons were now coming from the mine to gather near the room's only exit. I began pulling power from wherever I could feel water. There wasn't much due to the decades-long underground coal fires in this town. I stretched my senses further. My other nature roused, rattling the bars on her cage. As if I didn't have enough to deal with.

"Playing hard to get, Ashael?" Ian said, raising his glass as if he didn't notice the trap closing around him. "I'll make it *two* bags of jewels, but only if you get your arse here now."

Sure, keep trying to bring another powerful demon! I silently raged. *Forty or fifty demons against two are suicidal odds, but forty or fifty-ONE against two is a party!*

Michael leaned back, flashing Ian an arrogant look as the demons in the room now loomed around Ian's table, while new demons formed a barrier at the exit. Even the band abandoned their instruments to join the menacing crowd.

Ian eyed them as he set his empty shot glass down. "Wouldn't come any closer if I were you, mates."

Michael's brows rose. "Why is that?"

Ian smiled with luxuriant menace. "Because you won't like what I'll do. Moreover, from her scent, my wife is already brassed off, and you do *not* want to meet her when she's angry."

From her scent . . . Ian knew that I was here?

Michael laughed. "You, married? That's almost as funny as you threatening us with someone who isn't here."

"Oh, she's here," Ian replied, sounding amused now. "It's dangerous, and I told her not to come. That meant nothing could keep her away."

I wasn't even insulted. *So you* do *still know me,* I thought with dark appreciation.

Michael's expression hardened. "Enough stalling. We're going to collect that bounty on you now—"

"Not before I get my two bags of jewels," a smooth voice interrupted.

I hadn't seen anyone teleport in here, and I'd been watching. No, the tall man with the closely cropped hair, handsome features, dark brown skin, and a stubbled jaw had appeared as if all the room's shadows suddenly coalesced into a person. Power rolled off him, too, the kind I normally only felt from a Master vampire. If that wasn't enough, the demon then turned to stare right at the corner where Leah and I floated.

I didn't move. Maybe this demon knew our general location because he could scent me the way Ian had. But since he couldn't see me, he couldn't truly be sure where I was . . .

"You can drop the clever camouflage," the demon said, bowing in our direction. "I will allow no one here to harm you."

"Ashael?" Michael looked around. "Who are you talking to?"

"The person poised to slaughter all of you, should you make another threatening move toward Ian," Ashael replied silkily.

One of this demon's abilities is seeing the source of every person's magic, Ian had said. Was that how Ashael could "see" me even when I was invisible? If so, it also explained his other comment. *If he sees you, he'll spot your half-demigod nature before you can say hallo . . .*

"Hello," I said, dropping from Leah's arms. As soon as I did, I became visible. Every demon looked stunned except for Ashael, who stared at me with an inscrutable expression.

"My lovely bride," Ian drawled. "Good of you to join us."

Chapter 16

I told myself it was the tenseness of the situation that made me pick the bitchiest reply. "Oh, *now* you remember we're married? You didn't seem to recall that when you were giving your waitress the visual version of a mammogram earlier!"

Ian's chuckle rolled across my nerves as if it were coated in spikes. "Jealous? Good, I intended that. You don't consider our marriage an 'unfortunate technicality' now, do you?"

I was going to beat him bloody. I'd make it too painful for even him to enjoy. But not when we were surrounded by demons, the most dangerous one sizing up our exchange with interest.

"You must have no idea what she is, to anger her on purpose," Ashael stated.

"I know exactly what she is," Ian answered, staring into my eyes. "More importantly, I know she's mine."

The statement might have been romantic if we were alone. In a room full of demons, it smacked of male possessiveness. Then again, I'd just chastised him for *looking* at another woman, so I supposed I didn't have much room to complain. But I did give him a challenging arch of the brow that said, *Am I?* clearer than any words.

Ian's instant, sensual grin said, *Yes, you are.*

Then he tossed two velvet bags at Ashael. The demon tested their weight before putting them in his pocket with an appreciative grunt. "Whatever else you are, you're not cheap. This is enough to buy you an uninterrupted hour of my time."

"Not here," Ian said, with a languid glance around. "Hospitality seems to have waned."

I came toward Ian. A single glance from Ashael had the demons parting to clear a path for me. He must be formidable indeed to garner such instant obedience without even speaking.

"I'm coming with you," I said, my tone daring Ian to argue.

He only curled an arm around me while reaching out to Ashael with his other hand. "Shall we?"

"We shall," Ashael said, taking Ian's hand and lightly placing his other one on my back.

As soon as he did, everything blurred. If I didn't throw up from all this teleporting, I'd be amazed. Moments later, I blinked as bright sunshine met my eyes.

We were now on a balcony overlooking a densely packed city. I had no idea which city until I saw the snow-coated peak of a tall, very distinctive mountain in the distance. Wait . . . that couldn't be. But the curved roofs culminating in unique points on many of the buildings in the city confirmed it.

"Mount Fuji," I murmured in astonishment. Ashael had teleported us all the way from Pennsylvania to Japan in seconds.

The balcony had a shoji that was ajar. I pushed the paper-and-wood door aside to reveal a traditional Japanese tea room with a low ceiling, no furniture, and only an alcove with a calligraphy scroll for decoration. Ashael sat on the floor where the sun's rays couldn't reach him.

"Come," he said. "Join me."

I could think of a thousand reasons why a tea party with a demon wasn't a good idea, but I removed my shoes, nudging Ian to do the same. Another shoji opened and a lovely Asian woman with long black hair came forward with slippers. "Thank you," Ian said in Japanese. After we put the slippers on, we sat on the floor near Ashael.

"Safe to speak freely?" Ian asked, switching to English.

Ashael smiled at the woman, who set a platter with steaming teacups in front of him. That also broke from the formal tea ritual, but maybe Ashael wasn't a formal guy. "Yes. Mao and her family have been loyal to me for seven generations."

"Good enough," Ian said. "I need passage to Yonah's house."

Ashael's teacup had been halfway to his mouth. At that, he set it down and stared at Ian until my other nature lunged against her bars hard enough to darken my vision. She knew a death threat when she saw one.

Ian laced his fingers in mine. The simple gesture grounded me. *Stay down*, I ordered my other half. *I've got this.*

When my vision cleared, I saw Ashael smile thinly at our clasped hands. "You were wise to bring her with you. Otherwise, you'd already be dead for saying that name to me."

"I know you have to disown Yonah," Ian replied coolly. "Can't have it getting out that you're still friendly with the most wanted bloke in the demon world, can you?"

"Careful," Ashael replied in that dangerously smooth voice. "You've already used up almost all the goodwill you purchased."

Ian leaned forward. "You might not trust me, but you see what she is, so you know you can trust her. If she betrayed you over Yonah, you'd betray her to other vampires." A humorless smile edged Ian's mouth. "Just like the nuclear deterrent, no one fancies mutually assured destruction."

Ashael let out a short laugh. "I see you are no less bold for someone who has supposedly settled down."

"I'm married, not settled down," Ian countered, raising my hand to kiss it. "Never had someone take me higher, in fact."

My eyes began to sting. Ian might not remember what we'd had together, but when he said things like that . . . it *felt* the same. And despite knowing better, I'd missed that feeling so much, I wanted to dive into it until I drowned.

That's why I continued to study the teacup Mao placed before me. Ashael didn't need to see what I felt for Ian in my eyes. With luck, the demon would take my lowered gaze as shyness.

"Even if I did know how to contact Yonah," Ashael said after a long pause, "why would I risk doing so for you?"

I glanced up in time to see Ian's smile. "Because you hate Dagon, yet you can't kill him. Demons get right nasty when one of you murders your own, and Dagon's too powerful for you to send a regular vampire or ghoul after him. But she and I can kill him. More angry demons aren't going to frighten us; we've already got a bounty on our heads. Best of all, our only price is a meeting with Yonah."

Now, I met Ashael's gaze so he could see the cold purpose in mine. "We'll put Dagon in the ground, I promise you."

A thin smile stretched Ashael's mouth. "I believe you . . . Ariel."

Shock exploded in me. Only two people had known that Ariel was my real name: Tenoch, my long-dead sire, and pre-memory-loss Ian. Now, that number had just jumped to three.

Chapter 17

*I*t took all my control to keep my features frozen in their bland mask. "What a good guess. You'd be a hit at a carnival. Care to try for my height and weight next?"

Ashael laughed, reminding me that few things unsettled me as much as a demon finding me amusing. Unbidden, memories strafed my mind. *Blood coating my skin. My voice gone from screaming. Something wet and heavy spilling from my gutted midsection before coiling like scarlet snakes beside me . . .*

I blinked, banishing the memory of that torture and murder before hundreds more came to replace it. Dagon had used my ability to resurrect as the foundation for his own worship, claiming *he'd* been the one to raise me from the dead. For the first two decades of my life, I'd believed him. He'd murdered me over and over to gain power for himself, and I'd worshipped him for it.

Out of all the cruelties Dagon had inflicted on me, that was the most unforgivable.

"I don't know your height or weight because this image of a slip of a girl with blue eyes and yellow hair isn't the real you." Ashael all but purred at me.

I dropped my glamour. That was the least of my secrets now. My long silver-blue-and-gold hair streamed down my back as my body filled out until it strained the jeans I wore. My sweater had been bulky to help ward off the cold temperatures, so that still fit comfortably, at least.

Ashael's gaze raked me with a thoroughness that made Ian's scent sharpen with anger. *Good,* I thought crossly. I still wasn't over the stunt he'd pulled with the waitress yet.

"Stunning," the demon drew out.

"Impatient," I countered. "Do we have a deal or not?"

Ashael waved away Mao, then waited until she closed the screened door behind her before he spoke. Guess his trust of her had its limits. "Meet my terms, and we might," Ashael replied.

"Greed is natural for demons, but do try to restrain yourself," Ian said mildly. "Dagon's death is all you'll get."

Ashael shrugged. "You're going to kill Dagon anyway, so that's no incentive for me. But there *is* an ancient relic I'm interested in. Fetch it for me, and we have a deal."

Ian eyed him with all the wariness I felt. "Prove to me you can deliver us to Yonah first."

Ashael dumped the contents of his teacup onto the platter. Then he used his fingernail to slice open his wrist. When the cup was full of his blood, Ashael closed his eyes. He didn't speak, nor did his hands move, but magic flowed out until it made my skin crawl. When it crested, Ashael opened his eyes.

His blood rose from the cup, stretching to form the head of a middle-aged bald man with a Roman nose and deep-set eyes. When that head turned to see all three of us and his expression showed surprise, I realized the creation wasn't merely a magic-infused molding. This was a blood-coated conference call.

"Yonah," Ashael said to the head in Aramaic when he turned back to him. "I might be sending two sojourners to you."

Yonah looked back at Ian and me. "Are these the sojourners?"

Ashael flashed a cold grin our way. "If they meet my test."

Ian moved until he was facing the head. "If this is the true Yonah," he said, also in Aramaic, "tell me the name of the red-haired demon-branded bloke who met you a few years ago inquiring about refuge."

"Nathanial," Yonah replied at once.

Ian nodded as if satisfied. "Tell me about this relic," he said to Ashael.

The blood-formed head turned back into liquid that splashed down onto the platter. It reminded me that I was hungry, not that I'd feed from demon blood. Aside from my repugnance for their species, demon blood was also a vampire inebriant.

"It's an ancient horn," Ashael replied. "Guarded, of course, though the guards are vampires, so it should be easy for you to get past them. That's why you're going alone, Ian."

"Like hell he is," I said at once.

Ashael sighed. "Ariel—"

"Veritas." My voice was sharp. "I don't know how you heard that other name, but I don't answer to it."

Ashael inclined his head. "Veritas, then. You might not like this condition, but it's nonnegotiable. Besides, with the added benefit of Dagon's power, Ian should have little trouble overcoming half a dozen or so vampire guards."

Ian's expression didn't change, but he was still holding my hand, so I felt his temperature rise a notch. "See that, do you?" he asked in a careless tone. "Didn't know your powers included spotting evidence of a demon brand."

Ashael smiled. "You're not branded by Dagon anymore. Somehow, you have his power another way."

Ian's temperature spiked again; something that wouldn't be possible for a normal vampire, but Ashael had just confirmed he knew Ian wasn't normal. More significant, Ashael confirmed that a demon's power signature was as unique as we'd hoped. Now we *really* needed Yonah to do that tracking spell.

"Why do you want Veritas to stay here?" Ian asked, as if nothing of importance had occurred.

Ashael's smiled vanished. "I don't trust you. Yes, what I know about Veritas means she has every reason not to betray me, but I can see *you* keeping the horn and selling Yonah's location to the highest bidder while leaving her to pay the price."

I let out a contemptuous laugh even as Ian bit out, "That won't happen."

"Prove it," Ashael stated. "Steal a priceless artifact and give it to me instead of keeping it for yourself. Then I'll know you value her more than your infamous tendency to add yet another treasure to your vast collection of rarities."

"Done," Ian replied, letting go of my hand.

I muttered a curse in Sumerian, then picked up Ashael's cup and drained the demon's remaining blood from it.

Ian gave me an amazed look. "What are you doing?"

"Getting drunk," I replied tartly. "I can't take more of your eagerness to get killed while sober."

He snorted. "A few vampire guards will hardly kill me—"

"If this was this easy, Ashael would've done it himself," I interrupted. Damn demon's blood should have hit me with the potency of a bottle of tequila. Instead, it only felt like a few shots. "He's lying about the danger and you know it."

"Of course he is," Ian said in an exasperated tone. "But I can still handle it."

He probably could. I was the one who couldn't take this, and I didn't know how to make my constant, irrational fear stop. I hated being this out of control when it came to Ian! If I could rip my feelings out and murder them, I would.

"Is this the part where you're telling me to stay back only because you want me to follow you?" I asked in a harsh tone. Better to be angry at him than feel the borderline-panic coursing through me.

"If I'd told you Ashael needed to know what you were before he'd grant us passage to Yonah, you would have shown him whether you wished to or not," Ian replied, not flinching from my anger. "By telling you that Ashael would spot your nature on sight while also telling you *not* to come, I made it your choice to reveal yourself to him. Not mine."

My emotions ripped right down the middle, making me want to slap Ian, then kiss him until neither of us could think. He'd shamelessly manipulated me, but he'd done it to protect me. How could I, of all people, fail to understand that?

"She's a real bitch," I muttered.

Ian gave me a wary look. "Who?"

"Karma. Has to be a woman. Nothing else is that vicious, patient, or effective."

A smile tugged Ian's mouth. "How drunk are you, luv?"

"Not nearly drunk enough," I said grimly. "But if you're doing this alone, I need to give you something. In private."

Ashael rose. "I'll give you both a moment—"

"Not that kind of privacy," I interrupted, not looking away from Ian. "Take me where no one can see or overhear us."

Ian pulled me into his arms, saying, "Be back shortly. Don't go anywhere," to Ashael.

Then he teleported us out of there.

Chapter 18

I 'd seen Mount Fuji many times, but I'd never been to its summit. The snow was up to my knees, clouds turned the horizon into an endless expanse of white, and the cold slammed into me like a train smashing into someone tied to its tracks. Still, this more than met my requirements. *No one* was near us.

Ian turned his back to the freezing wind while tightening his arms around me so his body took the brunt of it. I leaned into him, feeling his chin rest on top of my head. I expected him to ask why I'd had him bring us out here, but he didn't. He only held me until tears stung my eyes, which I couldn't blame on the icy wind because he blocked most of it.

There were many reasons why I shouldn't feel the way I did about him. It was too soon, I was too old for him, the timing couldn't be worse, he'd lost over half his memory, I'd lost my immortality, Dagon was determined to kill both of us . . . and it all washed away when he bent and his lips covered mine.

I no longer felt the cold or the wind or the snow. All I felt was how tightly he held me, how his power sparked against my skin, and how he kissed me with delicate savageness, as if he sensed my turmoil and sought to turn it into raw need instead.

He would have succeeded. Our icy surroundings wouldn't have stopped me. My prior resolution to keep him at emotional arm's length wouldn't, either—I'd already failed at that. But there was one thing stronger than even my desire for him.

"Stop," I murmured, ducking my face away. "I told you, I have something important to show you."

The wind snatched away his groan. "What, my sad death from a terminal case of blue balls?"

I stifled my snort. "Being celibate won't kill you, but I don't trust Ashael not to send you into a trap. Yes, you can handle yourself, but I'm incurably paranoid, so humor me. Plus, a new memory *could* drop you at the wrong moment."

He shrugged. "Have your ghost friend tail me, then, if it'll make you fret less. For all I know, she's here now."

"Leah?" I called out, sighing when there was no response. "She probably couldn't keep up with Ashael teleporting us. Something about demons throws off ghosts, but that's off topic. If this relic retrieval *is* a trap, I, ah, wanted to show you how you can summon me."

He stared at me until more than the cold and bracing wind made me squirm. "Are you saying what I think you're saying?"

I shrugged as if I wasn't revealing my most dangerous secret. "Whatever my other nature is, it can be summoned the same way demons can. Good thing the ritual isn't as complex and dangerous as summoning my father. That's deadly, but to summon me, you just need my blood, my true name, and these symbols."

So saying, I pierced the tip of my finger with a fang, then drew the symbols across Ian's palm with my blood. The cold froze them into place and Ian's gaze drank in every curve of the symbols. When I was done, I shifted self-consciously.

"You can take a picture with your mobile, if you want."

"No need." His voice was thick. "I've memorized them."

Now, we both knew I couldn't run from him again. If he summoned me, I'd be pulled to his side no matter where in the world I was. But I hadn't been able to run before anyway. Not for long. What drew me to him was stronger than any ritual.

I wasn't ready to say that out loud, so I dragged my palm across a fang, then surrounded the falling blood with ice and shaped it into a small cylinder that I covered with magic. Now, the blood-filled ice cylinder would take weeks to melt instead of minutes. I handed it to Ian, still not meeting his eyes.

"Keep this with you."

He bent me backward with the force of his kiss. When I was burning on the inside despite the brutal cold, he released me.

"After I get back with that relic," he said in a tight voice. "You *will* be in my bed."

I hadn't been able to look at him before. Now, I couldn't look away. "Why? We never used a bed before."

The sound he made was too rough to be a groan. "Then it's high time that we broke one."

$\mathcal{I}$an borrowed weapons from Ashael when we returned. As he picked his deadly choices, Ashael told Ian that the horn was located inside an underwater structure off Japan's westernmost island of Yonaguni. Since that was beyond Ian's teleporting skills from our current location, Ashael teleported us to a condo in Taipei, putting Ian in range of the ruins.

As soon as we were there, Ian gave me a quick, hard kiss, then teleported away without another word. I was usually the one who led the charges, so I'd always assumed staying behind was the easy part. Wrong. I felt each tick of the clock as if it were an enemy's blade slicing into my most vulnerable parts.

To distract myself, I looked out at the city. Ashael's condo had a great view of the many high-rise buildings in Taipei. Here and there, glimpses of green peeked out from the urban landscape, but more natural formations like gardens or parks were few and far between.

I doubted I'd ever outgrow my dislike of high-rises. They still felt . . . wrong, probably because for most of my life, structures hadn't been much higher than the ziggurats that used to dot ancient Mesopotamia when I was human.

I stopped before I allowed myself to lament the other changes the industrial age had wrought, but kept pretending to be interested in the city. It gave me an excuse to stay in the sun's rays. Ashael sat on a sofa in the darkest corner of the condo, which was decorated all in marble, sleek metals, and wrought iron. The only nod to any formerly living organisms was the silk cushions and silk covering on the silvery-gray couches.

"Why would a group of vampires choose an underwater structure to hide a relic in?" I asked when I could no longer stand counting the minutes since Ian had left.

"For one, it's demon proof," Ashael replied, a smile curling his lips. "We can't teleport through significant amounts of salt water. Did you know that?"

I didn't, but I'd be sure to remember that. "What's the other reason?"

A shrug. "It was forgotten by history for thousands of years. Divers stumbled upon it a few decades ago, but none of the humans can agree if it was a man-made structure or a natural formation, so it's not being excavated. Its remote location, strong currents, and sharks also keep most humans away."

No wonder a group of vampires had repurposed it as a vault. It now also made sense why Ashael was so eager to send Ian after the relic. Any other vampire would have to beat their way through the thick stone, alerting the guards. But Ian could teleport in, get the horn, and teleport out. A simple smash-and-grab, if Ashael was telling the truth.

I still didn't trust that he was. Call me jaded, but the last time I'd trusted a demon, I'd ended up ritually murdered for two decades.

"Care for something to drink?" Ashael asked, pouring himself a glass of triple-malt Balvenie scotch.

"No thanks."

A silver knife appeared in Ashael's hand. I tensed, but all he did was press its tip to his wrist. "Something stronger?"

I gave him a level look. "No."

Ashael leaned back, toying with the handle of his knife. "Your concern for Ian is wasted, you know."

From his tone, that wasn't an endorsement of Ian's fighting skills. I let out a short laugh. "Won't you be surprised when he shows up with that relic, then? If you don't already have a spot picked out for it, might I suggest shoving it up your ass."

Instead of being offended, Ashael laughed. Then his chuckles died off and he gave me a sardonic look. "I've seen many women and men smitten by Ian. They all believed they were special to him, too. He's talented that way. He doesn't even have to lie. They simply infer what they want to hear from everything he *doesn't* say."

"Speaking from experience?" Ashael was gorgeous, dangerous, and powerful; a combination Ian would have found enticing.

Ashael let out an indulgent laugh. "No. My relationship with Ian was strictly business. He's shrewd about not mixing the two. You should have kept it strictly business with him, too."

Why did men always feel entitled to comment on a woman's sex life? "You must have me confused me with someone who gives a shit about your opinion."

The red lights in Ashael's dark brown eyes began to glow. "You might not, but Ian makes you reckless, and you have far too many secrets to be reckless if you want to survive."

I hadn't been lectured this much since my sire Tenoch was alive. "Once again, how is that any of your concern?"

He only smiled. "Have you figured out the real curse of longevity? Boredom. The monotony just wears at you, doesn't it? If you're lucky, every several thousand years or so, you'll find something that rouses your interest. If that something happens to be forbidden, well, all the more exciting, then."

Is that what he thought Ian was to me? An escape from boredom? If I cared, I'd correct his misassumption, but I didn't, so all I did was laugh. "As the kids say, what*ever*."

"I wasn't talking about you." Ashael's tone sharpened. "I was talking about your father."

Now he had my attention. "What about my father?"

His smile said he knew he'd scored a hit. "Did you never wonder how the embodiment of the river between life and death found himself acting as a lowly doorman by assuming the role of Warden of the Gateway to the Netherworld? Or did you truly believe your mother was the first to rouse his interest enough for him to stray where it was forbidden?"

The embodiment of the river between life and death . . .

Was that what my father was? Ancient Sumerians had worshipped him as Enki, the god of water. Egyptians had revered him as Aken, custodian of the boat that carried the souls of the dead to the underworld. Greeks had called him Charon, the boatman of the river Styx, and every time I'd seen my father, he'd helmed a boat on a river made of pure darkness.

But if that's what my father was, what did that make me? The supernatural equivalent of a Netherworld side creek?

I gave Ashael a measuring look. "How do you know so much about my father?"

Ashael flicked that knife across his wrist, filling the empty glass I'd ignored with his blood. When it was full, he filled another crystal glass with his blood. And another.

"I told you: I'm not drinking that."

"I thought you'd want to check in on Ian," he replied. "He isn't wearing a body camera, so this is the next best thing."

With that, Ashael's power blasted out and his blood rose into the air. It stretched into impossible quantities that took up half the room before forming into a red-coated image of Ian walking down a narrow hallway. From his movements, Ian wasn't underwater, so this part of the monolith's interior must be dry. Unlike with Yonah, Ian didn't seem aware that we were watching him. With his every stride, the blood changed, showing a real-time image of Ian and his immediate surroundings. It was breathtaking—and frightening.

Ashael could spy on anyone this way. Or was he limited in what he could see? Either way, it explained how Ashael knew the location of the relic and how many vampires were guarding it.

Two blood-coated figures suddenly formed and jumped Ian. "Eh, more of you?" Ian said in annoyance before he conjured up a tactile spell. Flung backward, his attackers twitched when they hit the ground as if severely electrocuted.

Ian stepped over them, pausing to kick one that reached out weakly for his ankle before he continued on.

"He didn't kill them." Ashael sounded surprised.

"Why would he?" I asked without looking away.

"They attacked him," Ashael pointed out, as if I hadn't noticed.

Did I really need to explain? Of course I did, mercy was an unfamiliar concept to demons. "They're defending their vault. Ian wouldn't take that personally. He also wouldn't kill people who've done him no wrong if he can defeat them by other means."

Even now, Ian's fingers were moving, forming another tactile spell. When he rounded a corner, another duo of guards lunged at him. This time, he knocked them unconscious before they even touched him, whistling as he hopped over them, too.

I'd worried for nothing. Ian wasn't being hampered by a new memory or overwhelmed by greater-than-expected opposition. He hadn't even bothered to draw his borrowed weapons yet.

He went through another five guards using magic before he entered a sacramental chamber. I'd been murdered on enough altars to know one when I saw it. This was on a raised stone dais, with a mummified-looking body on top of it. A black horn as long as a broadsword rested on top of the remains. Its tip was sharp while its hilt was as wide as my forearm. African bull kudu, I guessed, judging by the horn's double-curves in the middle. In ancient cultures, they'd often been used as weapons.

A quartet of new guards sprang out from the back of the altar. They circled Ian with the precision of hardened soldiers. Ian raised his hand, fingers weaving another spell. They must have realized what he was doing, because they abandoned their formation to lunge at him.

Ian flung the spell, then stopped, knocking only three of the four guards down. He stared at the fourth with his hand still raised.

"Timothy?" he asked in disbelief.

All I saw was a muscled male form coated entirely in Ashael's blood, but when he spoke, he also sounded stunned. And British.

"Ian? That you, mate?"

"A better question," Ian said, sounding angry now, "is why you've let me and the rest of your mates believe you're dead!"

$\mathcal{I}$ an and Timothy's forms suddenly disintegrated as the blood Ashael had used to form them splashed onto the condo's floor.

"Wait!" I cried out.

Ashael gave a diffident wave. "I'm not going to weaken myself by holding that up any longer. Besides, if this is Ian's friend, then he's in no danger, although if he tells Ian what they're guarding, you'll *really* never see him again."

"Is irritating me your version of masturbating?" I snapped. "Or are you this much of a bastard to everyone?"

Ashael gave me a genial smile. "I'm being nice. You don't want to see what I'm capable of when I'm being a bastard."

"Back at you," I said, using one of Ian's favorite lines.

"Oh, I know what you're capable of," Ashael said in a silky voice. "I've felt it both times you released your full power."

What? "How can you feel my other nature, let alone know how many times I let it take control?"

Ashael's smile widened. "You haven't guessed?"

Guessed what? Ashael knew what my father was and he knew my true name. The first he could have gotten from Dagon, but I had no idea how he'd learned the second. He could also see the origins of people's magic; something I didn't know any demon could do, but what did that tell me? Damned if I knew.

He could feel it when I used my power from my other nature.

Odd, but I could also feel his power, so we were even there. Drinking his blood hadn't intoxicated me as much as it should have. What would cause that?

Maybe he was a hybrid. If he was a vampire-demon one, that would explain his power-filled aura and less-intoxicating-than-it-should-be blood. What it wouldn't explain was how Ashael could manipulate blood with more skill than I could manipulate water. That wasn't a vampire trait. I owed my affinity with water to my other nature . . .

Ice suddenly skittered up my spine.

Did you never wonder how the embodiment of the river between life and death found himself acting as a lowly doorman by assuming the role of Warden of the Gateway to the Netherworld? Or did you truly believe your mother was the first to rouse his interest enough for him to stray where it was forbidden?

No. No. He couldn't be. Could he?

I bent down, dipping my finger in one of the many red splatters that coated the floor. This time, when I tasted Ashael's blood, I didn't focus on its less-than-expected inebriating effect. I pushed past that and the noxious taste of demons to search for something else. Something familiar.

When I found it, I closed my eyes with a mixture of despair and wonder. I'd always hoped there might be someone else out there like me. Now I knew there was, and he was a demon.

Or, more accurately, half a demon.

"Brother," I said, opening my eyes.

Ashael's smile turned into a smirk. "Little sister."

I didn't speak. Oh, I had a million questions, but who knew if he'd answer them, let alone honestly? Demons weren't trustworthy . . . and there was karma to bite me in the ass again. Out of every species, I had to be related to *this* one! It proved there was no point being bigoted. Whatever you looked down upon would eventually end up in your own family.

"When did you know?" I finally asked. "When you saw me at the mine earlier today? Or, like dear old Dad, have you known about me my whole life, but decided to ignore me anyway?"

He inclined his head. "When Dagon started telling stories of a Halfling with silver eyes that ripped the blood out of his fiercest soldiers, I wondered, of course. But I only knew for certain when I saw you earlier today."

"I ripped their water out, not their blood," I corrected.

He grunted. "Blood is over ninety percent water, so you ripped out both."

True enough. I searched his features, looking to see if we had any in common. He didn't have my gold-and-blue-streaked silvery hair, but he might have dyed his into showing only its pitch-black curls. His skin was rich dark brown, whereas mine was golden bronze, and his eyes were a deep walnut shade, while mine were silver. But he had our father's striking beauty, and Ashael didn't try to conceal his with glamour the way I did. No, Ashael flaunted his looks much the same way that Ian flaunted his.

Men. They had many strong suits, but subtlety was rarely one of them.

"Show me your real eyes," I said. All the facts pointed to him being my brother, but I still wanted proof.

"Untrusting," Ashael said, approval clear in his tone. "Good to know you're cautious about *some* men."

Another Ian reprimand. I was about to tell him where to shove that when the red glow in his eyes turned to piercing silver. Darkness also bloomed behind him, covering the condo's furnishings with a swath of fathomless obsidian—exactly how Ian had described my transformation. I'd never seen it as I didn't pause to stand in front of a mirror when it happened. But it proved Ashael was who—and *what*—he said he was.

Then the silver glow in his eyes darkened back to their natural color while that otherworldly swath vanished, all without the schizophrenic battle I would have had to wage first.

"How do you lock that half of you away without a fight?"

His brows went up. "You've kept your other nature locked away?" At my nod, Ashael began to laugh. "No wonder I felt it the two times you finally used your full powers! They must have had to explode out of whatever cage you've put them in."

I opened my mouth to reply—and Ian teleported into me, knocking me over because I hadn't braced for a large male body suddenly occupying the same space. He caught me using his right arm. His left arm was extended out and away from his body.

"Here's your sodding horn," Ian snapped at Ashael.

His head and clothes had gotten bloody since I last saw him. His shirt was also torn from shoulder to wrist, revealing that the formerly stiff horn had now curled itself multiple times around Ian's left forearm. How? Kudu horn didn't bend!

Ashael stared at the relic as if he, too, couldn't believe what he was seeing. Then he laughed, a sharp, grating sound.

"I fail to see anything funny," Ian said coldly.

"I do," Ashael said, still chuckling. "And the joke is on me. Clearly, the horn agrees with Veritas about you."

"I have nothing to do with this," I protested.

"You and the horn both think Ian is special." Ashael stopped laughing to give Ian a hard look. "I disagree, but magic as old as that horn chooses its wielder, and only rare, raw power plus the potential for more draws it."

Chooses its wielder . . . I'd heard of such objects, but had never seen one before. "Are you saying this horn was *made*?"

Ian looked at me as if I'd recently been hit hard in the head. "It's a ram's horn; a bloody ram made it."

"That's not what she means." Ashael's gaze held mine, confirming my suspicion. Then he turned to Ian. "Most weapons were forged by man, but a select few were made by the gods. You'll have heard of famous ones like Thor's hammer, Arthur's Excalibur, Poseidon's trident, and Apollo's bow, but there are lesser-known ones, like Hang Tuah's dagger, Ninurta's mace, Huitzilopochtli's ray . . . and Cain's horn."

Ian grunted. "Don't tell me *you* believe that dried-up corpse is Cain, too? Can't fathom how Timothy was deluded into joining a crazed Cain cult, but then he always was a dreamer—"

"The skeleton on the altar is Cain?" I interrupted, astonished.

"So my mate claims," Ian replied, derision coating his tone. "But even if that *was* the fabled first vampire cursed to forever drink blood as punishment for slaying his brother, Abel, he's now as dead as my virginity. Still, Timothy wouldn't leave him even after I took this"—another shake indicated the horn wrapped around Ian's forearm—"and *this* apparently has value."

Ashael arched a brow. "His acolytes think Cain will rise again, given the right mixture of blood. I've seen vampires regenerate from a skeletal state, so I suppose it's possible."

I stayed silent. Ashael didn't need to know that Ian was one of those rare vampires who could degenerate to bones and then regenerate. He knew too much already, family or no family.

Ian's eyes narrowed. "What do you mean, the right mixture of blood?"

A shrug. "His acolytes have tried many varieties. Blood of a virgin, blood of the slain, blood of the damned, blood of a vampire, blood of a ghoul, blood of a demon, blood of a demigod—I sold them that one—and countless combinations of all the above. Nothing worked. Some believe only the blood of a tri-bred will raise him since Cain also created the first ghoul."

I stiffened, then forced myself to relax. Good thing Ashael hadn't been looking my way. Ian hadn't moved so much as a muscle though he had to be thinking the same thing I was.

"A tri-bred?" Ian's voice was smoother than water. "You mean part human, part vampire, and part ghoul, like the little girl the vampire council executed recently?"

Ashael gave us a knowing look. "They were quick with that, weren't they? Almost like some on the council knew the rumor that Cain could rise if given that child's blood."

"Why wouldn't the council want a vampire with supposedly unrivaled powers like Cain back among them?" I countered.

Ashael snorted. "The same reason most people don't want their god among them, all protestations aside. Gods tend to point out their followers' hypocrisy, and few want that."

I didn't argue. History wouldn't be on my side. Instead, I said, "Best to let sleeping gods lie, then."

Ian extended his left arm to Ashael. "I don't care what the horn wants. I told you I'd fetch it for you, so here. Take it."

Ashael gave the horn a look I couldn't read. Then he met Ian's gaze and smiled as if he had never wanted it in the first place. "Who am I to argue with an ancient relic's preference? But you did fulfill your end of our bargain, so I'll fulfill mine, and take you and Veritas to Yonah's now."

"Wait." Both men turned. "We need to get Silver first," I told Ian. "He's already been alone too long."

Ashael's expression darkened. "I did *not* agree to transport anyone else."

"Believe me," I said with a dry laugh. "When you see Silver, you won't mind."

$\mathcal{T}$he small plane bounced like a stone skipping across a pond. If we got any closer to the ocean's surface, we'd soon sink like that proverbial stone, too. But Ashael seemed more concerned with staying below radar than keeping a safe distance between our aircraft and the Pacific.

Ashael teleported us everywhere else, so I'd assumed he'd teleport us to Yonah's, too. Wrong. After we picked Silver up back in Pennsylvania, Ashael had teleported us to a small, private airport in California. The Cessna Skyhawk he rolled out could have been his plane, or he could've been stealing it. With demons, either was a possibility.

Then Ashael had flown us out over the Pacific. The flight had been smooth until an hour ago. Now, another rough patch of air shook the Cessna hard enough to make us bounce in our seats. Silver whined. I reached over the short distance to his seat to give him a reassuring pat. Ashael glanced back at the Simargl and for a second, his gaze softened. Then, he caught me watching and his coolly arrogant expression returned.

Too late, I thought in amusement. *I saw that.*

Ashael's appreciation for celestial-created rarities like the horn obviously included Simargls. And Silver, who'd had a horrific experience being owned by a demon, seemed oddly at ease with Ashael. Maybe it was because Silver sensed Ashael's duel lineage? After all, Silver had loved my father on sight, too.

"You might want to hold on to your pet now," Ashael said. "It's about to get rough."

"Any rougher and we'll crash," I muttered, but picked Silver up and held him in my lap.

"Exactly," Ashael replied in a mild tone.

I waited for the punch line. When Ashael said nothing, I realized he wasn't joking.

"Explain," Ian drew out.

"If getting to Yonah's was easy, he'd be dead by now," was Ashael's reply. "Still, if either of you object to the risk, I'll turn the plane around, but then my part in this is done."

Asshole!

Not much could kill vampires, but a plane crash could. I couldn't even use the endless expanse of ocean below us to deter Ashael. The demon could teleport away before a drop of that salt water, burning to demons, touched him.

Ian pulled out his mobile. I couldn't see who he was texting because he was too quick. Then he turned it off.

"If we don't return from this flight, consider yourself marked for death by three of the world's strongest vampires," Ian said coolly. "That's only if I don't kill you myself first."

Ashael's scoff was both elegant and contemptuous. "As if you had the power to kill me."

Ian's arm slammed across Ashael's throat. The horn also shot out, its tip now elongated and very close to Ashael's eye.

"That a dare?" Ian asked.

Not a muscle on Ashael moved. Good thing, too, since one wrong slant on the yoke might slam us into the ocean.

"Ian," I said in as calm a tone as I could manage. "Please don't stab the pilot while we're still *on the plane*."

Ian kept staring at Ashael, the ram's horn a twisting, tangible threat between them. I didn't know how Ian had made it move, let alone in such a way. But he had, and Ashael acted as if the horn's tip was coated in demon poison.

"Veritas will not be harmed," Ashael finally said, his former mockery gone. "Neither will you," he added somewhat reluctantly. "You will both arrive safely. I give you my word."

Ian lowered his arm. The horn lost its rapierlike shape to coil back into the flexible one where it resembled a 3-D armband. Ashael gave the magic relic a look I couldn't read, then said, "Hold the yoke" and let Cessna's version of a steering wheel go.

Ian grabbed the yoke when Ashael closed his eyes and raised his hands. I didn't have time to ask what he was doing before his power blasted out. My eardrums ruptured from the sudden, explosive pressure shift. Ian ground out a curse I could no longer hear as blood ran from his ears, too. Still his hands remained rock steady on the controls.

Light exploded ahead of us, flashing in simultaneous bursts of colors that looked like lightning coated in rainbows. A tunnel formed amidst the dazzling display, showing a glimpse of something large and dark on the other side. Ashael opened his eyes and grabbed the controls from Ian with one hand. The other was still aloft, pouring more power into the tunnel/temporal anomaly/whatever it was. Then he steered us right into the circular kaleidoscope.

The small plane shook so hard, the metal sounded like it was screaming. I was tempted to scream, too. The plane couldn't take more of this without coming apart. I had to clutch Silver to keep him from hitting the roof from how violently we were thrown around. Still, my head bashed against the plane's side panel until I saw and tasted blood.

Suddenly, the dazzling flashes of color ceased, revealing a calm sky with a moon casting silvery beams on the ocean and island beneath it. The island was almost entirely taken up by the tall, imposing mountain I'd glimpsed from the other side of the tunnel. The punishing turbulence stopped, too, but my sigh of relief turned into a gasp when Ashael pointed us right at the mountain and increased speed.

"You see the big mountain in front of us, don't you?" Maybe he was temporarily blinded from all those flashing lights . . .

"Yes," Ashael replied, proving my ears had healed enough to hear again.

"Then why are you *aiming* for it?" I demanded.

"No one likes a backseat driver," was his airy response.

That was it. If we lived, I was committing fratricide—

We passed through the mountain instead of smashing into it. That's when I realized it was glamour designed to stop anyone from seeing the real island. A glance out the window now revealed a generous stretch of beach, lots of trees, and several buildings I could only glimpse before Ashael dropped the plane down and circled back, aiming for the beach.

I didn't bother telling him sand was too soft to land on. For all I knew, it wasn't sand at all. It was probably a runway glamoured to look like ordinary beach sand—

The plane landed hard, wheels ripping off right after tearing into the soft terrain that, yep, was sand, which I found out when it blasted through the broken windows while the plane was flipping end over end. Metal and glass also took turns pelting me, and I hit my head so hard, I was briefly knocked unconscious. When I came to, I was upside down, clutching Silver so tightly in my arms, he whimpered.

I let Silver go. He scrambled out of the nearest smashed-open window. The side door next to me suddenly tore free, revealing Ian. Blood dripped from multiple cuts as he bent to rip my seat belts off. He caught me before I fell out, ignoring my protests that I could walk. He refused to put me down until we were several meters from the smoking plane, which Ashael was now slowly crawling out of, too.

"This is your idea of her arriving here safely?" Ian asked in a blistering tone.

Ashael flicked a line of blood from his forehead once he was free from the wreckage. His cuts finished healing by the time he replied, "We're all fine, are we not?"

With that, the plane caught fire. Ian gave it a pointed look before replying, "Oh, right as rain," with scathing sarcasm.

Dammit, my luggage was about to burn! My head still rang from what had probably been a skull fracture, but I managed to pull a swath of water from the ocean and splash it onto the plane. The fire turned to smoke as the water doused the flames.

"Don't!" Ashael said, sounding appalled.

"Salt water in the engine is the least of your concerns," I replied, then stopped when all the water began streaming out of the plane and back into the ocean.

My eyes narrowed. Ashael wanted to play *that* game, huh? I pulled more water toward the plane, only to have it slam back down into the ocean so hard, it foamed.

"Stop it," I snapped to Ashael.

He paled, which was odd. He *was* getting on my last nerve, but I would hardly slaughter him over a watery version of tug-of-war between siblings . . . wait, what was he looking at?

I followed Ashael's gaze and saw something silver flash in the sea. Not a trick of the moonlight; its movements were too precise. It headed for shore, and the sea foamed in its path. Then that frothing part of the sea formed into a tall, humanoid shape that walked right out of the water to stand before us.

Oh, shit, I thought, staring at it. *What are you?*

Chapter 22

*T*he creature stared back at me. Silver growled, edging away from it. The creature glanced at the Simargl, and then it looked back at me again. At once, its body changed until it formed into an exact replica of my appearance.

"What is it?" I whispered to Ashael.

It reminded me of a water nymph, but water nymphs were tiny creatures that required constant contact with liquid to survive. This thing had been a head taller than Ian before it formed into a watery version of me, and it stood on the beach without needing to be within reach of the surf.

"Leviathan." Ashael's voice was a rasp. "They guard these shores, and no one touches the waters without their permission."

"That's information that would have been helpful *before*," I said through clenched teeth.

"How was I to know you'd break a cardinal rule within ten seconds of arriving?" Ashael shot back.

"Enough." Ian extended his left arm. The horn straightened until it resembled a long, dark sword. The creature's head swiveled toward Ian, and it smiled.

Ice coated my bones. If the grave could smile, it would look like that.

"Ian," Ashael said without looking away from the creature. "The horn might work on everything else, but it won't harm a Leviathan. Touch one of them, and you'll drown forever."

Okay, that sounded horrible. "How do I fix what I did to make it angry?" I asked Ashael in a low voice.

"Try apologizing and giving it an offering." I didn't like the new uncertainty in Ashael's tone. He might annoy me by sounding like an imperious prick most of the time, but if the Leviathan made Ashael afraid, we should all fear.

"Do *not* skimp," Ashael went on. "Leviathan are telepathic, so your offering has to be something very precious to you."

I stared at the Leviathan as I began walking toward the smoking plane, my sharp gesture warning Ian not to follow me.

"I am truly sorry for trespassing on your domain," I said as I reached inside the plane, using my hand instead of my gaze to find my luggage. Instinct told me that if I looked away from the creature, I'd regret it.

"It was a violation of your sovereignty," I went on. "I ask forgiveness only because I committed my crime in ignorance. Please"— more blind reaching, cutting myself on the twisted metal and glass until I felt the smooth sides of my biggest suitcase—"accept this offering as a token of my regret."

I pulled the suitcase out, kneeling to unzip it. I stayed in that supplicant pose as I felt around in it until my hand hit something large and hard. Slowly, I unwrapped the clothing I'd packed around the object to reveal the glittering bouquet of Faery Queen Crimsons I'd secretly brought with me.

Ian made a short, sharp sound. Now I was glad I had to keep my gaze solely on the creature. I didn't want to see Ian's face as I laid the magic-infused flowers at the Leviathan's feet. The roses seemed to add the moonlight's beams to their own blood-red radiance, shimmering as the Leviathan picked them up. It cocked its head at them in a very humanlike way, then it looked at me.

Leviathan are telepathic, so it has to be something very precious to you . . .

I let myself feel how badly I didn't want to give up the only gift Ian had given me. I opened my memory of seeing the roses for the first time, touching their petals in wonder while pretending not to want them because I couldn't bear for Ian to see how much I loved them. I also acknowledged the recklessness of taking them with me. If things took a wrong turn during our travels, I'd be caught red-handed with a magical object; something that could earn me an instant death sentence. But I hadn't wanted to part with the roses. They reminded me too much of Ian—rare, surprising, dangerous, and oh-so beautiful . . .

The Leviathan pulled the flowers into itself. They shimmered against the watery veil of its body for a moment, then both of them disappeared back into the sea.

Ashael let out an audible breath. "Whatever those were, thank the gods you had them."

Must mean my offering was accepted. "Anything else I should know about that could get me killed or drowned forever?" I asked while trying to smother my sense of loss over the roses.

Ashael gave me a sunny smile. "Not off the top of my head."

Ian gave Ashael a look that would have made anyone else back up a few steps. Then he went to the plane, grabbed his own suitcase from the smoldering remains, took mine as well, and returned to lay his free hand against my back.

"Let's head inland before the sea sends us any new visitors."

I DON'T KNOW what I expected from a magically cloaked island filled with people rejected from every supernatural species. Gloomy caves? Stone castles? Replicas of Superman's Fortress of Solitude? Whatever my expectations, they hadn't included something that reminded me of a Sandals Resort with a few medieval twists.

Bonfires made up the exterior illumination around buildings that could have been hotels or mansions, depending on your perspective. Multicolored tile roofs added vivid splashes of color atop their sand-toned walls, with plants spilling like green waterfalls over the residences' many balconies. Elaborate slides ended at mosaic-tiled swimming pools, with cabanas taking up space around the many aquatic recreation areas.

One thing was certain; I wasn't touching that water. For all I knew, those pools were day-care centers for baby Leviathan.

And all of the recreational areas were empty. The rows of windows on the hotels/mansions reflected the bonfires' glow back at us, making it impossible to see inside. I could hear the sounds of people within the buildings, though, even if few had heartbeats. The pool areas might be empty, but this place was far from deserted.

New arrivals must make the island's residents skittish. I couldn't blame them. If they were here, their species and others wanted them dead for reasons that basically amounted to "You're different, so you scare me." Funny how those same people rarely paused to consider how terrifying *they* were, handing down death sentences from their positions of power or privilege.

"Yonah's in this house," Ashael said, striding in front of us. "Come. He'll be expecting us—"

Ian had Ashael in a headlock before I could blink, that horn snapping out to draw a pearl of blood beneath the demon's eye. I knew I was bordering on the irrational side of exhaustion when I could only think, *What now?*

"What are you doing?" Ashael hissed at Ian.

"Testing a theory." Ian's voice was like silk sliding over daggers. "Earlier, my mate Timothy jumped back from this horn as if it were pure silver aimed at his heart. You also didn't move when it was near your eye on the plane, and you're not moving now even though it isn't made of demon bone. Means this horn is universally lethal, isn't it?"

My eyes widened when Ashael gritted out, "Clever boy."

The horn could kill vampires and demons? *And* form into different dimensions as if it knew what its wielder needed? No wonder Ashael had wanted it! Every warrior I knew would give their right arm for such a weapon, myself included.

"Pity you can't teleport yourself free," Ian continued. "This island's spelled against that, as I found out when I tried to get Veritas to safety after you crashed the plane, and multiple times again when that watery monstrosity threatened her. Still, makes sense. No telling who'd show up if just anyone could teleport in here, right?"

Ashael could still rip all the water out of Ian, and Ian didn't know that. "Ian, let him go," I began.

"He tried to kill me."

That cut my protest off. "What?" I said, fury slicing through me when Ashael glanced away from my accusing stare.

"Yes, by neglecting to mention something else important about the horn." Ian's tone was light despite the razor's edge of rage running through it. "Namely, that whoever takes it from its owner will get the back of their head blown off."

That's why Ashael had dropped his blood-generated spy cam right after Ian had found the horn! He hadn't been tired. Ashael hadn't wanted me to see the proof of his treachery when he could simply claim ignorance and call it an "accident" later.

"You bastard," I managed to say, my voice shaking with fury.

Ian let out a dark chuckle. "My thoughts exactly."

"Vampires can survive head wounds," Ashael hissed. "Getting captured and interrogated was the least you deserved for using Veritas as your latest plaything."

"Oh, the head wound wouldn't have killed me," Ian agreed. "But the other guards might have, when I was defenseless. Luckily for me, one of the guards was an old mate of mine. More than that, I sired him, and every vampire knows the greatest sin among our kind is betraying your sire unto death. That's why he kept me safe while I healed, so I woke up with the horn wrapped around my arm like a bloody pet. Must've decided it liked me after it nearly decapitated me. I knew Ashael had set me up when he refused to take the horn from me earlier. He didn't because he knew what would happen, didn't you, mate?"

Ashael's gaze slanted to Ian before it settled on me. One look, and I knew every word was true.

"Understand," Ashael said in a vehement tone. "I've known Ian for decades. He loves only himself. I will allow no one to take advantage of you, especially a man who will use and discard you the same way he's used and discarded so many others—"

Ian shoved the horn's sharp tip into Ashael's eye. Ashael shuddered and smoke poured from the blackening hole. My vision burned and my throat felt like it was trying to choke me. I wanted Ashael dead for what he'd done, but . . . I had always longed to have a sibling.

For a while, Tenoch had been my family, then his loss devastated me and sent me further into my shell. Now, suddenly, I had a brother. A twisted, chauvinistic brother, but in his way, Ashael had believed he was protecting me. If Ian killed him, he also killed any hope I had at seeing if there could be a real family bond between me and Ashael that went deeper than our secret blood tie.

"Ian." My voice was strained. "Let him go."

Maybe Ashael realized how much he'd fucked up. That would explain why he hadn't ripped the water out of Ian to stop him. No, Ashael was leaving what happened up to me, proving again that there was more to Ashael than his attempt to get Ian arrested and imprisoned so he'd stay away from me.

Ian looked at me in amazement. "You want this sod to live? Don't tell me you return his obvious interest."

"Asheal *is* interested in me, but not how you think." I cleared my throat to ease its tightness. "I'm his, ah, sister."

"You're *what*?" The horn's tip froze.

"His sister." Saying it out loud somehow made Ashael's betrayal hurt worse. I drew in a breath to get the rest of it out. "He realized that when he saw my father's lineage in me with his ability earlier. He . . . my father is his father, too."

Ian lowered the ram's horn and shoved Ashael away. The demon caught himself before he stumbled, a humorless smile curling his mouth. "Once again, you show more honor than I thought you capable of. She must bring out the best in you."

"Or you have no idea who Ian truly is," I corrected at once. "You believed the mirage, which caused you to underestimate Ian so much, you failed to imprison him with your horn retrieval trick. Instead, he almost killed you twice today."

Ashael inclined his head. "Point taken."

"Glad that's settled. This isn't." I landed a kick in Ashael's groin that doubled him over. Then he snapped back at the uppercut I delivered to his jaw. Bone crunched and my hand burned, but blood flew from Ashael's mouth. *Worth it!*

"Try to get Ian arrested or imprisoned again, and you're dead," I snarled. "You're only alive now because I always wanted a brother or sister, plus in your twisted demon mind, you thought you were protecting me. But *you don't get to choose* who I'm with, so I will kill you if you so much as plot to give Ian a stubbed toe in the future—"

Ian caught my next punch in mid-swing. "Think he gets it, luv."

I stared at him. "You were going to kill him two minutes ago! Why are you protecting him now?"

A grim smile flitted across Ian's mouth. "I'd still like to kill him, but if I had a sister, I wouldn't want a bloke like me near her, either. Can't murder my new brother-in-law for something I'd do myself, can I? Besides, he's not even fighting back."

I'd noticed that, and it only made me angrier. "Come on, you sexist demon, fight me! You think I can't take it?"

"I know you can, but I, too, have always longed for a sibling," Ashael replied, dark eyes now blazing red. "You are my only family this side of the veil. I've had twice your lifespan to feel abandoned, abnormal, and alone, so some blood and pain are nothing if they're the cost of my sister's forgiveness."

Damn him, damn him, damn him! How could I keep beating him after he said things like that? And how could I disown him when he was the only person who truly understood what I'd been through, since Ashael had lived it for twice as long as I had?

But he'd set Ian up to be imprisoned or worse. I couldn't overlook that, even if Ashael *had* acted out of a supernaturally demented sense of big-brother protectiveness.

Ian's arm slipped around my shoulders. "Family," he said in a conversational tone. "Can't live with 'em, can't kill 'em unless you really, *really* mean it."

A choked laugh escaped me. Ian should know; he'd killed his biological father over a far more terrible betrayal.

"I want you to leave, Ashael," I said. Pain flashed in his eyes until I added, "I need some time before I can look at you without wanting to smash your face in."

"Time as in decades, or a century?" he asked warily.

Now my laugh was even more ragged. To him, either probably didn't seem long. Guess I was still too young to measure time that way. "I meant a year or two. We'll see."

By then, I'd have tracked down the other resurrected souls and killed Dagon, or I'd be dead. Either way, my schedule would be clear.

Ashael's gaze flicked to Ian before he looked back at me. "Whenever you want to see me, raise a glass and call my name in any of the places I frequent. Ian knows where they are."

"Yes, I'm aware of your alcohol-based summoning ritual. Very millennial of you," I noted.

Ashael gave a brief smile at that. "Until that day, then," he said, and walked away.

I waited until I couldn't see Ashael before I turned to Ian. "I was going to tell you that he was my brother, but . . ." My gesture tried to encompass everything that had happened.

"The timing wasn't right until I nearly murdered him in front of you?" he supplied, a sardonic smile curling his mouth.

"Yes, that."

Ian's smile faded. "We've had terrible timing, but we're going to fix that."

I wanted to believe him. I just wasn't very optimistic. But I smiled as if doubt wasn't chewing at me like a school of ravenous piranhas.

"Let's find Yonah and get started, then."

Chapter 23

I could start a joke with, "A vampire, a demon, and a ghoul walked into a pool area," but the looks the approaching trio gave us didn't lend to humor. After needing to open a temporal rift to see a glamour-concealed island you had to crash-land onto before traversing past Leviathan-filled seas, I rather thought that anyone who wandered onto the back patio of Yonah's house had already passed the security test, but from the three guards' expressions, they disagreed.

"Names," the ivory-skinned vampire said, a Russian accent coloring the word. I didn't let her delicate build, sarong-style dress or the pretty seashell comb in her thick brown hair fool me. Her appearance said *lovely and breakable*, but the power vibrating from her aura said, *Test me at your peril.*

"Ian," he replied, his brow faintly arching at me.

"Ariel." I could hardly use my vampire Law Guardian name. I also wasn't wearing any glamour, which caused the blue-eyed, blonde-haired demon's gaze to linger over my appearance.

"Body like Beyoncé, hair like Daenerys Targaryen," he murmured with open lust.

"Temper like the Punisher," I countered. An appreciative look was one thing, but I felt like I needed a shower after that vigorous eye-fucking. "With a husband that's imagining ten different ways to kill you before you even take your eyes off my ass," I added, seeing the new, lethal flare in Ian's gaze.

"Twenty," Ian corrected, tone as smooth as a well-thrust blade. "And so few only because she just admitted to something she's been denying for weeks."

What? Oh, damn, I *had* called him the "h" word! Where was a Leviathan to endlessly drown me when I needed it?

"We're here to see Yonah," I said, as if that could erase the new, crackling tension between me and Ian. "Ashael told Yonah to expect us, so point the way or move aside."

A smile quirked the Russian vampire's mouth. "Follow me."

Silver trotted behind us as we went into the room overlooking the pool. The only decoration or furniture it boasted was plants on various stands. The bareness highlighted the large stone fountain with a carved Medusa in the middle of the room. She didn't look ugly or monstrous the way legend claimed. This Medusa was beautiful, the snakes gently haloing her head with devotion instead of their reputed mindless menace.

Our guards led us past the fountain room into a library. Shelves covered the walls to the ceiling, while leather couches were arranged around the open stone hearth in the center of the room. First fountains, now fire pits. If we passed a mud shrine in the next room, all the elements would be represented.

"Wait here," the Russian vampire directed, indicating one of the generous-sized couches. "I will bring Yonah to you."

I sat, weariness urging me to stretch out until I was lying flat. I resisted the temptation even though dawn now bathed the windows with streaks of gold. If I were a new vampire, I'd have no choice but to sleep, but I was thousands of years past the anesthetizing effects of the rising sun.

Silver sat on the floor near me, while Ian folded his long, lean frame into the opposite corner of my couch. He looked completely relaxed, arms resting on the back of the couch and legs stretched out in front of him, but his eyes told a different story. They moved over our surroundings with tactical thoroughness, gauging threats and assessing advantages.

I didn't know why I wasn't doing the same. Ashael had promised we'd be safe here, but his word had hardly proven to be infallible. I was tired, but I'd remained on high alert while practically dead on my feet from exhaustion before. So why wasn't I scoping the place out while coiled and ready to fight the way Ian was?

You don't have to.

The truth of that hit me, as unexpected as a sniper's bullet. Tenoch had taught me to rely only on myself, but I wasn't fighting to be at my best now as I knew that Ian would alert me if things took a dangerous turn. Until then, I could take a moment to relax, knowing I was safe because he wouldn't let anything hurt me while I was vulnerable.

Was this . . . was this what trust felt like?

If so, it was like sinking into a warm bath after an achingly brutal day. I wanted to wrap myself in the glorious, unfamiliar feeling, but it was also an indictment on everything I'd done since Ian had come back from the dead. I thought Ian couldn't survive the threats I still had to face, yet he'd proven more than able to meet every challenge I'd feared plus several I hadn't even thought of. Now, I was the one leaning on him, not the other way around.

I'd ripped my heart apart these past several weeks for nothing, hadn't I? For *nothing!* If it wouldn't look severely psychotic, I'd start punching myself in the face.

Footsteps jerked my attention to the far corner in the room. Our three guards reappeared when one of the book shelves suddenly slanted open, revealing a door. A hidden passageway: how very old-school. A new, bald vampire of medium height also came from the secret bookshelf entrance. He had sand-colored skin, a Roman nose, pleasant features, and a swimmer's build. Ian leapt to his feet when he saw him. I followed suit, smiling to indicate friendly intentions, because I recognized him from Ashael's blood-soaked conference call yesterday.

"Yonah," I said. "Pleased to finally meet you."

Ian's hands flashed with rapid movements. For a shocked moment, I thought he was conjuring a spell. Then a smile wreathed Yonah's face and his hands moved with similar speed.

Sign language. Not ASL or any of the other sign languages I was versed in. I didn't know this one. No surprise, Ian did.

"Imperative that this remains between us," Ian finished out loud while still signing. The verbal part must have been for my benefit, then.

Yonah's gaze raked me, lingering over my hair. Recognition sparked in his eyes before he hooded his expression. Still, it was enough. He'd either seen my father in his true form, or someone had told him about me. Which was better? I had no idea.

"You've clearly encountered difficulties in your travels," Yonah noted, also out loud this time.

Right, Ian's clothes and hair were still a bloody mess. At least that made it harder to see the horn between his ripped shirt and the drying brownish blood staining Ian's pale skin.

"We also had a disagreement with our escort and parted ways with Ashael shortly after arriving," I said, still smiling as if nothing of importance had occurred. "But we're glad to be here."

"I am pleased to have you," Yonah replied, which made the three guards who'd been lurking by the room's exits relax. Guess that was Yonah's way of telling them to stand down. "You'll want to refresh yourselves before our festivities this evening, so I'll have Katsana show you to your rooms. Our ball in honor of our island's new member begins at dusk."

Ian signed what I hoped was a polite decline. Now that we were finally face-to-face with Yonah, I wanted to see if he could isolate Dagon's power so we could formulate a tracking spell. Not attend a ball—

"Truly?" Yonah interrupted out loud.

More signing from Ian. Yonah's expression creased into a frown as he signed back. Then, he shrugged, a gesture that required no interpretation.

"See you at dusk, then," Yonah said, giving me a little nod.

I nodded back. Katsana, the brown-haired Russian vampire, hooked her thumb in the universal gesture for "follow me."

We did. Katsana led us to a staircase at the back of the manor. Instead of going up, we went down. Once below, the unusual decorations vanished, replaced with maintenance corridors, utility rooms and other things you'd expect in the basement of a large manor/small hotel. We continued until even those vestiges of comfort disappeared, leaving nothing except a dark hallway that was starting to smell of mold and the sea. Silver pressed close enough for me to feel his feathers against my legs. He didn't like this new setting any more than I did.

Where was a great place to murder unwanted guests? Beneath the manor where no one would see and where body disposal was very convenient, considering the large furnace we just passed.

If I was reluctant, Ian's strides were long and swift, until Katsana had to quicken her pace to a near trot to keep Ian from barreling into her. I gave a mental shrug. I'd trust Ian in this, too, then. Besides, only one vampire against me and Ian? That was no threat, Katsana's formidable aura or no.

"Here you are," Katsana said, stopping at a metal door.

Ian pushed it open, revealing a small, poorly lit room with a concrete floor, an empty desk, a half-made bed and a shower that would incite panic attacks in anyone with claustrophobia.

"This will do," Ian said, stunning me. This wasn't close to his usual high standards. It looked like the place where maintenance workers caught a nap while on break.

"Take our pet to the kitchens; he'll be hungry," Ian continued. "He's on a special diet, so vegetables only."

I stepped between Katsana and Silver when she bent to pick him up. "He stays here." No way was I letting some unknown vampire take Silver when the vampire version of a narcotic ran through his veins.

Ian grunted. "This is the last place someone would harm him, but very well. Bring him a plate of vegetables here, then."

Katsana's nose wrinkled. "I'll send someone else to do it."

"Good enough." I was stunned when Ian all but pushed me into the room, saying "Stay" to Silver before shutting the door with him still in the hallway.

"What the hell?" I demanded.

Ian turned, a wild kind of darkness glittering in his eyes. "Hell is what you've put me through, but it stops now."

$\mathcal{I}$ made no effort to hide my confusion. "What happened to make you angry at me all of a sudden?"

His laughter sounded like knives sharpening against each other. "What happened? You left me naked in a whorehouse."

That was hardly recent. "And?"

Emerald blazed from Ian's gaze as he grabbed the horn and ripped it from his upper arm. It landed on the floor and instantly straightened into an upright position, like a sword on an invisible stand. I backed away from it, not wanting to touch the deadly magic relic even by accident.

Ian stalked toward me. With the small size of the room, he quickly closed the space between us. "Know what else this little beastie did, aside from 'choosing' me as its new owner? It gave me all my memories back."

Shock made me sputter. "What? *How?*"

He grabbed my shoulders. Green blazed from his eyes and his aura sparked with so much angry energy, being near it felt like standing beside a swarm of stinging bees. "Whatever else it is, the horn's also a power amplifier. Felt it making me stronger the moment I woke up with it. Then it bashed down the walls in my mind. Thought my head would explode again when all the memories came rushing back, but it didn't. Maybe the horn protected me, but either way, for the past several hours, I've remembered every secret we shared, each moment in each other's arms, all the promises we made and the last words I said, all while knowing that *you left me naked in a bloody whorehouse!*"

Shame slapped me, but his anger made mine rise to the surface, too. "I didn't want to leave you, but what was I supposed to do? Say 'Hey, Ian, you don't remember me, but we're technically married, and guess what? I *didn't* help the council execute your friend's child! I helped save her because I'm a secret cross-species, double-agent Law Guardian! And sure, you already got killed once by being with me, but want to risk getting murdered again to see if the second time's the charm?'"

"Yes." His tone was more scalding than a splash of boiling water. "That's exactly what you should have said. Then I would have told you I *did* remember you. Perhaps not all the specifics, but enough to chase you even after you threw me away as if I were yesterday's rubbish."

My anger fled at the flash of pain in his gaze. I'd caused that. Me and no one else. My throat closed off and my chest tightened until it felt like it was being crushed. I was grateful for the sudden, blurring sheen of tears because I could no longer bear to meet Ian's gaze. I hadn't known that regret could manifest as physical pain until this moment.

"Ian . . ." What could I say? Nothing could take back what I'd done, and worse, now I knew I hadn't needed to do it at all. But I had to explain, this time without anger, sarcasm, or rationalizations. I owed him that.

I met his eyes, hoping he could see the anguish in mine as I dropped all the defenses that had shielded me. "I thought I could never hurt as much as I did when I lost Tenoch. Then you died and . . . it broke me. Literally, as it turned out. I didn't know I *could* do what I did after you shoved that bone knife through your eye. If I had, I would've done it sooner to save you."

I let out a bitter laugh as I dashed away the tears that started to run down my cheeks.

"After you died, I would've let that half stay in control. She registers loss, but she doesn't *feel* it. It's all cold logic with her. Then

Dagon said he could bring you back, and I had to see if he was right. So, I wrestled back control. For once, Dagon wasn't lying. My father brought you back and I was so happy, I didn't even care that it meant Dagon was going to live, too. But then I was told you wouldn't remember me."

My breath shuddered past my lips. Ian's hands flexed as if he'd been about to reach out to me, but then stopped himself.

"I lost you again," I summarized, voice cracking. "Only this time, my other half wasn't in control to shield me from the pain. I really *did* think leaving you was the best way to keep you from getting killed again, but I—I did it to protect myself, too. Like someone on fire, I ran, even though that only made everything worse. I know every reason why I shouldn't feel what I do for you," I added more briskly, struggling for any semblance of control. "But I can't help it. I love you—"

He yanked me close and his mouth crushed mine. I kissed him back, clutching his head as if I'd never let him go. He tasted like salt from all my tears, but I couldn't stop them. I couldn't stop anything. Everything I'd shoved down before was bursting out of me now.

I only let go of his head to yank his shirt off. Then my nails scored a path down his back while my other hand stayed tangled in his blood-stiffened hair. He shuddered with lust, tongue lashing mine with sensual brutality.

I groaned when a hard rip tore my sweater from neck to waist and his bare chest pressed against my skin. I wanted to feel all of him but my damn bra stopped me, and I hated my jeans more than anything in life except his pants, which I *loathed*. If I were pyrokinetic, all our clothes would've immediately burned to ash. I needed his naked body on mine, and I needed it now.

I grabbed his waistband and ripped.

The sound he made had me tearing at my own pants until he gripped my hands and held them at my sides. He dragged his mouth from my throat to my chest before one sharp bite severed my bra clasp.

It split open, baring my breasts. I gasped when his mouth closed over my nipple, swirling the tip before sucking strongly. Pleasure rocketed to my core, growing until I was wet and aching. I strained to free my hands so I could tear the rest of our clothes off, but he didn't let me go. He moved to my other breast, laving it before he sucked harder, longer, until my skin felt too tight, heat bathed me, and I couldn't think about anything except having him inside me.

"Forget foreplay, I need you now," I gasped.

Breath hit my hypersensitive nipple from his low laugh. "You call this need? You're not even begging yet."

Begging? That would take too long!

I tangled my legs in his and swept them out from under him. He fell and I landed on top of him, ripping his pants with a triumphant swipe. He rolled, trapping me beneath him with a wicked grin. At once, I held him with my thighs and arched, crying out when his hard flesh rubbed me where I ached the most.

His eyes closed, a guttural sound escaping him. Then they opened, glowing so bright it hurt to stare into them.

"You'll beg later." A threat that thrilled me as much as the hard yank that split my jeans from waist to ankle. "Right now, you're mine."

Every nerve ending jumped when he moved between my legs. I arched upward, so desperate to have him, a whimper escaped me. His mouth captured it as a hard thrust blasted pleasure all through me. His silver piercing burned in the sweetest way, its friction heightening sensations that already had me thrashing beneath him for more. My nails raked his back at his next thrust, and when he ground against my clitoris while buried deep inside me, the double blast of ecstasy tore a shout from me.

His kiss muffled that. His next thrust was just as hard, but slower, drawing the pleasure out until my skin felt too thin to contain it. I gripped his hips and cried out as another slow, deep thrust made inner bands convulsively tighten within me. The bunching of his muscles beneath my hands, each claiming kiss, his body against mine, and those hard, sinuous thrusts . . . I'd been dying of thirst, and now I was drowning.

It only took one more thrust before I came with a shout his mouth couldn't completely muffle. His hips twisted, prolonging the rapture that shook me while all my limbs suddenly felt languorous and heavy. He muttered something I couldn't make out, then his mouth and the blissful weight of his body was gone.

I didn't have time to protest before he slid down between my legs. Then I gasped as his tongue seared over flesh that still pulsed and tingled from climax. I tried to sit up, but he pushed me back, grip tightening on my hips to hold me down.

I could barely think with his tongue moving over me, proving his memory had indeed returned because he found my most sensitive spots with ferocious accuracy. My hips rocked beneath the erotic barrage and soon, I was gasping until I sounded like I was hyper-ventilating.

"You *are* going to make me beg, aren't you?" I moaned.

A dark laugh teased my quivering flesh. "Told you I would. Besides, I missed your taste."

A breathless sound escaped me. "I missed everything."

Another firm swirl of his tongue had my back off the floor as if he'd yanked on it. "With how fast you came, I believe that," I heard him mutter.

Not even the explosive sensations his mouth elicited could stop me from telling him he'd misunderstood me. "As great as sex is with you"—my voice choked from emotion—"it's the least of what I missed about you, Ian."

He stopped, barely leashed wildness lurking in his gaze. I sat up and he didn't stop me this time. I grabbed his hair and slid down as I pulled him forward. His body covered mine and I opened my legs, welcoming the thrust that filled me with the sharpest kind of rapture. Then I kissed him until I could no longer taste the salted honey of my pleasure on his mouth.

"I should never have left you." The truth left me in a rush when I finally pulled away. "I am so, so sorry."

His grip had been tight before. At that, it became bruising. His new roughness only made the pleasure more intense. I gave myself to it, telling him with my raking nails and the fangs I sank into his shoulder that I wanted more.

He gave me more, until I was lost in sensations that danced between incredible pleasure and quicksilver pain. His blood painted my nails and lips, while mine coated his mouth when I swore, "I'll never leave you again," with a drawn-out moan.

He grasped my hair, stopping with a suddenness that made him feel like he'd been turned into a statue. "Swear that on more than what you're feeling in this moment."

My body pulsed from an overload of sensations and I was slightly buzzed from drinking his demon-tainted blood, but at that, my mind cleared as if he'd thrown a bucket of icy water onto my brain. He wanted a promise I couldn't later say I'd been forced to make, or try to brush off as a mere "technicality." Whatever I said next, I'd better mean it.

I stared into his eyes as I dragged my palm across a fang, letting the blood that dripped down fall onto both of us since I was still on his lap, straddling him.

"By my blood, Ian, I swear I will never abandon you again."

Determination bordering on ruthlessness flashed in his gaze. "I'll hold you to that. Now"—his immobility ceased with an arch that rolled heat though me like a fire wave—"let's see if I can make you scream loud enough to find out if this reinforced room is as far away from everyone as Yonah promised."

Laughter bubbled out of me. Was that why we were in this ratty hole instead of the mansion's much nicer accommodations?

My arms tightened around him. "Let's," I said, adding huskily, "after all, you promised me a broken bed."

Chapter 25

We were late for the ball. Not just because we were having sex, though the bed *was* in pieces and the walls now had several body-size dents in them. No, we were late because I hadn't realized how exhausted I was until I drifted off in Ian's arms and woke up a full eight hours later.

Ian had let Silver inside at some point during my slumber. I would've felt horrible if he'd been stuck in the hallway this whole time. He was in the corner of the room farthest away from the horn and bed debris, sleeping as Ian and I got dressed.

I'd brought many things for this trip, but I hadn't thought to bring a ball gown. No matter, as it turned out. Katsana brought me four to choose from. I picked the strapless one with the tight square bodice and wide, swaying skirt that met in the middle with the elegance of a swan's wings closing gently together. It was deepest indigo from the bodice to mid-thigh, then it had been dip-dyed into a shimmering silver. It reminded me of the sea when bathed by moonlight; dangerous in these parts, but lovely nonetheless.

Ian had packed a tuxedo, so his foresight meant he had no need to borrow one. His was black with a white tie, leaving just his auburn hair and his ruby cufflinks as color accents. He looked unapproachably gorgeous in the elegant ensemble. Only I knew that his cufflinks matched his new silver-and-ruby cock piercing. Ian could never be tamed, even at his most refined.

"I'd rather we spent the rest of the night here, but Yonah was emphatic about our attending the ball," Ian remarked as I put the finishing touches on my appearance. "Said they're celebrating the arrival of a newcomer to the island. Guess making a party out of it helps newcomers feel less like they've come to a prison for rejects and more like they've found a new home. We'll make nice with everyone for a couple hours before we corner Yonah and convince him to do the spell."

I swept my hair into a knot that was formal enough for the occasion. It also allowed me to bring a thin, sharp silver stick to the ball. Few people noticed a woman's hairpin even if it could double as a weapon. "You're confident Yonah can do the spell, but you never told me why."

"Yonah's a former demon prince." Ian's tone was so casual, he could've been discussing me wearing my hair up or down. "It's why he's got a staggering bounty on his head. Demons don't fancy their own betraying them, and Yonah left his brethren in such a blaze of backstabbing glory, they killed everyone who knew him, trying to contain the humiliating fallout."

That explained why I hadn't heard of Yonah before! And wow, how wrong I'd been, thinking that Yonah was a vampire. How had he managed to conceal it so that he felt like one species when he was another? That was a trick I needed to learn.

"'Course, it's impossible to completely erase someone when they're still around," Ian went on. "Despite the mass slaughter, rumors of Yonah still made the rounds. So did stories of him having a secret hideaway. One of my former lovers shared those stories with me. Shared them with other people, too, which is how she got her eyes stabbed out," he added offhandedly. "Demons still don't fancy hearing Yonah's name bandied about."

No wonder Ashael had reacted in such a visceral way when Ian first mentioned Yonah. Anything less would've cast suspicion on him, if Ian had been sent by another demon to test Ashael. *I know, you have to disown Yonah,* Ian had said. *Can't have it getting out that you're still friendly with the most wanted bloke in the demon world, can you?*

But my half brother *had* befriended his world's most wanted fugitive. Moreover, Ashael must have ferried other people to Yonah's island, judging from how easily Yonah had accepted Ashael bringing Ian and me here. Despite our very different upbringings and the thousands of years that separated us, we'd both ended up doing the same thing: sheltering people unfairly condemned by laws that governed the other half of our species.

Maybe one day, Ashael and I might have a friendship in common, too. Oddly, I found myself hoping so. In the meantime . . .

"What do you think? Sapphire, or the pearl earrings?" I asked, holding up one of each next to my ears.

"Neither," Ian replied, drawing a slim, rectangular box from his suitcase. "I recommend these."

He opened the box. Triple-tiered diamond chandelier earrings caught the light like they'd been chasing it until that very moment. Each flawless stone was set in platinum, the largest ones at the base before narrowing to a smattering of glittering drops at the tip. My mouth suddenly felt dry. The jewelry box looked and smelled new. This wasn't something that Ian had just happened to have lying around.

"When, ah, when did you get these?"

"A few weeks ago," he replied, a glint of something I couldn't name in his eyes.

Shame smacked me again. He'd gotten me the Faery Queen Crimsons *and* these earrings, all while I was refusing to even read his texts. How did I begin to make up for that?

I'd find a way. I put my other earrings back in my travel case. "They're stunning, Ian. Thank you."

He fastened the earrings onto my ears himself. When he was done, I looked in the mirror. My upswept hair displayed them to maximum effect and they were so gorgeous, I decided against a necklace. Anything competing with these earrings would lose.

"If you don't want to return that dress to Katsana in pieces," Ian said in a casual tone, "take it off as soon as we've concluded our business. I swore when I bought these that I'd see you wearing them and nothing else. I intend to make good on that promise tonight."

I almost took the dress off to make that happen now, but it was already an hour past dusk. If we dallied any longer, we'd miss the "fashionably late" window and end up insulting the same host we needed a large favor from.

I was still tempted to rip the dress off.

Ian leaned down, taking in a deep breath before his lips brushed my throat. "Whatever you're thinking, keep thinking it," he murmured. "Desire sharpens your scent until it's like standing in the middle of a storm, rain whipping me while lightning crashes all around . . ."

"Stop," I breathed, need making my voice breathy. "Or we're going to miss the ball, piss off Yonah, and lose our chance to track Dagon and the other resurrected souls."

He backed away, but the heat in his eyes made it impossible for me to move. Ropes couldn't have held me more securely.

"One hour." His voice was tight. "Then find the nearest loo. I'll meet you there."

I merely nodded, then set a reminder on my mobile for sixty minutes. Heat still smoldered in his gaze, but he held open the door as if he were a perfect gentleman.

"To the ball, then."

$\mathcal{I}$ quickly learned that "ball" was a flexible term. "Extrava-ganza" would more accurately describe the sight that greeted us when we ascended back to the main level of the mansion. The bon-fires were still lit outside, but little else had stayed the same.

All the cabanas and most of the slides were now gone, leaving ample space for the silk swaths that formed several open tents around the pool area. Champagne fountains and blood fountains floated off the ground, while stationary towers of roasted meat, pastas, cheeses, vegetables, fruits, and desserts made up the edible decorations. The towers never toppled over no matter how many people helped themselves to their bounty, either, and there were a lot of people. Hundreds.

This was only one level of the party. We followed a line of for-mally dressed people to the second floor, where an orchestra played one of the most famous musical scores, from *The Phantom of the Opera*. That wouldn't have been unusual, except the orchestra consisted of instruments playing themselves while floating near the ceiling. Vampires, ghouls, demons, and humans danced, laughed, and mingled below them, interacting with an ease I had never seen when so many different species were present.

They weren't the only supernatural beings here. I didn't know what the blue-skinned people with the tiny white lights in their hair were. Or the tall, winged people who reminded me of carvings of Sumerian Anunnaki deities from my childhood, but they also chatted with the others as if there was nothing unusual about different supernatural species getting along.

A burst of applause directed our attention to the end of the ballroom, where an immense balcony opened up to views of the sea. A crowd gathered there to watch something beyond our view. Ian and I went over to see what they were looking at.

Once on the balcony, we saw Leviathan dancing above the waves. Their watery bodies moved in perfect unison to the music, illuminated by spotlights pointing at that section of the water. They leapt and whirled, while other Leviathan formed into different sea creatures that effortlessly glided between them. I had never seen anything so stunningly graceful. It was as if the soaring music manifested into the Leviathan's beautiful, fluid forms. I watched, riveted, until the final crescendo from the song "The Music of the Night" faded into silence and the Leviathan melted back into the waves and disappeared.

Applause broke out from the onlookers. I joined in. Next to the Leviathan's riveting aquatic display, the statue of Medusa walking around while filling her champagne glass from one of the many floating fountains paled by comparison.

I paled by comparison, too. Here, my half-celestial nature didn't make me someone to be feared, loathed, admired or even noticed. I was simply one of many unusual creatures, more interesting than some and far less remarkable than others.

"You're trembling," Ian said, and drew me away from the crowd on the balcony.

"I've needed to hide what I am for my entire life, and suddenly, I'm ordinary." I couldn't suppress the wonder in my voice. "Even if I went into full daughter-of-the-underworld mode, I don't think these people would be afraid. Some might even yawn!"

Ian snorted. "I doubt that, but I see your point. Must feel very freeing."

"Yes," I said with such emphasis, his brows went up.

"Are you saying you'd like to stay here permanently?"

I opened my mouth to deny that . . . and stopped.

Did I? I could, as the island's entry requirement was rejection by your own species. I had that covered as soon as I showed Yonah what I was. Ian did, too, now that he was a vampire with partial demon powers. For all I knew, Yonah thought both Ian and I had come here to seek asylum. Ashael had told Yonah that he was bringing two sojourners. He hadn't said he was bringing two people who only wanted Yonah to do a spell for them before they quickly left.

What if Ian, Silver, and I *did* stay here, safe from Dagon and everyone else trying to kill us? What if we made a life where none of us ever had to hide what we were again?

"You like the idea," Ian said, no surprise on his features.

My sigh came from the deepest part of me. "I love it, but I can't. I made a vow to my father. Even if I hadn't, Dagon will try to kill the other resurrected souls to regain the power they absorbed from him, and some of them might have been innocent like you were."

"I was no innocent," Ian said, his smile sardonic. "But I *was* tricked, and I can hardly begrudge those people their chance to live if Dagon tricked them, too. Besides"—his gaze turned knowing— "you spent most of your life putting yourself in a position of power so you could help the powerless. You won't give up on them just to hide out here."

"Probably not," I agreed, then a wry smile tugged my mouth. "But a girl can dream, right?"

His laughter wrapped around me like a tempting embrace as he led me to the dance floor. The floating instruments had switched from opera's songs to a waltz. No surprise: Ian moved as if he'd been born to dance to it.

"Are you bad at anything?" I teasingly asked.

"Celibacy," he replied, with a mock shudder. "Thought neglect would rot my parts off these past several weeks."

I rolled my eyes even while something warm glowed inside me. I hadn't asked if he'd sought comfort with anyone else during our time apart because I'd half expected the answer to be yes. Not that I would've had cause to criticize. You don't abandon someone while simultaneously demanding their fidelity.

"Going without sex for weeks is nothing," I said to mask my deeper feelings. It hadn't escaped my notice that I'd told him I loved him earlier, and he hadn't said it back. Yes, Ian cared for me, but he wasn't where I was emotionally, and I didn't need to keep reminding him of that.

"I've gone without for years at a time," I added just to see his reaction. "Sometimes, even decades."

A look of horror crossed his features. Then it faded and a predatory light shone in his gaze. "I hope you enjoyed your appalling sexual fasts, because they're over. In fact, you won't last the next ten minutes."

I made a show of checking the alarm on my mobile. "Sorry, but I have twenty-six more minutes of celibacy left."

He leaned down, his mouth sliding over my throat until it reached the tender hollow where my pulse would have been. "No, you don't." His fangs lightly grazed the spot. Shivers raced over me. "I spotted two loos on this level," he went on, moving up until his breath touched my ear like the brush of feathers. "Pick one and go. I'll be right behind you."

"We could always go back to our room," I said, stifling a gasp as his tongue traced the sensitive strip behind my ear.

"Too far." A growl that swept heat through me.

Without another word, I left his arms and headed to the nearest bathroom. Ian wasn't the only one who'd marked their location when we first came into the ballroom.

Two human women were inside, one applying lipstick, the other toying with her hair. "You both look stunning," I told them, lighting up my gaze with green. "Leave now and have a wonderful night."

They turned on their heels and walked out, one saying, "You *do* look stunning," while the other replied, "I know, so do you!" with the kind of confidence women didn't often enough allow themselves to feel. I didn't hear any more heartbeats, but I bent to glance beneath the bathroom stalls to check for people anyway. Empty.

When I straightened, Ian was behind me, already turning the lock on the door.

I stared at him as I reached beneath the wide skirt of my dress to pull my undergarments down. He unbuttoned his jacket and unbuckled his pants, his gaze burning as my panties landed near his feet.

"Just this once," he murmured, picking me up and setting me on the countertop. "Don't release your control."

I wrapped my legs around his waist, already wet with anticipation. "We'll see."

$\mathcal{I}$ 'd never used a stranger's semi-public bathroom stall to freshen up after impromptu sex before. No one had aroused me to the point that waiting for privacy wasn't an option. Most cultures would expect me to be embarrassed, especially since the women who'd been waiting outside had no doubt as to the reason for the locked door when Ian flashed them a satiated grin as he opened it and left. But I wasn't embarrassed. I practically took a bow before slipping into the nearest stall to clean myself up.

Ian was so gorgeous, those women should more than understand. If they didn't, that wasn't my problem. We hadn't even broken a single fixture in this room, and the countertop had escaped with only a new crack in the marble. They had no idea the amount of control that had taken. We couldn't have been more restrained if we'd both been bound hand and foot.

And it had been mind-blowing. He'd tried bondage on me before his memory loss, but shadows from my past had ruined that. Now, I couldn't wait for Ian to break out the magic ties. I'd loved being restrained while everything inside me was seething out of control, and he'd had to restrain me to keep this room in its borderline-pristine condition.

I finished cleaning up, then came out and washed my hands. The bathroom was empty now, the other women taking less time than I had. I'd just finished fixing my makeup and securing my hair back in its knot when the door opened and a lovely black-haired woman wearing a deep-purple ball gown came in.

She gave me a polite smile before she disappeared into the stall. I smiled back, but it froze as my brief, disinterested glance suddenly set my brain on fire with recognition.

Even after all this time, I knew that silky swath of long black hair, those clear brown eyes, and the skin that was the same golden-bronze shade as my own. But it couldn't be. Ereshki had died thousands of years ago, and the woman in the stall was most assuredly human. Her heartbeat more than proved that, as did the sound of her urinating.

Still, memories I'd done my best to suppress slammed into me. *Ereshki's hesitant smile when she was first thrust into my cage. I'd been often taunted with smirks, leers, and grins, but no one before her had ever smiled at me with kindness.*

A flush sounded, then the woman came out of the stall. She seemed surprised to see me standing between the sinks and the door, staring at her as if transfixed. But then she began to wash her hands as if nothing unusual was going on.

"Do I know you?" I forced myself to ask in a calm voice.

She looked up and smiled again, more faltering this time. Her heart rate had sped up, too, indicating her new nervousness. Not that I could blame her. A vampire was blocking her path to the door while staring at her with unblinking intensity. If that didn't make her nervous, she wouldn't be smart enough to have survived whatever had forced her to take refuge at this island.

"I don't think so," she replied, then screamed.

I don't remember making the decision to cross the room and grab her by the shoulders, let alone to hoist her up. But she was now in my hands, screaming while her high-heeled shoes kicked at the air since I'd lifted her off the ground.

That *voice*. Higher than mine but devastatingly familiar and with my same accent Ian said he couldn't place when we first met. Few people could. Ancient Sumerian had died out as a language thousands of years ago.

"Who are you?" I snarled, just as the bathroom door burst open. The deadly magic horn had already exploded from Ian's sleeve, but it retracted when he saw I wasn't the one in danger.

"Veritas," he said in a guarded voice. "What's amiss?"

"Please, stop her!" the woman beseeched Ian. To me, she screamed, "Let me down, I've done nothing to you!"

She stopped, giving me a shocked look as I started cursing her in the first language I'd ever learned. From the way her eyes widened, she'd understood what I was saying, too.

"Who are you?" she breathed, speaking in Sumerian now, too.

I didn't have time to reply when she began pounding on my arms and aiming her kicks at my body instead of the air.

"Who are you?" she shouted again, rage and frustration twisting her pretty features. "Do you know who did this to me? Was it you? Was it?" she finished in a roar.

Ian spun around, horn whipping out again at the crash as someone else flung the bathroom door open. Yonah strode into the room, red pinpoints gleaming from his moss green eyes.

"Who dares abuse my hospitality?" he thundered as the air in the room thickened until it felt like a tangible weight.

I dropped the woman only because I didn't trust myself not to crush her to death in front of Yonah. "This woman," I said through gritted teeth, "is not whoever she claims to be."

"Ereshki is our guest of honor. This ball is in celebration of her being our newest member here." Yonah's tone sliced the air like a killing blow. For an instant, black wings spread out behind him, so large they touched the ceiling and pressed against each side of the hallway before they vanished.

The sight would've awed me, but it was nothing compared to hearing her name spoken aloud by someone else for the first time since I'd been human. For a moment, the past swallowed me so completely that I wasn't Veritas, Law Guardian for the vampire council, any longer. I wasn't even Ariel, beloved adopted daughter of Tenoch and secret biological daughter of the Warden of the Gateway to the Netherworld.

I had no name. I wasn't worthy of one. I wasn't even worthy to suffer and die for my god, Dagon, but he permitted it so others could see his magnificence when he raised me from the dead. After that, it was their turn to die for Dagon. If they truly believed in him, Dagon would raise them back to life, too. He'd proved that by raising Ereshki, and he'd gifted me with her presence so I was no longer alone in my cage. If Dagon didn't raise his other sacrifices back to life, then they hadn't truly believed in him. Perhaps the people in the next town would . . .

"Ereshki?" The harshness in Ian's tone snapped me back to reality. "The bitch who conned you into continuing to believe in Dagon so he could keep torturing and murdering you?"

"What?" Yonah said.

At the same time, Ereshki screeched, "I did not do any of that! I don't know you! Why would you say such things?"

Rage and regret over all the lives Dagon had brainwashed me to help him take made my voice hoarse. "If you're not the same person who helped Dagon murder thousands by pretending to be his victim while all the time you were his ally, then you *won't* have a birthmark shaped like a crescent moon on your left hip."

I should have been satisfied to see her face pale when I ripped her purple ball gown to expose her hip so Yonah could see that the mark *was* there. But I didn't. I still felt so choked by her betrayal when I'd been at my most helpless that my throat felt as if it had been suddenly stuffed full of razors.

"I never got the chance to ask you why," I rasped. "Why did you bother to befriend me first? You could have convinced me of Dagon's deity without pretending to love me as a sister. It's that cruelty I can't forgive, let alone understand."

She'd backed as far as she could into the corner of the room, her heartbeat sounding like a drummer banging away on steel lids.

"I don't know you." An anguished whisper as she frantically glanced between me and Yonah. "I have never seen you before now. I have no idea who Dagon is, either. You know I don't!" she wailed, directing that, oddly, at Yonah. "I remember almost nothing before waking up in that ditch five weeks ago!"

I felt the color drain from my face while my stomach dropped as if I'd come to a sudden stop after a long fall. She had almost no memory beyond the past five weeks? No. No. She couldn't be one of the newly resurrected souls . . . could she?

She *could*. Ereshki had bargained her soul away to Dagon before we met. I'd overheard that when I learned of her betrayal on the same day that Tenoch rescued me. Of course Dagon would've collected on Ereshki's debt a long time ago, and how like him to bottle her soul as his own personal resurrection fuel instead of delivering it to its intended destination.

That meant she was probably telling the truth. She *didn't* know me because my time with Ereshki had been tied to Dagon, and my father had yanked all Dagon-related memories out of her when he brought her, Ian, and the other souls back to life. She wouldn't have had cause for those memories to linger the way they had for Ian, either. She'd cared nothing for me.

"Bugger," Ian said, echoing my suspicions.

I forced a neutral expression onto my features even though I was close to screaming at this cruel twist of fate.

"Yonah," I said in an admirably controlled tone. "We need to talk."

Chapter 28

*Y*onah, Ereshki, Ian, and I stood on opposite corners of the elegant drawing room on the third floor of the mansion, one full level away from the festivities. Of course, things were less festive now that the ball's guest of honor had been hustled upstairs by Yonah's guards. Yonah had summoned them because he hadn't trusted me or Ian to secure her.

Wise of him. Despite her memory loss, a part of me still very much wanted to kill Ereshki. From the glares Ian shot her way, so did he. The only reason Ian probably hadn't slaughtered Ereshki himself was because he wanted to watch me do it.

"We appear to be in a quagmire," Yonah said, starting with the obvious. "Ereshki was brought to me three weeks ago by a loyal ally who'd found her in an Iraqi marketplace, screaming in terror at the planes overhead and the vehicles around her."

A harsh snort left me before I could stuff it back. I suppose that would be terrifying, if the last thing Ereshki remembered before that was camels for transportation.

"This ally quickly realized Ereshki was suffering from more than normal mental health ailments," Yonah went on. "Her last memories were from ancient Mesopotamia. Ereshki also exhibited mild supernatural abilities as well as having altered blood. All the above put her in danger from Law Guardians, demons, and Red Dragon dealers. Thus, this ally sent her to me, and she has been nothing but gracious and grateful—"

"Oh, she's good at that act," I interrupted, bitterness sliding like venom through my veins. "I fell for it, too, even when I was being repeatedly tortured and murdered."

Yonah stared at me for a long moment. Then he sighed. "Many refugees over the centuries came to me with the same story: a beautiful vampire-witch named Ariel with silver eyes and white-blonde hair streaked with gold and blue saved them. As if there was any doubt that this was you, no fewer than six of them recognized you at the ball tonight. For all that you have done on behalf of those who are now my people, Ariel, I thank you. But"—now his tone hardened—"my gratitude does not include giving you Ereshki as a sacrifice for your vengeance. Whoever she was when she wronged you, she is not that person any longer."

The rational part of me agreed with his logic. The rest was screaming, *That's for ME to decide!* I'd bought that right with my blood, and I was all that was left of Ereshki's other victims, too. They also deserved long-denied justice being served to her.

That's why I couldn't trust myself to speak at Yonah's arrogant declaration that I had no say in Ereshki's fate. Worse, I could feel my other half stirring, drawn by my rage. It wouldn't take much for that half to assume control again. She looked for weaknesses to exploit all the time now.

Ian glanced at me, then settled into his high-backed antique chair as if he had nothing more important to do than make himself comfortable. "You're being shockingly naïve," he said to Yonah in a companionable tone. "No wonder you couldn't stand living in your former world. Must have been hell."

With how Yonah's face darkened, he didn't appreciate the quip. "I know who you are, too, boy," he replied coldly. "Unlike Ariel, nothing I've heard commends you."

Ian grinned. "Then you heard exactly what I wanted you to hear. No one suspects a scoundrel of allying with righteous causes, so I'm not on any of the wrong radars. Let me tell you what you don't know—Dagon is coming for this girl, so you endanger everyone on your island every moment that she is here."

Yonah gave a diffident wave. "Someone is always coming after my residents. If they weren't, they wouldn't need to be here."

"Not like Dagon." The grin never left Ian's face despite his gaze hardening into turquoise-colored diamonds. "He absorbs souls to burn through them as power sources when needed. Ask Ereshki if she has nightmares of being drowned in darkness. That's from being one of Dagon's former soul batteries."

Ereshki's hand flew to her mouth. "I do," she gasped.

"'Course you do," Ian said, showing his teeth the way a tiger did before a kill. "I, too, was trapped inside Dagon that way. Then Ariel arranged for all of us to be yanked out of him and resurrected—"

"How?" Yonah interrupted.

I didn't mind revealing my secret to Yonah, but I had no intention of telling Ereshki. "Do you know what Ashael is?"

Yonah's expression shuttered like a house battened down for a storm. "Assuming I know what you're speaking of . . . what of it?"

Yonah might be protecting her, but he was being careful with what he revealed around Ereshki. Good. And he absolutely knew what Ashael was. He wouldn't have reacted this way otherwise.

"Ashael and I have much in common," I said, and pulled a small trickle of bloodied water from the palm of Yonah's hand. With my other nature so close to the surface, it barely took any thought at all, and that worried me as much as it should.

Yonah's eyes widened as he felt the water being pulled from his skin. He didn't look down, though, and his fist closed, hiding it so Ereshki didn't see. Ian noticed, however. His nostrils flared as he scented it.

"Ah," was Yonah's only reply.

Ereshki looked even more confused, not that it mattered.

"As I was saying," Ian went on. "Dagon's coming for Ereshki because he wants to reclaim the power she consumed from him when she was released and resurrected. He's coming for me, too, which is why I'll do you a favor and remove both of us—after the smallest of favors. You're right: a normal demon is of no concern, but one who's hyped-up on souls for extra power?" Ian tsked. "That's no fun, is it?"

"Assuming I'd agree about the danger," Yonah said, holding up a hand at Ereshki's frightened squeak. "What is the favor?"

Ian's smile was charming and lethal at the same time. "So glad you asked."

Chapter 29

*E*reshki was no longer in the drawing room. It was just me, Ian, and Yonah. The former demon prince's wings were clearly visible now, the obsidian arcs made of something that was neither shadow nor night but whatever darkness had existed before those. They grew and stretched as Yonah poured the largest amount of power I'd felt on this side of the veil into the blood-drawn symbols before him.

The blood was Ian's, pumped out directly from his heart. I'd done that myself after Ian stripped off his tuxedo jacket and shirt so only his gleaming, bare upper body bore the stain. He'd taken the horn off, too. It stood upright in the corner of the room the way it had the last time he'd removed it, though this time, it was swaying as though in approval of Yonah's power.

At a nod from Yonah, I drew another stream of blood from Ian's heart so he could paint it over the last of the symbols. "Now," Yonah said without looking up. "Use some of the power you stole from Dagon, Ian."

How? He couldn't teleport with the wards here and . . . oh!

Not a muscle on Ian moved, but his whole body began to shimmer until it looked like he'd been bathed in a silver haze. New magic filled the room, twining around Yonah's power until it felt like I was watching an invisible dance. Nothing on Ian moved, so this wasn't a tactile spell. He also wasn't speaking. Not even breath escaped Ian's lips. Still, the power grew until it grated across my skin. I half expected dents to appear in the floor from the weight of it.

With a sense of awe, I realized that Ian could now create spells by drawing from his power alone. Or, more accurately, by drawing from Dagon's stolen power in him.

Yonah gave Ian a surprised, if satisfied, look. Then he began chanting in a language I'd never heard before.

With a snap, all the blood-drawn symbols suddenly caught fire. Then they lifted into the air, their shapes now drawn by fire instead of blood. That fire brightened, merging with Ian and Yonah's power, before it coalesced into a long single swirl that suddenly rammed into Ian's chest with enough force to drive him more than a meter through the demon's hardwood floor.

"Ian!" I gasped, about to run to him when one of those long wings blocked me. Its weight belied its non-corporeal appearance and touching it felt like plunging my arm straight into hell.

"Don't," Yonah gritted out. "Not yet."

Ian's body bowed while muscles stretched and tore as if trying to contain something fighting to get out of him. That shimmering glow turned to fire and a shout tore from Ian that had me beating against Yonah's shockingly immovable wing despite the burns that ate through my skin.

"Stop it, stop it!"

"Too late," Yonah said in a pitiless tone. "Ian will either absorb the spell or it will kill him."

Why did we *ever* trust a demon? This was the second time one was putting Ian's life in danger!

Another howl tore from Ian as blood suddenly coated him as if his capillaries had erupted violently enough to burst through the surface of his skin. Then he shuddered with such violence, I could hear as well as see his bones break.

I let my other half free with a ferocity that made my vision turn black and my own skin feel like it had split open. For once, my other half and I were in complete agreement: If Ian died, Yonah was going to die with him.

I spread out the darkness haloing me until I felt its width surpassing the demon's curious wings. Then my power sought the energy in the water surrounding this island. Once it found it, I felt the Leviathan, their sinuous bodies cleaving through the sea as if they were lethal, sentient waves. But something else felt me touching them, and it snapped back my power like the retracting coil of a whip.

Ah, the Leviathan had a ruler. One that walked on land, too. Intriguing but at the moment irrelevant. There was more than enough water on this island to fuel my power, and . . . had my vampire finished screaming? Good. The sound had been grating.

I opened my eyes. The demon had stayed in his corner, his wings now tight against his body as if he were about to charge me instead of run. A worthy opponent, then. Did I owe him death?

I glanced at Ian. My vampire no longer shuddered from agony and his bones no longer broke. He lay still, eyes closed, that former silvery glow and the fiery one now nowhere to be seen.

"Are you alive?" I asked, crossing over to nudge Ian with a foot. No answer, but he wasn't shriveling into a state of true death. Then again, being killed by magic might preserve his body. I'd seen that before. My nudge turned into a kick.

"Stop," Ian muttered, opening one eye. Then both eyes opened and widened. "Why hallo, my lovely demigod," he said in a careful tone as he slowly sat up. "We've never been properly introduced. I'm Ian."

Did he think me simple? "I know who you are," I said, giving him a raking look. "And you should be running. Didn't *she* make you promise to flee if you saw me?"

Ian held out a hand to Yonah, who started to circle me in a predatory way. "I've got this," he told Yonah in a crisp tone.

His confidence was amusing, if misplaced.

"If she breaks free and threatens any of my people—" Yonah began, stopping when I swung to give him an icy smile.

"She won't," Ian said with that same confidence.

My gaze swung back to him. "You believe you could stop me?"

Ian smiled, lifting himself out of the hole in the floor with surprising grace. Then he brushed the shards and splinters from his bloodied torso as if dusting lint off a suit.

"I won't have to." Another smile, this one crafty as well as charming. "It's also why I lied when I promised to run if I ever saw you. There's no need. You quite like me."

Impertinent. Perhaps I should rip the blood out of his body and slap him with it. "Do I?"

He came closer, that smile never slipping. "Oh, you do. You burst free whenever I'm in danger, and I also see you lurking behind Veritas's eyes when she loses control in other ways."

His caressing tone left no doubt as to which ones. Then he reached out, trailing his hand down my arm. The sensations that followed weren't unpleasant, so I allowed it.

"She thinks you're not her, but you are, aren't you?" Almost crooned as he continued to stroke my arm as if gentling a wild beast. "You're just another side to her. We all have our different sides. Yours is simply more . . . well-defined."

"She thinks me evil." Saying it made something sting as if I'd been poked with a clumsy stitch. Bitterness, she'd call it.

"I've seen evil." Now his hand was in my hair. I tilted toward it to see if I enjoyed that more. If I didn't, I could always rip his hand off. "You're not even close."

I did enjoy his hand in my hair. It was even more pleasant than the strokes on my arm. His body would be more pleasant, too. I knew that because he was right—I had, on occasion, watched through her eyes when she shared her flesh with his.

"You may leave," I said, flicking my fingers at Yonah. "Or you may stay. Either way, he will pleasure me now."

The demon muttered something I didn't care enough to catch. Then he left. Ian laughed, a low, sensual sound that—surprisingly—affected me as much as his touch.

"Saucy little half-celestial minx, aren't you?"

I pressed my mouth to his before he could say anything else. Yes, very enjoyable. His tongue was even more so, and his body created sensations I wanted more of. I had only watched this before. Now, I wanted to feel it.

I let out a hiss of disapproval when he caught my hands before I could rid him of his unnecessary pants.

"Hate to disappoint," he murmured, "but we can't do this."

"Why?" To see if I'd misunderstood his interest, I grabbed his cock. Harder than a block of ice. Certainly no impediment there. "You want this."

Another laugh, this time edged with something rough. "Oh, I want this all night and into next week, but your vampire half would object, so it's not happening."

"You said I *am* her," I argued, not liking the feeling of being denied. "Begin the copulation!"

He brushed my hair back before tracing my lip with his thumb. Somehow, I felt that touch deeper than my skin. *Sorcerer.*

"You are," he said softly. "One day, she'll realize that, but right now, she still sees herself as two separate people. She's wrong, but until she realizes that, I can't accept your invitation. So again, with regret, this isn't happening."

Then he kissed me, ending with a nip that was hard enough to draw a drop of blood that he caught with his tongue. I liked that as well, which made his refusal all the more frustrating.

"Now," he said thickly, "show her she's wrong about you by willingly relinquishing your control back to her."

I shoved him away, feeling stabbed by an enemy I could neither see nor destroy. This must be what betrayal felt like. "She will cage me again."

"For a while," Ian agreed. "She was taught to fear this half of herself, but what was learned can be unlearned. Besides," his voice deepened, "the cage is only an illusion. You're always there, aren't you? When she frees you, she's really only freeing herself."

A sigh hissed through my lips. If he knew that, why did she not know it, too? Even still, I debated ignoring his counsel, but with each brush of his hands, her power grew. Soon, she would break free unless I stayed away from him.

Did I want to do that? My jaw tightened.

No. I did not. *Sorcerer.*

"Very well," I said, and let her rise.

Chapter 30

$\mathcal{I}$ snapped forward as if I'd been slingshot back into control. For a moment, I could only stare at Ian. His hands were still in my hair and he was standing so close I could feel the heat from his body, elevated from the stress of fighting for his life in Yonah's dangerous spell.

"You talked her out of it," I finally said in disbelief.

Ian's mouth curled in a knowing smile. "No. I talked *you* out of it."

I realized with a jolt that he was probably right. I'd experienced decades of extreme trauma by the time Tenoch saved me, and he'd been adamant that I keep my other half locked away because it was too dangerous. Anything Tenoch feared, I feared, too, so I'd spent my life shunning that part of myself. It wasn't such a stretch to imagine that my past trauma combined with incessant self-alienation resulted in a partial other identity, which was really me trying to continually disassociate from the parts of me that my beloved sire had feared.

If so, I had a lot of therapy in my future. But first . . .

"Does the spell work?" I asked, trying to stuff down my rage over how Yonah could have killed him with it. That rage was like rolling out the welcome mat for my other half . . . or the part of me I felt more comfortable calling my other half even though it really wasn't? Gods, this was confusing.

If Ian sensed any of my inner battle, he didn't comment. All he did was take my hand while also holding out his other arm. The horn flew over to wrap itself around his bicep as if it were a giant slap bracelet from the nineteen eighties.

"Let's find out," he said.

The spell embedded in his body led us out of the drawing room and all the way down to the basement level of the house. We were only a few doors away from the room we'd stayed in when Ian stopped and opened another door. Yonah, Ereshki, and Katsana were inside, and from their expressions, only Yonah wasn't surprised to see us. He merely gave Ian a sardonic look.

"That took much less time than I expected."

Ian ignored the slur to his supposed sexual stamina. "This proves what I warned you about," he said. "This spell traced Dagon's power right back to Ereshki. What's to stop him from using one just like it to find her and the others he's seeking?"

"It also proves Ereshki is telling the truth," Yonah countered. "She doesn't remember Ariel or any of her former crimes despite being one of the souls Dagon hoarded inside himself, which she must be or she wouldn't have specks of Dagon's power in her for the spell to trace now."

I hated that I agreed with the demon. I might not be capable of believing Ereshki after what she'd done to me, but spells didn't lie. The question was, where did that leave me and the many, many other people who had only me left to speak for them? Should this Ereshki pay for the crimes of her former self? Or did having all memory of *that* Ereshki ripped from her mind make the woman standing before me technically innocent?

I was still wrestling with that when Ian said, "It also proves Ariel's version of events, so we'll take Ereshki and go now," with such deadly silkiness, it was clear *he* wasn't suffering from a crisis of conscience.

Ereshki burst into tears. Hearing it tugged at a place in my heart I'd thought was long dead when it came to her. Even Yonah gave her a sympathetic look. Then he stared at Ian.

"Unaccept—"

He never finished the word. The floor heaved, then a huge crack appeared that the sea immediately filled. Water was up to my knees before I could even react.

Silver! If I didn't get him out of here, he'd drown! I dashed out of the room, then ducked because Yonah flew over me with Ereshki clasped in his arms. That's right; she was human again so she was susceptible to drowning, too.

I flew down the hall, ignoring Ian's shout to stop. By the time I reached our room, the water was already higher than the doorknob. I kicked it open right as a tremendous quaking caused multiple cracks to appear in the ceiling. Silver flew out as if he'd been fired from a canon. Now, the only dry space left was around my head. I clutched him to that while fighting to fly above the water line. More horrible crashing sounds above had me glancing worriedly at the ceiling. Whatever catastrophe had happened—an earthquake, maybe?—it sounded like the roof would cave in any moment.

"Ian!" I shouted, not seeing him in the hallway with its rapidly rising water and ominously increasing roof debris.

I thought I heard his voice farther ahead, but I couldn't be sure. The water was now so high, I could no longer fly, and walking through it while holding Silver's nose above the water would take too long. More collapsing sounds proved that. We only had seconds before this entire hallway crashed in on itself.

I yelled, "Hold your breath!" to Silver, prayed he understood me, and dove beneath the water, holding him.

I kept one arm in front of me to punch aside any debris as I swam as fast as I could. My other arm protected Silver's head and the rest of him was tucked against my body. I fought panic as new crashing sounds reached me even through the churning water. More debris began to pile up, blocking my path. Silver could be dying right now, and where was *Ian?* Vampires couldn't drown, but he could be trapped under something while the house collapsed upon him with enough force to rip him apart—

Something hard slammed into me, yanking me up. I thought I felt someone's body next to mine, then there was nothing except pain from the multiple concussive impacts and noise that made the previous sounds pale by comparison. When I could see again, it was through a sheen of blood that turned my vision red.

Red Ian had me clutched against him while flying us free of the house, which pancaked onto itself with horrifying rapidness. Red Silver coughed out water while blood dripped from his soaked feathers. Then red sand met our feet as Ian set us down on the beach, which heaved from the aftershocks of whatever had brought the house down.

"How did you find me in all that wreckage?" I gasped out.

"Locator beacon in Silver's collar," he replied. "Slipped it on him back at that villa in Athens."

I choked on the laughter that bubbled up. "That's how you found me at the Mycenae ruins."

"I'll always find you," he swore, giving me a hard kiss.

Another round of aftershocks shook the ground, breaking our kiss. Gods, *the house*, filled with hundreds of people celebrating a ball when the walls came crashing down! How many had gotten out like we had? How many were still trapped?

I set Silver down. "Stay," I told the Simargl. Then I grabbed Ian's hand. "We have to go back and help!"

Something like a snort escaped him. "Knew you'd say that."

We flew back to the house, me wiping the blood from my eyes, Ian muttering something I couldn't catch due to the wind and the continued sounds of concrete smashing and people screaming. In the short seconds it took to get back to Yonah's, his four-story mansion had crumpled to barely one level, with the sea pouring into a huge fissure that went from the ruins of his home all the way to the night-darkened surf.

Ian dropped down near a group of vampires who were digging in the rubble where the pool area had been. It was gone now, replaced by huge pieces of the house that had slid off and an even deeper hole that seemed to swallow the remains. I was about to join him when fresh screams sent me flying past him to the collapsed section of what had been the second-floor balcony.

"You take that section, I'll take this one!" I yelled.

The balcony was on the ground, crushing anyone who'd been unlucky enough to be underneath it. The scent of blood and death was choking, but from the moans and screams, there were also some survivors beneath it. I began throwing aside the pieces of the former balcony, careful to aim them at the sand behind me instead of what could be more buried people around me.

"I'm coming!" I called out, digging and throwing even faster. I soon lost my grip on a hunk of railing because my hands were dripping with blood, but I would heal. The people trapped might not have that chance, if I didn't hurry.

Something large and heavy landed next to me. Yonah, wings nowhere to be seen, pulling at the debris with a single-minded determination that matched my desperation.

"Stop," he said, shocking me. "I can do this, but only you can halt the sea. Pull back the waves from the fissure, Ariel. Now, or we'll never reach the human survivors in time."

"I can control *some* water, but I can't hold back part of an ocean!" I protested.

"Then do what you can!" was Yonah's impatient reply before he disappeared to begin tunneling beneath the debris.

I was still furious with Yonah, but he was right; the biggest danger to mortal survivors now was the sea. Manipulating these waters might be against the Leviathan's rules, but I couldn't value a mere threat to my life more than the guaranteed deaths of the trapped human survivors if I did nothing.

I raised my hands and sent my senses down to find the water that I knew was churning beneath the rubble of Yonah's house. *Besides,* I thought grimly. *These parts of the sea had crossed onto* here *without permission. I was only sending them back.*

I closed my eyes. Sight wouldn't help me. Only senses, and I let them wrap around the energy in the water beneath the house's ruins until I felt it pulse through me. Then I wrapped my power around that energy and pulled, trying to force it back from the countless crevasses it had filled while also trying to hold back the sea's relentless flow into the main fissure.

But almost instantly, I was swamped by the crushing force of more power than I could ever understand, let alone bend to my will. *Run!* a shrieking, primal part of me urged. *Run now or die!*

At the same time, my other nature reached through the bars of her cage. Not only was she unafraid, she was intrigued by the potential of all the uncontrollable energy roiling around her.

I didn't think. I grabbed at her hand and pulled.

Chapter 31

When my other half finally relinquished control, the vampire, ghoul, and demon survivors had plugged the largest of the fissures with multiple pieces of debris from the house. It wasn't a permanent fix, and seawater still ran through the cracks, but it was no longer the massive deluge that had overwhelmed me with its power before.

And I was so exhausted, I couldn't even pull myself into a sitting position as I watched bloodied survivors wait at the edge of the ruins. Some were crying, some were praying aloud that their loved ones would be among those still being pulled out from under the collapsed house. I couldn't hear heartbeats beneath the rubble, but I hoped that was because of all the noise those digging through the ruins made. I wanted to join them to help, but I couldn't seem to move yet.

When something foaming and deep blue rose up from the sea, for a moment I thought it was a rogue wave. Then I realized it was several Leviathan forming out of the waters. Of course, once they did, they came out of the surf and headed right toward me. I couldn't even summon the energy to be afraid. All I could think was, *Took you long enough.*

Then ripped black pants filled my vision. I followed them upward to see a muscled, pale back and soaked auburn hair. Ian raised his arm, and the horn that had been wrapped around it stabbed at the air as if wishing it were flesh.

"I chalked up the first threat to her life as a cultural misunderstanding, but now I'm all out of fucks to give," he said in a loud, chipper tone. "So if *any* of you water-logged sods comes near her, I'll shove this horn so far up your arses, Poseidon himself will be screaming from his new hemorrhoids!"

If that was the last thing I ever heard, at least it was memorable.

"That will not be necessary," a smooth voice stated.

I don't know why I thought it would be Yonah. Probably because I'd saved at least some of his people, so I'd hoped the demon would speak up in my defense, if it came to this. But the man who stepped into my vision had long white hair instead of a shiny bald pate, and his skin . . . *Wow,* I thought hazily.

He must've had it covered up by an elegant tuxedo at some point, but deep rips in the fabric revealed skin that at one moment was so pale it resembled moonlight resting on the waves, while in the next it was deep blue shot through with silver. Staring at it was like watching light refract and diffuse as it penetrated through water, and now I knew what his hair reminded me of: the roiling froth that formed when seas were at their stormiest.

"The Leviathan ruler," I mumbled. I might not have seen him when my other nature took control earlier, but I'd felt him, and that was enough to recognize him now.

Ian turned, placing himself now between the stranger and me. "You don't say?"

Ian's drawl didn't fool me. His aura burst out like the detonation of a bomb; a warning as clear as the deadly horn now pointed at the tall, white-haired Leviathan ruler.

"As I said, that won't be necessary," the stranger replied. With that, the Leviathan melted back into the sea.

Ian didn't relax his stance. "Do I owe you thanks, or did you call off your sea dogs to take a crack at Ariel yourself?"

"Ariel?" The Leviathan ruler's lips twitched as he looked past Ian to me. That's when I finally noticed that if his skin wasn't so unusual, he'd look like a normal, handsome young man. "You of all people named yourself after a fictional mermaid?"

I summoned up the energy to reply. "That book wasn't written until the thousands of years *after* my sire named me, but the irony of it isn't lost on me now."

Another smile touched his mouth. Then he looked back at Ian. "I mean her no harm." *But you couldn't stop me if I did*, his newly hardened stare added.

Ian's smile made me drag myself into a sitting position. I'd seen that same smile right before Ian threw himself into a gleefully violent fight to the death.

"I could use some help," I said to distract Ian. It wasn't a lie. My body felt like a wet rag, and now Yonah was striding toward us with his wings out. That couldn't mean anything good.

"I've finished taking the wards down, so I and my people are leaving," Yonah announced, seeming to speak more to the Leviathan ruler than Ian or me. At his declaration, everyone stopped working with a suddenness that made the new silence eerie. "I will give you our new location when it is safe," Yonah went on, again seeming to speak to the Leviathan leader alone.

They grasped upper arms in the ancient form of a handshake. Since Yonah didn't immediately start spewing water from his mouth, the Leviathan leader must not have the same "drown upon contact" limitations that his fluid-formed kinsfolk had.

"Safe journey, Yonah," he said in his unaccented voice.

"To you as well, Indus," the former demon prince replied.

Indus. The name of a river not far from my homeland in ancient Mesopotamia. Coincidence? Or had the cradle of civilization birthed much more than I'd realized?

Ereshki distracted me by limping up to our pile of debris. "Please," she said. "Please, Yonah, do not leave me behind!"

"Rules state that only the most trusted members are brought to a new sanctuary after an attack," Yonah replied in a harsh tone. "You are the newest, so you are the least trusted. Even if you were not, this place has been a haven for over five hundred years, but less than a month after your arrival, an earthquake levels half the island when it is nowhere near a fault line? No! Dark magic was afoot. I can sense it, meaning this one"—he stabbed his finger at Ian—"is right. Your enemy tracked you here, and I cannot allow him to track you to where we are going."

Ereshki tried to cling to him. Yonah shoved her away. She sank to her knees, weeping with a hopelessness that caused a poignant stab of remembrance. I knew how hopelessness that deep felt. I wished it on no one, not even her.

"How are you getting your people out of here?" Ian asked, ignoring Ereshki's tears. "As you might know, our plane is no longer functional, so we could use a ride."

"Not with me," Yonah replied curtly. "You can call for help, if you find a working mobile phone. Or start flying. Or swim; the Leviathan will be gone soon, too. I care not which. With the wards down, I can now teleport all my people out of here, even those still trapped beneath the ruins. But that also means this island is now completely unprotected."

With that, Yonah unleashed a shockwave of power. It threw Ian backward and must have knocked me out, because when my eyes opened, only Ian, Ereshki, and I remained.

Ereshki's sobs turned into wails as she realized Yonah had made good on his promise to leave her behind. Then she scrambled to her feet and ran, but soon tripped on a piece of sliding debris and fell.

"I'll deal with you in a moment," Ian muttered before raising his voice. "Silver! Get over here, mate, we're leaving!"

I was relieved to see a streak of gray flying toward us. Then all I saw was Ereshki when Ian teleported her over and dropped her in front of me. "Need to make it quick—we have to leave before this island is overrun with Yonah's enemies."

For a second, I didn't understand. Then I did. So did Ereshki. Her sobs became frenzied, and she looked at me with a bleakness that transcended despair.

She expected no mercy. I certainly owed her none. Dagon didn't merely slit my throat before claiming he was the one to raise me from the dead when I came back to life later. No, Dagon had all the flair of a showman combined with the ruthlessness of his ambitions. The more prolonged the suffering, the more grotesque the method of execution . . . the godlier Dagon looked when I came back from the dead, thus the more power he derived from his worshippers.

And I'd loved Ereshki so much, I *begged* Dagon to make me the object of his cruelties instead of her. When he did, I was relieved for her sake because until the day Tenoch rescued me, I thought Ereshki loved me as a sister, too. But on that last day, I recovered from a beating faster than my captors anticipated and overheard Ereshki laughing with Fenkir and Rani over how easily she'd deceived me. She wasn't a helpless captive. No, Ereshki was Dagon's willing demon-branded acolyte, there only to keep me loyal to him through her deceit.

Finding that out had hurt worse than anything Dagon had done to me.

Now, I could finally get my revenge. In many ways, I *needed* to, not only for myself, but for all her other victims, too. But even as my hands shook with the urge to choke the life from her, I couldn't. The Ereshki who'd betrayed me and all those other people wasn't here. Only this one was, and she couldn't remember her many crimes.

Murdering this Ereshki wouldn't be justice. It wouldn't even be vengeance. It would be cruelty for cruelty's sake. That's why I couldn't do it. If I did, I wouldn't be much better than the monster Ereshki had been back then, and I *was* better, dammit! She'd taken a lot from me, but she wouldn't take that.

"I'm not killing her," I said.

Ian shrugged. "If you're too tired, then I'll do it."

"No." Now my tone was steel. "We're taking her with us."

$\mathcal{I}$'d never argued with someone while teleporting before. I can't say I recommend it. Whenever Ian didn't want to hear what I was saying, he'd blink us another hundred kilometers or so over the expanse of the ocean. Between that, we flew. Or, more accurately, Ian flew while toting me, Silver, and Ereshki because I was still too weak to carry myself, let alone anyone else.

I'd never heard such a litany of curse words in different languages during the hours it took us to fly, teleport, rest, and repeat before we finally reached the mainland, which turned out to be the coastline of Santa Monica, California. Many times, I expected Ian to leave Ereshki behind to drown, but despite his clearly stated objections, he kept her with us. In the end, I wasn't sure if that was out of respect for my wishes or because of my colder assertion that Ereshki was worth more to us alive.

That's how the four of us stumbled into the first gorgeous beach house we saw after swimming the last couple hundred meters to shore. It wasn't empty, but a few flashes from Ian's gaze later, the rich middle-aged Caucasian couple was all too happy to host us as their unexpected guests. Demons couldn't enter a private home unless invited and we were well into midday, so for the next several hours of daylight, we were safe.

I took a long, grateful sip from the husband's wrist while his wife busied herself asking Ereshki if she wanted something to eat. Ian, to my surprise, went straight to the couple's phone and started dialing.

"Crispin," he said moments later. "Something urgent has come up. Need you to meet me at my favorite house tonight, and I know you like to keep her close, but whatever you do, do *not* bring the girl with you."

I heard Bones's snort through the phone. "You know Cat won't agree to staying behind—"

"Not that girl," Ian interrupted.

A tense silence followed, then Bones said, "See you tonight," and hung up.

I was intrigued. Was Ian finally asking his friends for help to take Dagon down?

Ian put the phone down. Then he sprawled onto the nearest sofa without care that he was still soaking wet. Ereshki scrambled to get as far away from him as the stunning ocean-view room allowed. I caught her glancing at the side door that led to the deck and its stairway to the beach as if estimating her chances of reaching it in time.

"You're safer with us than on your own. Dagon will rip you apart to get what he wants from you." I couldn't kill her in good conscience, but I wasn't about to coddle her, either. "All we'll do is be rude and keep you confined. Be wise, Ereshki. Take rudeness and confinement over death."

"*He* still wants to kill me," she said in a shaking voice.

The grin Ian flashed her said she wasn't wrong.

"He won't," I replied, ignoring Ian's challenging arch of the brow. "You're the perfect bait. Dagon has clearly found a way to track you; Yonah's destroyed island sanctuary is proof of that. We arrived less than twelve hours before the earthquake, and a spell that powerful would've taken much longer to implement, so Dagon followed *you* there. Not us. But Dagon's not at full strength yet. Plus, he'll be struck with crippling pain as soon as he's near Ian, so we're going to finally set a trap for him that he can't escape from."

We only had the element of surprise and the results of whatever my father had done to Ian to combat Dagon's wild-card ability to burn through souls to increase his power, but it would have to be enough.

"Why will being near Ian harm him?" Ereshki asked at the same time Ian said, "Do go on," in a dangerously silky tone.

I stiffened. Had I not mentioned that to him before? From Ian's darkening expression, I hadn't. I sighed.

"My father put a spell on you that only activates when Dagon is near. You saw what it did when Dagon crashed our date at the amusement park. He dropped to his knees screaming."

The memory warmed my heart, but Ian's fingers began to drum against the armrest of the sofa hard enough to send bits of fluff from its inner stuffing into the air.

"Once, I thought the most awful thing I'd heard was Vlad's witchy wife cursing me to fall for someone who insisted on monogamy." Ian's tone was deceptively jovial. "I must not have heard the part where she added that the object of my affection would also have an enraging set of scruples combined with insane protective instincts that led to repeated suicidal tendencies!"

I must not have drunk enough from the rich husband. If I had, I might have known what the hell Ian was talking about. "Is this your way of saying you don't want to be monogamous?"

An end table went sailing through the window. Glass shattered and the wife let out a frightened squeak that Ereshki echoed. Ian was in front of me before I could speak, those strong fingers now digging into my shoulders.

"No." His voice was harsher than a growl. "It's my way of saying I can't believe you avoided me for weeks for my supposed protection when all the while, doing so put you in more danger because *I* was spell-bound into being a bloody Dagon-repellant!"

"I wasn't thinking about *my* danger," I snapped, weariness turning to anger. "I wasn't much thinking at all, as I've tried to explain to you over and over. Yes, I handled things badly, but after you hold *my* dead body in your arms, you can react with all the cool rationality you want. Until then, excuse me for *not* acting with my best cold logic right after holding yours!"

"We should leave," the husband said, edging out of the room.

Ereshki must have agreed. She started to follow him until Ian snarled, "Stay!" with his eyes lit up.

At that, all of them froze.

Was Ereshki susceptible to mind control like regular humans now? Or had she frozen in place because she was afraid to make Ian any angrier? I didn't have time to find out which. Ian's eyes closed, and he drew in a breath as if to steady himself.

"No," he said in a grating tone. "I wouldn't have reacted logically or rationally to you being dead in my arms, either. Now, is there anything *else* you neglected to mention to me?"

I stared into his eyes, my anger leaving as fast as it had come. There was too much raw feeling in them for it to remain. Or, as my brother had warned me, was I only seeing what I wanted to see? Was I drowning in the same quicksand many, many others had by assuming Ian felt more for me than he did?

"No," I replied hoarsely. What Ian did or didn't feel for me was a conversation for another time. Right now, survival came first. "That's the last of my secrets, I think."

A sardonic smile curled Ian's mouth. "I hope so, but I won't be surprised if it's not. Now"—back to our silent audience—"Mr. and Mrs. Rich, invite over half a dozen of the wealthiest sods you're mates with. Don't take no for an answer, either. I don't know about my lovely wife, but I'm famished."

Chapter 33

*M*r. and Mrs. Rich, as Ian had ironically titled them, had several wealthy—and tasty—friends. One of them even had a company jet. That saved us the trouble of trying to get Ereshki through security at a commercial airport. She might appear to be susceptible to vampire mind control at the moment, but that could change. Who knew which of Dagon's powers she'd absorbed but hadn't shown, or perhaps didn't even know about yet?

We left the wealthy group with a lower red blood cell count and a memory of loaning the company jet to "friends." That would buy us a day or two before the mogul snapped out of Ian's compulsion and went after his plane. We made it easy to find by leaving it at the White Plains Airport in New York, then took an Uber to Manhasset.

One glance showed why Ian had described this as his "favorite" home. It was as large as Yonah's sprawling mansion, but Ian's three balconies were adorned with various carved creations instead of flowing plants. It didn't surprise me that Ian's taste ran the gamut from the fantastical to the erotic. I caught a glimpse of stone gargoyles cavorting with women, men, and satyrs—or were those centaurs?—before Ian hustled me, Silver, and Ereshki inside. Night had just fallen, making it safe for demons to roam again. How quickly could Dagon track Ereshki? Or Ian, if Dagon was tracing his power in Ian the same way the spell embedded in Ian now traced others? We'd soon find out. I only hoped we would be ready.

I'd barely had time to admire the ornate woodworking on the

walls of the grand foyer when we heard a car pull up. I stiffened even though I knew Dagon would have another demon teleport him here if he'd found us and intended to ambush us. Dagon wouldn't drive up and slam the car door when he got out. When I heard a second car door close more softly, I relaxed.

"Cat and Crispin," Ian said. "Prompt, for once. Take her," he added to one of the two vampires who came into the hall, then pushed Ereshki toward them. "Keep her secured and don't underestimate her. She's not a normal human."

With that, Ian flung open the double doors before the couple walking up to them could knock. "Have a demon problem, so you'll understand why I won't invite you in," he greeted them.

Bones—whose birth name was Crispin, but only Ian called him that—gave Ian a pointed look as both he and his wife, Cat, strode inside. Cat's red locks were still dyed that hideously drab shade of brown and Bones's hair was still so long, it hid half his face, but their auras made the air crackle. When they walked over the threshold without hesitation, another knot in me eased. No demon could walk inside a private residence without being invited first, so this wasn't Dagon and another demon wearing glamour in an attempt to fool us.

In the next moment, I realized I'd relaxed too soon. Something large and dark thudded onto the front grounds with such force, the stone fountain next to it sloshed water over its sides. Perimeter alarms began to blare, but over their loud din, I caught Ian's curse . . . and understood when that large, dark form was instantly illuminated by multiple spotlights from the roof.

Mencheres.

"Don't worry, I won't wait for an invitation, either," Ian's sire said as he strode up to the house.

Ian gave Bones an evil look. "Low of you, Crispin."

Bones's brow went up. "As you would say, paybacks, Ian."

I FOLLOWED IAN into the drawing room, fighting flashbacks of the last time I'd met with his closest friends. We had presented ourselves to them as besotted newlyweds. They hadn't bought it then, but they'd been more restrained in their disbelief, and I was including their death threats to me in that descriptor. Now, the gloves were clearly off.

"I know why you sold your soul," Mencheres said as soon as Ian shut the smoked glass drawing room doors behind him.

"Of all the times to be out of heroin," Ian muttered. Then he went to the crystal decanters on the shelf and poured himself a large glass of whatever the dark amber liquid was.

Mencheres stared at him before his obsidian gaze landed on me. The weight of it made me feel like I was being restrained with layer upon layer of thick chains. Then he looked at Silver, who flew over and began to sniff the former pharaoh's legs.

"Silver," I said in reprimand.

"He smells my mastiffs on me," Mencheres replied, his look turning sardonic. "Though none of my pets have wings."

"Who else wants whisky?" Ian said, ignoring that. "I know you're a yes, Crispin. Cat? Veritas?"

"I'll have some," I said, thinking, *And I wish you had some demon blood to spike it with.*

He handed me a glass as full as his own, then gave a half-filled one to Bones before taking the chair next to mine.

"So, Vlad or Leila finally let my secret spill," Ian said in a conversational tone.

"Incorrect," Mencheres replied with the same faux pleasantness. "Both she and Vlad refused to tell me, but Vlad did say to watch my fake execution video more closely. I did. You're almost out of the camera's range, but after Vlad supposedly blows my head off, you come toward him with a knife. Vlad says, 'Don't,' and you say, 'Oh, I'm not going to kill you. I'm going to let Mencheres do that.' Then the video ends."

I hadn't been there that day, but I knew what happened next: Ian had cut off the warding tattoo that had been blocking Dagon from finding him. And Dagon had come running.

"Now, I finally understand what you meant." Mencheres's voice lost its amiability and became a harsh rasp. "You were vowing to bring me back so I could avenge my own death, and there's only one way you could do that—by selling your soul."

"Except you weren't dead." Ian's tone was light, as if he hadn't paid in misery, death, and worse for his selfless act. "Gave Dagon a right good belly laugh, telling me that after our bargain was struck."

Pain was etched into Mencheres's features so deeply, for an instant he looked all of his true age despite his unlined, handsome features. "I promise you that I will fix this."

"You don't have to."

Mencheres's head, which had bowed with grief, snapped up at that. Ian continued with a wave in my direction.

"My wife is full of surprises. Yanking me back from the grave after my death voided my soul debt to Dagon is merely one of those surprises."

"How?" Cat's disbelieving outburst was echoed by her husband. Mencheres looked too shocked to speak.

"The same way I do everything else," I said, hoping vagueness would be enough. "Bibbity-bobbity-boo."

Mencheres finally found his voice. "Magic can briefly reanimate flesh or bones, but it cannot pull a soul from the afterlife and restore it back to their body. Only a demon deal can do that . . . or, perhaps, a demon herself."

Revulsion touched Cat's features. From Bones's hardening expression, he'd suspected that, too.

"Don't insult me," I snapped before realizing I was insulting my own half brother with the comment. "Though not all demons are evil," I amended. "Besides, I'm"—*the daughter of the embodiment of the river between life and death, to hear my half-demon brother describe it*—"Something else," I finished.

"A demigod," Ian said with the same casualness that he'd offered them whisky with.

Mencheres gave me a look that wasn't entirely surprised. Bones, however, rose to his feet.

"Your hair." He'd actually started to recoil from me before he caught himself and stopped.

Ian rolled his eyes. "Really, Crispin? Act your age."

Cat was more succinct. "What the hell, honey?"

Bones sat back down, a flash of embarrassment crossing his features. Then they hardened and his aura flared as if arming itself. "Your. Hair." Each word was an indictment.

"Rude," Cat hissed to him before saying, "I think your lowlights are cool," in a louder voice to me. "Granted, I'm a Buckeye fan, and blue and gold are Michigan colors, but—"

"They're not a Wolverines tribute, Kitten," Bones interrupted. "Remember the Angel of Death I told you about? When I caught a glimpse of his true form, his hair was just like hers."

Cat's eyes bulged until they looked as if they were attempting to escape her face. "I thought *my* family tree was fucked up," she breathed. "Wow."

Suddenly, the air felt like it was squeezing me; a warning from Mencheres. "Ariel, daughter of Aken," he said, voice low and resonant as he true-named me. "Is Ian truly free from his soul debt to that demon?"

At last, something I could answer without hesitation or vagueness. "Yes."

"She also had a ghost secretly guard me *and* set a spell on me that boomeranged any malicious magic off me and sent it back to its caster," Ian said, resulting in Mencheres giving me his first real smile. "But none of that is why I called Cat and Crispin here," he continued. "I just found out that Timothy's alive."

"My friend Timothy?" At once, Cat gave Bones an accusing look. "You didn't tell me you thought he was dead!"

"Because I didn't," Bones began in an exasperated tone, then stopped when he saw Ian's face. "You don't mean . . . ?"

"I do indeed," Ian replied grimly. "Saw him myself while I was stealing this," a swipe indicated the bulge beneath his sleeve. Right, they hadn't seen the horn yet. "And you'll never guess why he'd hidden himself away from us all these years."

"Oh, you mean *your* friend Timothy from when you were all human," Cat said, cluing in. "If he's alive, that's great!"

Bones gave Ian a measuring look before turning to her. "If this were only good news about Timothy being alive, Ian wouldn't have insisted on giving it to us in person." To Ian, he said simply, "What's Timothy done?"

Ian leaned back with a sigh. "It's what he could do. You remember Timothy left because he was looking for Cain? He and the cult he joined believe they've found him, or Cain's remains, as it were. More importantly, they believe those remains can be raised back to life if given the blood of a human, vampire, and ghoul tri-bred to drink."

Light suddenly exploded around Cat in twisting, diaphanous forms while an unearthly wail made me want to clutch my ears. Just as quickly, it was gone, leaving Cat haloed in nothing except the artificial glow of the room's subtle high-hat lighting, while the only sound came from Silver's contented grunt as he settled near Mencheres's feet. I looked around, amazed that no one else seemed to have noticed that for an instant, Cat had been surrounded by deadly wraiths.

"Your old friend wants to bleed my daughter?" she hissed.

"If he knew about her, yes," Ian answered bluntly. "Granted, Timothy didn't kill me when he had the chance, but I'd never bet on friendship against zealotry, and Timothy is a zealot now."

Bones reached out to take Cat's hand. "Then I hope we never see him again," he said, his tone no less deadly for its new softness. "Now, what's this thing you stole from him?"

I got up, not needing to see Ian demonstrate the horn's remarkable abilities. I must have still had a grudge against the relic for blowing Ian's head off and nearly killing him.

"I'll check on Ereshki," I said as Ian took his cashmere jacket off. Ian had arrived at the beach house this morning wearing only ripped pants, and Mr. Rich had been a similar size, so Ian had raided his closet. I wasn't judging; I was now wearing a cashmere sweater and slacks, courtesy of Mrs. Rich.

"I'll go with you," Cat said, surprising me.

We were halfway to the door when Mencheres suddenly blocked my path. I tensed, but all he did was fold me into his arms.

I was startled. Even at our friendliest, Mencheres and I were not huggers. Only when Mencheres whispered, "Thank you," in a voice vibrating from emotion did I realize why he'd done this.

Ian. Of course. We had loving him in common.

"You're welcome." *Though I didn't do it for you . . .*

Mencheres released me. "As long as I've known you, Veritas, I've either admired you as an ally, respected you as an equal, or been wary of you as an adversary. Now, it is my great honor to welcome you to my family as a daughter."

Ian's smirk said, *Told you he'd do this.*

I was touched, but I couldn't show how much without revealing feelings Ian didn't yet reciprocate. That's why I covered my deeper emotions with a wry smile.

"That's sweet of you, Mencheres, but considering I'm more than a hundred years older than you . . . I'm not calling you 'Dad.'"

He chuckled. So did everyone else, which covered up the vulnerability of the moment for me. Or so I thought. Out of the corner of my eye, I caught Cat giving me a knowing look. Was she very perceptive, or were all my efforts futile because what I felt for Ian was written all over my face?

I didn't want to find out. "Ereshki," I said, as if reminding them of where I was going. "Where is she?"

"Ask any of my guards," Ian replied. "They'll show you."

I looked at Cat, wishing I had an excuse to avoid her now. "Still coming?" *Please say no . . .*

"Right behind you," she replied with a quick smile.

Shit.

$\mathcal{I}$ intended to avoid conversation with Cat by quickly finding one of Ian's guards to take me to Ereshki. However, we'd barely left the drawing room before Cat began tugging me across the formal hall to one of the many rooms beyond it.

"The library," she exclaimed, as if she'd never seen one before. "The last time I was here, I almost killed Ian in this!"

She kept tugging on my arm to get me to follow her. I gave the glass-domed ceiling above the foyer a longing look. If I flung Cat through it, she'd get the hint that I didn't appreciate being pulled along like a reluctant toddler, though that would be a bit extreme. And rude, I supposed.

Thus, I let her lead me into the library. It was an impressive, two-story room with thousands of old and new volumes lining the walls. Another section housed glass-encased scrolls. I could have browsed the books for hours, but Cat seemed more interested in the room's only piece of artwork, a collection of bones formed into a mosaic of the Australian outback.

"I can't believe Ian put this back together," she marveled. "It crashed into pieces after I threw it at his head years ago."

She clearly wanted me to ask about this fight, so I did. "Why did you throw it at him?"

"For distraction. He'd just chucked me into a wall, and I was determined to kill him even though I was surprised by how strong he was." Then she gave me an arch look. "But Ian heard my heart-beat, and like all vampires, the sound lulled him into believing I was far more fragile than I appeared. Being underestimated in a fight gives you the best advantage ever."

More conversation was only polite, I decided. Besides, she'd intrigued me. "Why were you so determined to kill him?"

"It was my job." She cocked her head. "I was once on the Law Guardians' watch list, so you must know that I used to work for the government, killing vampires who indiscriminately murdered humans. I thought Ian was one of those indiscriminate murderers because my boss sent me after him. I only found out later that my boss's reasons were personal. Ian had turned my boss's brother into a vampire, and shortly after that, the newly fanged motherfucker wiped out most of my boss's family."

Now I knew who she was talking about, and how literal of her to describe that vampire as a "motherfucker."

"You're speaking of your father, Max." Making Cat's former boss her paternal uncle. I hadn't known that before now.

"Yep," she said in a harder tone. "The other thing Max did right after getting his fangs was hook up with my mom, and he was so newly undead, he still had viable sperm. To make matters worse, right afterward, Max green-eyed my mom into believing he was a literal demon. Know what it's like to grow up afraid of yourself because you were told that half of you is evil?"

I flinched, then cursed myself along with my far-too-perceptive companion. I thought Cat had dragged me in here only to brag about a long-ago fight, but her real goal had been to confront me about a struggle she shouldn't know I was having.

"I saw your face when Ian told us what you were." Her voice softened. "Don't worry, the others didn't catch it. They'd have to have lived it to do that, and they didn't. But I did."

If I'd suddenly been stripped naked, I would have felt less exposed. Ian had caused me to feel this way many times, but I trusted him, while I barely knew the woman across from me. Once again, I threw up my Law Guardian front as if it were a shield.

"I don't know what you're speaking of." My voice sounded cool and composed, to my relief.

She snorted. "Bullshit. You're barely holding it together, and I don't blame you. I thought I had it rough, hiding what I was for a couple decades. You've been hiding for thousands of years while masquerading as a stick-up-your-ass vamp cop. Falling in love and then nearly losing Ian was the last straw, wasn't it?" Another too-knowing look. "Twice, I thought Bones had died, and I lost my shit to epic degrees both times. No matter how tough we think we are, loss like that cuts too deep to handle, doesn't it?"

Each word smashed through my defenses faster than I could rebuild them. Worse, she wasn't done.

"I don't know how you brought Ian back from the dead, but I bet it took all the power from the part of yourself you've been hiding to do it. There's no putting *that* genie back in the bottle once it's out, either. I remember that from when I was fighting against my vamp side. The scariest part was how much I loved giving in to that power when I finally did let go . . . and let everything in me out for all to see."

"What are you, the half-breed whisperer?" I snapped, too rattled to continue hiding behind my stick-up-the-ass vamp cop persona, as Cat had described it.

Her dark-gray gaze glinted with green. "I'm not, but after all this time, *you* should be. The fact that you aren't means someone told you that your other half was bad when you were young enough to believe them. I don't know who that was—"

"Stop," I ordered, horrified to feel tears start to well. How had she reduced me to this so quickly? Or had I done it to myself? Was I still as out of control as she'd insinuated?

"But you must have trusted that person, to believe them this long," she went on, her tone turning flintlike despite the new sympathy in her eyes. "Must have loved them, too. Only someone you love could mess you up this bad, this long. My mom sure did a number on me, but she was wrong, just like whoever worked you over emotionally was wrong, too—"

"You know nothing!"

Now I was shouting, and my vision turned ominously dark. I would tolerate her filleting me, but I would rip her blood out and bathe in it before I allowed her to disrespect my sire.

"Tenoch was *not* wrong. He *never* would have changed over the world's most ruthless warlord right before he died unless he *knew* that part of me was so dangerous, there had to be someone equally dangerous to stop me if I ever truly let that half of myself free!"

Wetness hit my cheeks. I thought it was my tears until I saw the drops flying from Cat's eyes before feeling more tiny splashes on my skin. I hadn't meant to yank her tears from her, but I had, and from the flush filling her skin, her blood was also rising to the surface faster than she could've directed it.

I spun around, squeezing my eyes shut while trying to force my other nature down before I did bathe in her blood. *Go away, go away, go away!* I chanted at it.

It wasn't enough.

Desperately, I sent my senses out to the fountain in front of Ian's house. Then I blasted my rage into the water it contained instead of the woman who'd cut through centuries of scabs to effortlessly stab me in my deepest wound. I felt the water boil before it iced over so fast, the extreme temperature change shattered the stones. The sound of the fountain exploding was so loud, it masked the crash the library door made when Bones flung it open.

"What's wrong?" Bones demanded. "Felt a burst of power coming from this room."

I turned to see Ian right behind Bones. Cat was still staring at me, but at least she wasn't covered in blood. Neither was anything else in the room. The only damage was what Bones had done to the wall with the door.

Good. I'd caught myself in time.

"Oh, that was just me, being totally *not* dangerous," I said in a scathingly bright tone. "Now, I think I'll go check on our prisoner by myself, thanks."

I would've left, if one of Ian's guards hadn't run into the room in the next moment. He was covered in blood, making me think I *hadn't* directed all my rage at the fountain outside. Then his panted words made me think again.

"She escaped!"

"How?" Ian demanded, already shoving past him.

The guard ran to catch up with Ian. I did, too, which meant I caught the guard's reply.

"We don't know! One minute, she was chained to the chair. The next, the three of us were bloody and she was gone!"

"Sound the alarm," Ian ordered. "She needs to be found!"

"Don't you feel where she is?" I asked him, surprised.

Ian's mouth tightened. "No, I don't."

Yonah's spell had given Ian a significant range. Even if Ereshki had somehow gotten free the moment after she'd left our sight, she couldn't have run *that* far in such a short time.

Ian led us downstairs to a solid concrete room that looked like a new vampire holding cell. Its door was the length of my forearm in thickness, and it had no windows. It should have been more than enough to hold Ereshki, but the chair that was bolted into the floor was empty of everything except heavy chains.

Ian bent near the chair, then straightened so abruptly, he nearly ripped it free from its welds. "What is this?"

The room's two bloody guards gave a guilty glance at each other before the black-haired one replied, "Pen and paper."

The look Ian gave them should have sent them to their knees begging for mercy. "*Why* did you give her that?"

"She was crying about how she wanted to write a good-bye note," the other guard said, hunching as if feeling the blows that were certain to come. "We only loosened one wrist. Her arms and legs were still chained. What could a human do with only one wrist, some paper and a pen?" he added defensively.

I closed my eyes. *Ian heard my heartbeat*, Cat had said about their first fight. *And like all vampires, the sound lulled him into believing I was far more fragile than I appeared.*

Ian had warned his guards about Ereshki. They still hadn't listened, and she'd used that to her advantage. But how?

I took the piece of paper Ian had had clenched in his hand. Then my jaw tightened until I heard cartilage snap as I recognized the symbols. "She drew a knockout spell and a teleporting spell."

That's why Ian couldn't feel her any longer. The teleporting spell might only work once, but it would be enough to take her far away from here.

Ian inhaled sharply. "She shouldn't have known either, if her memories were limited to only what she knew thousands of years ago as a Mesopotamian peasant."

He was right. Moreover, a teleporting spell normally required a high-level practitioner *and* potent spellbinders such as magic-infused gemstones to anchor it. Ereshki had only a pen and paper. Even if she somehow knew magic of that caliber, it should have been impossible for her to perform, unless . . .

Once again, Cat's words rang in my mind. *Being underestimated in a fight gives you the best advantage ever.*

All at once, I knew how she did it, and my rage made every water pipe in the house instantly burst. "That *fucking bitch!*"

Ian looked more concerned over how I'd started to tremble than he did over the water that immediately began to stain the walls outside this cell. "What is it?"

"She was never one of the other resurrected souls." I could barely get the words out past my fury over how completely Ereshki had deceived me, *again*. "She only appeared to have your spell confirm that because she *does* have some of Dagon's power in her. She's had it ever since Dagon branded her when she sold her soul to him, but unlike you, Dagon never collected on that debt. He didn't have to. This whole time, Ereshki's been on his side as his demon-branded servant!"

Chapter 35

*I*an hustled me upstairs after ordering his friends and staff to evacuate. Private, demon-proof residence or no, we were no longer safe here. We'd seen what had happened to Yonah's island. Now, we couldn't be sure if that was Dagon's doing or Ereshki's. Dagon's power had been growing in her for thousands of years, all while keeping her as youthful as the day I'd met her.

I should find it comforting that Ereshki's resurrected-human-amnesiac-act hadn't fooled only me; she'd also fooled an eons-old former demon prince. But I wasn't comforted. Yonah hadn't known what Ereshki was capable of. I had, yet I was the one who'd refused to kill her when Ian had given me the chance.

How many people would now die because of that?

I was so burdened by the thought that it took a moment to notice that Ian had hustled me into a bedroom. It was a huge space with dazzling white woodworking covering the walls and inlays that showed off paintings by Michelangelo and Edvard Munch that were supposed to be in a museum. Eighteenth-century Chippendale settees were stationed around a modern crushed-glass fireplace, and the skylight above was decorated in a stained-glass motif that looked ripped right from the Vatican.

But the room's most impressive aspect was the bed. It looked hand-carved from one enormous tree, with a canopy that was easily three times my height. Naked nymphs adorned the domed top;

then more gorgeous carvings curved down the elevated sides to end at gargoyles, where thick, turquoise silk draperies flowed from their extended wings. Mischievous-looking cherubs perched on either corner of the foot of the bed, holding the draperies' tasseled ends off the floor. Not that those tassels were in danger of touching the floor. The bed's base was almost a meter tall and was adorned with so many intricate carvings that it reminded me of wedding-cake decorations.

"My bedroom," Ian said, a casual swipe indicating the magnificent space. Then his brow arched. "Not what you were expecting?"

"Unless you have a sex dungeon hidden behind one of these walls, no," I replied bluntly.

He let out an amused grunt. "This room is for privacy and sleeping. I have other rooms for those activities."

I bet he did. In another mood, I might have even wanted to explore those, too. But rage and a sickening sense of guilt made me want to beat these walls down while simultaneously throwing up. Even at Ian's kinkiest, I didn't think he'd be into that.

Besides, the items in this room were far too rare and valuable to destroy in a futile display of denied vengeance.

Silver flew into the room. Then, he dropped down to curl around my legs as if he were a house cat instead of a celestial creation. He always tried to comfort me when I was upset.

I spent a few moments petting him for his efforts before I said, "Why are we here instead of leaving?"

"We need supplies," Ian replied, pressing a button beneath the crushed-glass fireplace. A hidden wall *was* revealed, but it didn't contain a secret sex room. Instead, drawers slid out, revealing an assortment of weapons, two black bags, tactical apparel, and several brightly colored stones.

Not stones, I realized as a wave of power hit me like an invisible slap. Magic-infused gems. In the right hands, they'd be more deadly than the knives, swords, hatchets, mallets, and various guns Ian had in the other drawers.

"If you see anything you like, take it," he said as he began tossing his selections into one of the black bags.

I went right to the set of knives that appeared to be made of ivory, if you didn't know what demon bone looked like. The knives had steel glinting up their pale backs and handles made for gripping, not throwing. That was fine. When I killed Ereshki, I didn't want to do it from a distance. I wanted to be up close. Ian sheathed one of the larger pairs of demon bone knives, then tossed those into his bag, too.

"Where did you get so much demon bone?"

He gave me a sardonic look. "You left a lot to choose from at that former amusement park."

True. Cat had told me she'd get rid of the bones. Guess she'd given some to Ian first, which had been smart of her.

Ian finished his bag off with six pairs of handguns, two pairs of automatic weapons and lots of ammunition rounds. Then, he put two sets of tactical apparel and a closed briefcase into the second bag. Finally, he swiped a yellow and blue vase off the mantel and smashed it against the fireplace.

That was one way to decide you were sick of an eighteenth-century Peking vase. Then I saw a large, glittering gem amidst the glass shards. The stone was deepest blue at its center, but brightness flashed from its every finely cut facets.

Ian shook the glass from the gem. Then, mouth curling with an emotion I couldn't name, he held it out to me. "Doesn't look as if it's worth being chased by a demon for decades, does it?"

Now I knew what stone this was. It was the catalyst that had started Dagon's hatred toward Ian after Ian had led the demon on so he could get close enough to the gem to steal it. Considering the size of the diamond, I knew more people than Ian who'd chance a demon's wrath to possess it.

"It looks like starlight formed around its favorite part of the ocean to keep it forever," I murmured, taking the diamond.

As soon as it touched my hand, I gasped. My arm felt numb from the instant surge of power that kept climbing through me until my very teeth ached from the force of it.

"*That's* why you stole this from Dagon back when he was trying to seduce you!"

It hadn't been mere greed because the diamond would fetch millions on the human market. The gem's real value went beyond its vast number of carats. It was so soaked in magic, I could barely stand to keep holding it, and the most impressive part was that I hadn't felt anything at all until I touched it. I could wave this gem under the vampire council's nose, and none of them would realize it was a magic object unless they held it.

"Yes." Ian's voice was a lethal caress. "Fitting to use it to help kill Dagon now, don't you think?"

I didn't know how he intended to do that, but considering the number of spells something with this kind of magical energy could power, he had a lot of options to choose from. And we'd need all the help we could get, now that I'd royally fucked things up by letting Ereshki live.

"Yes," was all I said, handing the diamond back to him.

His brow rose at my abrupt tone, but he said nothing as he tossed the blue diamond into the second bag, then zipped it up.

A knock sounded at the door even though it was open. I turned. Mencheres was in the doorway, his expression strained.

"Let me come with you on this journey, Ian. I want to help you destroy the creature who took so much from you."

Ian turned around with a sigh. "Thank you, but Dagon knows what you mean to me. He'll come at you with everything he has because of it. You might be able to best any vampire alive, but you can't win against a time-freezing demon."

"I can if he's headless," Mencheres said darkly.

Ian grunted. "Think I haven't tried that already? Dagon's either immune to telekinetic spells, or he's got something that deflects them. No. If you come, you will only endanger me because Dagon will kill you, then use my reaction to his advantage."

"What about me?" Bones appeared behind Mencheres, his half

smile belying the deadly look on his face. "I've faced a demon before and come out on top. Let me come."

Ian let out an amused snort. "You needed my help to defeat that
demon, or did you forget that part?"

"Did you forget I was an undead hit man for decades?" Bones
countered. "Murdering rotten blokes is what I excel at."

Ian zipped the bags shut. "Don't want to be insulting, Crispin,
but Veritas is an unkillable demigod and I'm juiced up with both
magic and demon power. If we can't do this without your help,
then we won't be able to do it with you, either."

Ian still thought I could resurrect after I died? I opened my mouth
to correct that, then shut it. Why burden him with information that
would only cause him to lose focus? Worrying over my new mortal-
ity would distract him, so it was better for him to remain ignorant
of it.

"Besides," Ian went on. "If you die, Cat will go on a grief-driven
revenge rampage, get killed in the process, and then your daughter
will end up being raised by Justina and *Tate*." Ian shuddered as if
in horror. "You can't do that to an innocent girl. It's inhumane."

"If you won't accept my help because of my love for you, then
accept it because I owe you." Bones's tone became flat. "For much
more than your latest warning about my daughter. Without you
turning me into a vampire over two centuries ago, I wouldn't be
here now, and I also owe you the greatest of debts for betraying
you."

"Eh, that." Ian waved. "I'm over that now since karma, as my
wife likes to say, is a vindictive bitch."

Bones's brows rose. "Come again?"

Ian hefted the two bags with one hand. "I mean, I understand
why you did it. You went barmy when Cat left you, so when you
finally found her and believed I was a danger to her, you did whatever it took to protect her. Brassed me off something awful at the
time, but now"—Ian saluted him with the suitcases—"I say, well
done! Can't take any chances with those we love, can we?"

Bones stared at Ian, then very slowly looked at me. "Lucifer's bouncing balls," he breathed. "You've done the impossible with Ian. If I hadn't seen it myself, I would never have believed it."

Would his friends never give Ian credit for who he was? "I've done nothing. Ian is this honorable all on his own."

"That's not what I meant," Bones began, but Ian's sharp whistle for Silver cut him off.

Silver flew over and landed on Ian's arm. Then, Ian pulled me to him and said, "I appreciate your offers to help, my friends. Truly, I do. But I can't accept, and we don't have time to keep arguing. All of us have to leave before demons crash this party, so until again, mates!"

With that, everything slid into white noise and a blur as Ian teleported us away.

Chapter 36

When the blur from Ian's teleporting stopped, we were in a new home. The white-framed windows revealed a wooden boardwalk, a beach and night-darkened waves outside. This room had a stone fireplace, exposed beams in the high ceiling, hardwood floors and comfy-looking suede couches.

"Mencheres's cottage in the Hamptons," Ian said by way of explanation, tossing the bags onto one of the couches. "He won't mind, and this area's almost deserted in the winter, so we won't have to fret about any nosy neighbors."

Aside from the protection of being inside a private residence, the continuous salt spray also acted as a natural demon repellant, plus that same sea offered me an endless supply of water-fueled energy. Ian clearly wasn't taking any chances.

"It's great," I said, setting Silver down. He immediately flew onto the couch and snuggled into the soft-looking cushions. Within moments, his eyes were shut. I must not be the only one who'd had enough of this day.

Ian came over and began to smooth my hair from my face, but he couldn't get far since it immediately tangled around his fingers. Teleporting was hell on a hairstyle. My hair would look less disheveled if I'd been repeatedly electrocuted.

"None of this is *great*, Veritas."

His hand stayed in my hair, while his gaze filled with an empathy I couldn't stand to acknowledge. I tried to swallow away the new tightness in my throat. I didn't deserve what was in his eyes. Not when I'd failed so badly by letting Ereshki fool me again. I'd put both of us in more danger than before, and that had already been in the you're-probably-going-to-die category.

"I should start on a new protection spell," I said, turning away to stride into the next room. It was a conservatory, and in another mood, I would have loved its windows-for-walls and bright white trim. Now, I hated it because the windows bounced my reflection back at me everywhere I looked. Still, it was better than Ian giving me none of the anger I deserved—and needed—to shield myself from the enormity of what I'd done.

Before I took my next step, Ian was in front of me.

"Veritas," he began.

I grabbed him and yanked his head down to mine. Then I jumped up to wrap my legs around his waist. If I couldn't avoid Ian, I could at least be sure he wasn't in a talking mood.

He caught me, holding my hips while his mouth opened to give me a blisteringly sensual kiss. I sucked on his tongue, then dug my fangs in until I tasted the coppery-flavored wine of his blood. He rolled his hips, sending a sweet ache into my loins. Now I was thoroughly distracted, too.

"I'm going to bite you everywhere," I breathed, dragging my fangs across his lower lip to suck the ruby drops that welled.

"Are you?" he growled as he untangled my legs from his waist, then dropped to his knees while holding my hips. He pressed his mouth between my legs and exhaled until his hot breath penetrated my clothes with its own touch.

An exquisite clenching had me gripping his head to hold him closer. He chuckled, and it went right through me as well, teasing flesh that throbbed to feel more of him. I tried to unzip my pants to give him better access, but he stopped me, chuckling again as he held me more firmly while releasing another deep, tantalizing exhale.

A cry left me when he ended that exhale with a lingering bite. My pants kept his fangs from piercing skin, but their skillful application of pressure sent ripples of ecstasy through me. His response to my cry was a deep lave that was somehow as erotic as if it had seared bare flesh. My hands trembled as they fisted in his hair. Now, I wanted him with a ferocity that made me feel as if I'd turned feral, and he hadn't even gotten my pants off yet.

He wouldn't anytime soon, either. I could see it in the sensually taunting glint in his eyes right before he lowered his mouth again. Another deep, molten exhale combined with more tantalizing friction had me shuddering against him. No, he'd tease me until I was mindless from desire, and as glorious as that usually was, I couldn't wait for it. I had to have him now.

I closed my eyes, focusing on the part of him I needed deep inside me. Then I wrapped my power around that long, thick member and very gently pulled.

His surprised hiss felt like it went all through me.

"What are you doing?" he asked in a strangled voice.

I smiled without opening my eyes, pulling on that power gently again. Why had it never occurred to me to do this before? Erections were only possible when the member filled with blood. I could call that blood closer to the surface, until Ian was awash in sensitivity, making the barest brush of fabric from his pants feel the same as my mouth sliding up to engulf his cock.

Or my fangs sliding into its tip, if I focused that power more selectively while pulling on it a little harder . . .

He let out a hoarse shout, his grip on me tightening until I heard a rip and felt the give of fabric around my hips.

I stopped. "Too much?" He liked pain, but I was new to this, so I might have pulled too hard . . .

He rent my pants open and buried his mouth between my legs. Fireworks went off inside me, so consuming and continuous, everything else melted away. When the last orgasm faded enough for me to think again, I was on my back with my clothes in tatters and Ian was rising from my open thighs. He'd also removed his clothes and the horn, allowing the moonlight streaming in from the windows to cling to his body as if it was making love to him, too. His skin was almost as pale as those ethereal beams, making my thighs a far darker contrast as I lifted them to grip his hips when he slid forward to cover my body with his.

A strong arch of his hips tore a gasp from me as he filled me in one stroke. The pleasure was so intense, I dug my nails into his back, while my eyes closed from bliss.

"Don't," he said in a throaty voice. "Open your eyes."

I did, seeing his tightly sculpted muscles bunch before another deep stroke cascaded more bliss into me. Then I looked at his face. Pleasure parted his lips, which were fuller from bringing me to multiple orgasms only moments before. His dark brows framed glowing emerald eyes and his auburn hair swung to brush his cheekbones with every nerve-sizzling stroke. If beauty could be poured into skin, it would look exactly like this.

"I'm going to come just from watching you," I breathed.

His low laugh was filled with everything that made Ian addictive. "Not yet, but soon. You didn't think I'd let you off without repaying you for making me cream my trousers with the naughty side of your powers?"

A smile teased my mouth. "So you *did* like that."

Another twist of his hips briefly cleared my mind of thought. ". . . loved it," I vaguely caught him saying. "Just like you're going to love this."

His hand left me as he raised it, fingers working a complex yet rapid spell. When he stopped, his outline blurred for a moment, then a second Ian pulled away from his body while the real Ian grinned at me.

"What?" I said with disbelief.

A grin lit Ian's face before it was mirrored on the second, slightly shimmering Ian who now slid behind me.

"Temporary duplication spell," Ian said, picking me up and settling me across his lap. That bared my back to the second Ian, who began to caress it. "He's controlled by my desires, so everything I want to do, he does."

He proved that by kissing me while his double's hands wandered over the parts of my body Ian's weren't already caressing. Soon, his double's mouth did, too, heightening pleasure already skyrocketing from those ceaseless thrusts.

If one Ian was insatiable, two were relentlessly, gloriously overwhelming. Nothing else existed because nothing else could get through the barrage of pleasure. When I finally sagged against him, too sated to move, he let out an amused grunt and gave a complicated snap of his fingers.

His duplicate vanished. I used the last of my strength to lie back and pull him fully on top of me. His gaze was almost a blindingly bright shade of green, but his expression was worth the effort to keep my eyes open.

If I could freeze any moment in time to live in forever, it would be this one. Not because of the rapture that had completely exhausted me from this unexpected astral threesome, but because of what I saw in Ian's eyes now. Seeing it, a surge went through me that had nothing to do with the way he gripped me tighter and increased his pace.

Before Ian, I'd never wanted anyone to look at me this way. I had too many secrets, and being loved meant being pursued to degrees that would endanger me. But staring into Ian's eyes, I wanted what I thought I saw in them more than anything I'd wanted before it.

At the same time, I was terrified that it might only be the reflection of what *I* felt for him, and not what he felt for me.

Another thrust brought a distracting clench of ecstasy. I gave myself to it, letting it chase away my fears. Right now, Ian was mine and I was his. Tomorrow was uncertain for many reasons, so right now, this was enough.

*M*encheres's house had four bedrooms. We didn't use any of them, though Ian did take the bedding from the nearest one to wrap us up where we lay. We'd gone back to the room with the beachfront view. The stone fireplace was gas, but despite its slightly acrid scent, it gave off a pleasant amount of heat.

Silver slept on the couch above us. Poor thing had barely bothered to pick up his head when we came back in. I'd rummage in the kitchen for vegetables for him later, but right now, I wanted a few more minutes curled up with Ian.

He'd brought pillows, but my head rested on his arm while his free hand traced the curve of my shoulder. I reached out to brush the spot on his arm that the horn normally wrapped itself around. At some point during our first encounter in the conservatory, he'd taken it off. I hadn't even noticed.

"Glad the horn didn't violently react to me touching it," I mused. "Or I would've left brain bits all over the conservatory's pretty driftwood floors."

Ian snorted. "I had it on in the bathroom with you at Yonah's the other night, or was that only yesterday?"

"With all the teleporting, time-zone changes, and everything else, I can't remember," I replied.

"Neither can I, but the horn either likes you or it knows you're not trying to steal it from me. That must be why it doesn't harm you when you touch it."

"Probably the latter," I said, adding dryly, "it's obviously a possessive little relic, to blow the head off anyone who tries to take it from its current owner."

Another chuckle, this time with a touch of grimness. "I'll never forget the headache that gave me, and that's when the horn decided it fancied me enough to keep me."

I didn't remind Ian that "fancying" him hadn't been part of the horn's decision. Only raw power and the potential for more drew it, Ashael had said. If so, I understood why it had been drawn to Ian. As a vampire, he'd already been far more powerful than normal, as his beating me in our first fight attested. As a vampire highly skilled in tactile magic *and* imbued with additional power after what Ian had consumed from Dagon? I had no idea the heights Ian could attain.

Lofty ones, the relic choosing him seemed to indicate.

"Wasn't trying to eavesdrop earlier." Ian's tone turned serious, which warned me that I wouldn't like what was coming. "But you *were* screaming, so it was hard to miss hearing why you believe Tenoch turned Vlad into a vampire right before he died."

I stiffened, pulling away from him without realizing I'd moved until I felt cool air where his body had been. I would rather pull out all my teeth than talk about this. No—I would rather pull out all my teeth, swallow them, then fish them out of my stomach with a sharp hook than talk about this.

But Cat had nearly brought me to a full meltdown by merely mentioning it earlier. How much of that had Ereshki overheard? If she'd caught any of it, she'd share it with Dagon, and I couldn't afford to give the demon such a powerful weapon against me. That meant I *had* to talk about this. Sometimes, the only way to clear the infection out of a wound was with a sharp knife.

"I don't know what you've heard about Tenoch." My voice was abrupt. If I was doing this, I had to be as cold as possible. "Many people talk about his powers, but more than anything, Tenoch was a good man deeply burdened by his concern for others. It's partly what drove him into his grave. You can't care like that without it taking a toll."

"Mencheres always believed that Tenoch's death was caused by more than an ambush by marauding ghouls." Ian's voice was neutral, as if he knew I couldn't handle anything more.

I gave a brisk nod. "Mencheres was right. The ghouls who killed Tenoch were happy to believe they'd overwhelmed him by their greater numbers, but I knew, as Mencheres did, that Tenoch still could've escaped. Incredible strength aside, Tenoch was telekinetic *and* pyrokinetic. He could have alternated between ripping their heads off or exploding them off, if he wanted to . . ."

Ian finished what I couldn't bring myself to say. "Instead, Tenoch let those ghouls kill him."

"A mere two weeks after turning the fiercest human in the world into a vampire." I let out a laugh that sounded as broken as the memories made me feel. "For the first several decades, I was too grief-stricken to wonder why turning Vlad was the last thing Tenoch did. Then Vlad began exhibiting powers he could have only if Tenoch had poured the remainder of Cain's legacy into Vlad when he turned him. That's when I knew that Tenoch had designated Vlad as my new murderer, if the need arose."

"Perhaps Tenoch emptied his remaining portion of Cain's legacy into Vlad because he knew that soon, he'd have no need of it?"

I gave Ian a look he didn't deserve. "Then he could've given it to me, but he didn't. Not then and not thousands of years earlier, either."

Ian propped himself up on his elbow. "You're referring to Tenoch giving Mencheres that power, after Tenoch turned Mencheres into a vampire."

I gave a brisk nod. "Soon after Tenoch turned me into a vampire, there was . . . an incident involving my other abilities. What I did terrified him, but he loved me too much to kill me. So, he made me vow to always keep that part of myself locked away, then bequeathed Cain's legacy of power to Mencheres." I gave a humorless laugh. "Mencheres was my intended executioner, if I broke my vow and let the other half of me take over. Mencheres didn't know it, but I always did."

Rage blasted across Ian's features before it vanished. In a carefully controlled tone, he said, "Tenoch told you that?"

A surge of defensiveness made me sit up. "You don't understand. What you've seen of my powers is only a little slice of what I'm *actually* capable of. Tenoch didn't make this decision lightly. He was thinking of the greater good—"

"The greater good." Scorn dripped from Ian's tone. "I'd have to think long and hard to find three words more widely twisted to excuse the infliction of needless pain and suffering than those."

"Maybe," I said. "Tenoch believed it when it came to me, though. I—I thought he'd stopped fearing me because we'd been through so much. Then he died, and Vlad began manifesting powers he couldn't have on his own." I tried to laugh, but it came out as a strangled sob. "Tenoch must've thought Mencheres wouldn't be enough to take me down. Mencheres *had* sunk into a depression after his first wife left him and began plotting against him. So, Tenoch dumped the last of his legacy powers into Vlad, then killed himself with a horde of ghouls two weeks later."

Leaving me reeling with grief, guilt and a resounding sense of culpability, once I'd put it all together.

"No wonder you refer to your other abilities as a separate person." Ian's voice was very soft. "It's how you compartmentalized the pain when it was too much to bear."

Once, I would've argued. Now, I closed my eyes. "Perhaps."

"Tenoch was still a bloody fool."

My eyes snapped open in time to see my vision flash with black. Ian didn't flinch from the rage he had to see as well as scent.

"He might have been well-intentioned, but like millions of parents who reject their children over things they don't understand, Tenoch was wrong. You are exactly as you should be, and it's Tenoch's loss that he never realized that."

Anguish tightened my muscles until it felt like I was being beaten from the inside. "You didn't see what I did—"

"As a new vampire dealing with incredibly heightened senses and emotions that doubtless activated the abilities in your other nature?" Ian made a contemptuous noise. "I don't have to see it to know a slip of supernatural control doesn't make you a monster that needs to be exterminated. Yes, your power can be dangerous, but the same can be said for your vampire side. Or your human one, when that applied."

"Tenoch would never have gone to such extremes unless he knew it was the only way!"

I'd repeated that to myself countless times over the centuries. Otherwise, the knowledge that Tenoch had still considered me a threat to be eliminated when he died would break me.

"Fear can make people do terrible things, even to the ones they love," Ian replied in a softer tone. "You know that. You just can't bring yourself to admit it when it comes to Tenoch. Makes you feel disloyal, and that's just the beginning. When you realize it was Tenoch who was wrong, not you, you have to confront the fact that you stuffed half of yourself into a cage merely to appease the fears of a man who should have loved you unconditionally because that is a parent's bloody *job*."

"He did love me! He just knew the other half of me could never be trusted—"

"Bollocks," Ian said crisply. "He never bothered to find out. He saw your father, shat himself in terror, then made up his mind that something that powerful had to be evil. That's why he shat himself again when he saw those same powers in you, but whatever you did was no more innately evil than a new vampire losing control from blood cravings. Are all of them evil, too?"

"No, but . . ." Dammit, now he was confusing me!

"No is right. They're simply untrained. You were, too, and instead of training you to control your power, Tenoch made you fear and suppress it."

"Because I *hurt people* with it," I snapped.

"Did they deserve it?" he countered. "I'll wager they did, because when your other nature broke free after I died, you didn't hurt innocents. Instead, you took out the demons who'd tried to kill us, and you forsook eons of vengeance against Dagon in order to pull me back from the grave. When that half of you grabbed the wheel again, you repeatedly protected me, propositioned me—my favorite part—*and* saved dozens of humans from drowning beneath a toppled house. Show me the evil in any of that."

Well . . . I couldn't, if I was looking at it objectively. But if Ian was right, Tenoch had punished me for simply existing, and the man who'd rescued me, protected me, and loved me when no one else had *couldn't* have made such a colossal mistake. Could he?

No. Ian hadn't seen what Tenoch had seen back when vampires from a rival clan had kidnapped me in an attempt to force Tenoch to side with them. What I'd done had made Tenoch fear me for the rest of his life. How could I discount that?

"You're ignoring the fact that I *wanted* to do those good deeds." My voice was flat. "What happens if I want to do something terrible when my other half is in control?"

Ian snorted. "Then the person you do it to will richly deserve it. You wouldn't even murder your second-worst enemy when you thought she hadn't remembered her foul deeds. *I* would've cheerfully slaughtered Ereshki, and I don't have your supposedly malevolent other nature. Don't blame it on Dagon's power in me, either. I know what I am capable of without it."

Each point bashed at walls that housed my long-buried doubts, hurt, and anger. I hadn't always taken Tenoch at his word about me. It hadn't seemed right that everyone else could mold their character based on their actions, while I had to accept that I was born defective. But, as Ian predicted, wondering if Tenoch had been wrong made the ground feel like it disappeared beneath me. Believing Tenoch had been the basis for almost everything I'd done. If I ripped that belief away now, how did I put myself back together? In many ways, it was easier to continue to believe Tenoch than confront the possibility that I'd lived my entire life based on a lie that the sire I adored had told me.

"That's different," I said to cover my roiling emotions.

He sighed. "It isn't. You are one of the finest people I've met, to my great exasperation. If you were more selfish, you wouldn't have stayed away from me after I was first brought back from the dead. You also wouldn't have spared the little bitch we now have to track down, and you wouldn't have caged half yourself away to the point that you damn near have a split personality. But you *are* ridiculously unselfish, which is one of the reasons I so enjoy holding you down to pleasure you before allowing you to touch me," he added almost offhandedly. "You're so used to putting yourself last that I truly savor making you come before I'm even inside you."

This must be what emotional whiplash felt like. One moment, I was frustrated over his flattering but incorrect portrayal of me, and in the next, I was looking at his mouth and thinking of all the ways he *had* used it on me.

"You're maddening," I finally said, too jumbled on the inside to come up with anything more articulate.

He laughed. "Back at you. Leila cursed me right and proper when she bade me to fall in love with someone like you."

"Good thing Leila isn't a real witch or that curse might've stuck," I muttered without thinking.

He cocked his head. "Whatever do you mean?"

I hadn't intended to bring this up. With everything else we'd touched upon, the last thing I needed was to confront Ian with what he didn't feel for me. "Never mind."

He came closer, that relentless gaze pinning mine. "Don't put me off. What do you mean?"

Fuck it, why not? I thought despairingly. I'd have to spend years processing all the points he'd brought up about me. Why not give him something to think about, too?

"I mean you *don't* love me." I squared my shoulders. "It's fine," I added. "Things are still very new between us, even if the past couple months feel like years, and . . . why are you laughing?" I demanded, seeing his chest shake with mirth.

"Because you might be spectacular in bed, but no one's *that* spectacular," he got out between infuriating chuckles.

Anger shot through me. "What's *that* supposed to mean?"

His mirth faded as his expression sobered. "You're serious? But you told me you remembered my last words."

At that, pain arced through me enough that I looked away. "I do. You, ah, said that you could have loved me."

"No. I didn't."

My gaze snapped back up. "What?"

"You misheard me," he said, ripping my heart apart. This whole time, I'd clung to the hope that one day, "could have" would turn into "did," and this whole time, I'd been wrong?

"Not really a surprise," he went on, heedless to how he was shredding me. "Half my brain was pronged end to end with one bone knife while the other half was partially skewered by a second. Not a recipe for intelligibility, is it?"

I sucked a breath in and held it so I wouldn't scream. "What did you say, then?" I managed to ask in a calm tone.

He closed the space I'd put between us. "Not 'could.' I didn't chase you all over God's green earth before branding myself a married man in front of the whole bloody vampire council because I *could* have loved you. I did it because my actual last words were 'should have told you I loved you.'"

I froze with such suddenness, it was as if I'd used my abilities to make time stand still. I knew I should say something, but I was too shocked . . . and too afraid that somehow, this wasn't happening. I'd wanted it too much for it to be real.

His lips curled as he yanked me closer. "Heard me properly this time? Or do you need to hear it again?" His mouth lowered. "Should have told you I loved you," he said against my lips. "Whether you're Veritas the Law Guardian, Ariel the vampire-witch, or Death's scary demigod daughter. Doesn't matter. In all your forms, in every manifestation of yourself, *I love you.*"

Then he claimed my mouth with a kiss that made me glad I was sitting down, because otherwise, it would have leveled me. He didn't stop kissing me for the next several hours, but I managed to speak between them, and it was the same four words.

"I love you, too."

$\mathcal{I}$ never wanted to leave Mencheres's beach house. Not when I would forever associate this place with where I'd truly discovered happiness—all internal conflicts about Tenoch and the other half of myself aside. In fact, I was already formulating an offer to buy this place from Mencheres when the water I'd cupped in my hands suddenly shimmered and a familiar, feminine voice said "Ariel" from it.

I was so startled that I dropped the water and jumped back from the sink. I was alone in the bathroom since Ian had left after our long, very enjoyable shower. I'd stayed to comb the tangles out of my sex-tousled hair and brush my teeth. I'd been in the process of rinsing my mouth out when the water in my hands suddenly began talking in Ereshki's voice.

Either I'd just experienced a complete psychotic break, or Ereshki really had been trying to communicate with me through the water. I gave both possibilities fifty-fifty odds.

No point wondering which. I cupped my hands beneath the sink's still-running faucet, filled them, and waited.

No voices, no strange shimmering. Psychotic break, then. I sighed. Well, I'd lasted nearly five millenniums without one. Guess I was overdue. It could be worse. I heard that writers had psychotic breaks every decade or so—

"Ariel," a voice said before Ereshki's shimmering image formed in the water cupped in my hands. "Don't drop me this time," she added. "This spell is quite taxing."

The only reason I didn't hurl her watery image into the mirror was because I was curious why she'd dared to contact me.

"I'm sorry," I said with heavy sarcasm. "Wouldn't want to *tax* you. I want you hale and hearty when I rip you to pieces."

She laughed. It hit me like a physical blow when I saw the corners of her eyes crinkle with her mirth. When I was human, that sight had been one of the only joys in my life. Now, it filled me with enough rage to make my hands quiver.

"You did surprise me with how vicious you've become," she remarked. "I had no idea you'd go right for my throat when you first saw me. I thought you still had a sister's love for me. If I'd known you learned of my duplicity back when you were Dagon's, I never would have followed you into that bathroom."

"I was never Dagon's," I spat. "But you have been since the moment we met, and every single moment after that."

I saw a hint of her shoulder as she shrugged. "Famines were common when I was young. I didn't want to die of starvation like the rest of my people. Dagon offered me an alternative."

An "alternative"? That's how she brushed off what she'd helped Dagon do to hundreds of men, women, and children who, unlike me, *didn't* come back from the dead after they were sacrificed to him? I wished she were in my hands right now. I'd squeeze the life from her while smiling the entire time.

"Why are you contacting me? This spell is too complicated for you to use only because you want to gloat."

She allowed herself another smile before it faded. "I didn't realize the depth of your power until I saw you hold back part of the sea. Dagon told me you could tear blood and water from people, but that . . ."

"Is the least of what I'll do to you," I said pleasantly.

"That's why I'm contacting you." A hint of aggravation filled her voice. "I don't want you to kill me. Do whatever you want to do to Dagon, but leave me alone."

Laughter broke from me in harsh peals. "I had no idea you were so funny, Ereshki! Please, tell me another joke."

Even through the unsteady sheen of the water, I saw ice fill her clear brown eyes. "Dagon long suspected that Ashael was hiding something. How amusing would you find it if I told Dagon that Ashael was the one who brought you to Yonah's? Or that the two of you had 'much in common,' as you told Yonah?"

I stiffened. If she did that, Dagon would repeat it, and Ashael would be hunted by other demons for his allegiance to their most-wanted fugitive. Add in the speculation that Ashael wasn't a "real" demon, and he would be marked for death by every species that feared mixed-race people, which was all of them.

Shit.

A knowing look crossed Ereshki's face. "I thought you cared for the handsome demon. I was too far away to hear what was said, but you appeared to be pleading for Ashael's life when your lover threatened him right after you arrived at Yonah's."

Dammit! That *had* happened within full view of Yonah's house. With the mirrorlike quality of his windows, I couldn't tell if anyone had been spying on us. Clearly, at least one person had.

"You must have been shocked to see me," I noted.

Another shrug. "Not then. I didn't recognize you until later. It had, after all, been a very long time."

For some reason, that made me angrier than everything she'd said before it. When you helped torture and murder someone for a decade, the least thing you could do was *recognize* her!

Ian suddenly filled the doorway, but a sharp shake of my head kept him from entering. "So, you're offering to keep quiet about Ashael if I don't hunt you down like the filthy scrap of vermin you are," I summarized in a hard tone. "And I'm supposed to believe in your sincerity about this why?"

Her brow rose. "I grow tired of doing Dagon's bidding. His last task, sending me to destroy Yonah's island so he could claim credit afterward, nearly killed me, as you know. But, if you kill him and agree to spare me," her smile crinkled the corners of her eyes again, "I'm free. Is that sincere enough for you?"

Was she capable of such back-stabbing selfishness? Of course she was. I knew that better than anyone. But I didn't trust her. Still, that didn't mean she was without usefulness.

"Sweeten the deal. Give us a location on Dagon first."

"He doesn't report his whereabouts to me," she scoffed. "When he wants me, he uses the tie in my brand to find me."

"Then tell me where *you* are so I can find him that way."

She gave me a look that was so worldly, it reminded me that she'd lived for as many years as I had. "So you can kill me and lie in wait for Dagon next to my bones? I think not."

I gave her a savage grin. "Worth a try."

Her image started to fade. "The spell is nearly depleted. Accept my terms, Ariel. Unlike Dagon, I am not trying to kill you, so killing me would only be salve to your pride. Is that truly worth more to you than Ashael's life?"

Yes! part of me wanted to shout. I wished that part came from my other half, but no. I owned all of it.

My sigh exploded out of me. When I spoke, it was through teeth clenched from long-denied rage. "Tell no one of Ashael," I gritted out, "and I vow that I will never kill you, Ereshki."

The last thing I saw was her smile. To anyone else, it would look like the carefree grin of a pretty Middle Eastern woman in her twenties. To me, it was venom sliding through my veins.

I threw the water into the sink, then pushed past Ian without speaking. I couldn't stand to hear his recriminations or have him urge me to go back on my word. I already knew why Ereshki didn't deserve a shred of my honor, but if I only kept my word when it was easy, then it was as worthless as she was.

I was so agitated, I walked out of the house and onto the boardwalk. The sun was up, its bright rays warming the cold wood beneath my feet. I didn't stop until I'd left that wood for sand, then left the sand for the icy embrace of the waves.

Ian, no surprise, joined me. I had on a robe that floated around me in the waist-deep water, but he wasn't wearing anything except an oddly satisfied smile.

"What?" I said. "Going to tell me you were right about me being too stupidly honorable for my own good?"

"Not at all," he replied in a cheery tone. "I'm too busy envisioning how I'm going to thank Ereshki."

"Thank her?" I repeated in disbelief.

His smile slid into a grin that rivaled the freezing waters for its coldness. "Before, I couldn't fathom how I'd get to kill her without robbing you of your well-deserved vengeance. Now, she solved that problem, so I fully intend to thank her before I slaughter the little bitch."

I started to laugh, which I wouldn't have thought I was capable of only moments before. But this truly was funny, in a karma's-coming-for-you way.

Ereshki had gotten free before because Ian's guards had made the mistake of underestimating her. She'd just made the same mistake with Ian. Ereshki thought she was safe because *I'd* vowed not to kill her? Wait until she saw what Ian could do.

"I'm suddenly in a good mood," I said.

"So am I," he replied, his grin turning wolfish. "Because thanks to her contacting you, now I can also feel where she is."

Chapter 39

The blur that made up my surroundings stopped with the same nauseating abruptness I'd grown used to with teleporting. We'd driven to Dummerston, Vermont, but left our car at a gas station to teleport the rest of the way. Now, Ian stopped a full half kilometer short of where he said he felt Ereshki.

We stayed at the edge of Route 30. The narrow, north-south road was mostly free from cars despite this being the hour where most human workers would be on their way home. Still, this section of Dummerston looked like it hadn't been clogged with rush-hour traffic in decades, at least. I pulled out a pair of binoculars from Ian's bag and aimed it where he pointed.

Winter had stripped many of the trees bare, allowing me to see past them to a three-story white lodge with a rust-colored fence. There were two tiny shacks on either side of it, but the lodge was the main structure, with the mountain towering up behind it. A faded sign out front proclaimed that this had once been a ski mountain, but from the empty slopes, lack of lights, and missing ski lifts, it had been closed for many years.

It might have one resident inside, though. I couldn't tell. The windows I could see were all boarded up.

"I can't see inside, and it's too far away for me to hear a heartbeat," I told Ian, lowering the binoculars.

"Ereshki's in there," he said with absolute confidence.

Then she'd chosen her hideout well. The former ski lodge wasn't near any rivers, and when I sent my senses out to check the ground for water reservoirs, the lack of energy that bounced back practically screamed *Parched!* to me. There wasn't even snow on the ground despite this being the height of winter.

"I suppose the Sahara was too far for her to travel," I said, only half joking. With the earthquake spell at Yonah's, the teleporting spell to leave Ian's house, and contacting me through the water spell, Ereshki might not have had the energy to go farther than Vermont. Thousands of years demon-branded or no, that was still a lot of magic for her to wield.

Ian let out a grim snort. "If she wanted to live, then she should've conjured up another teleporting spell."

"She's probably out of juice," I replied.

He flashed me a predatory look. "Then this will be easy."

If it was, it would be the first easy thing that had come our way since we teamed up months ago. Still, I could hope.

"Let's find cover," he said, hefting our three heavy bags.

We chose the remains of a large tree for our hiding place on the opposite side of route 30. It was a hundred meters farther from the lodge, plus the surrounding patch of evergreens blocked our view, but Ian assured me that he could feel it if she tried to leave. I hadn't seen a car in the lodge's parking lot, but Ereshki could have hidden one in the back. Or she could have done what we'd done and left her car elsewhere—assuming she'd driven to this section of Vermont. This could have been where she'd teleported to when she escaped from Ian's. That had only been a day ago, even if it felt much longer.

"Ready?" Ian's casual tone belied the new flare in his aura as he held out a pouch containing several magic-infused stones.

I gave him a level look as I took it. "More than ready."

Ereshki had said if I knew where she was, I'd murder her and lie in wait for Dagon next to her bones. To give her credit, it was a good idea. I was just changing up the order of events.

We waited until it was so dark that only another vampire or demon could see. This section of road lacked streetlights and the lodge's exterior illumination had long gone out, allowing blackness to swallow the area. Only the occasional headlight bit through the darkness. Thus concealed, Ian and I began placing the stones around the perimeter of the former ski lodge. Ian set his at the five tips of the pentagram's star. I placed mine at the five vertices of the inner pentagram. I didn't have the stealth advantage of teleporting, so in case I was spotted, I wore my usual glamour. Ereshki had only ever seen me in my true form, so she wouldn't recognize me while I was wearing my slim, blonde Law Guardian appearance.

When we finished placing our stones, we drew a magic circle around the entire pentagram, then went back to our hiding spot. There, I began to fill the double-enclosed space with more magic, taking my time so the spell would be undetectable to all but the most attuned sorcerer.

"Done," I said over an hour later.

Ian's aura flared again. "Now, we wait for Dagon to use his tie in Ereshki's brand to find her."

Ereshki had said that Dagon checked in personally with her for updates when he wanted one. After everything that had happened, he'd want an update, all right. I only hoped he hadn't already gotten one in the eighteen hours since Ereshki had escaped.

"If we're lucky, it won't be long until you get to kill her," I said, trying to stay optimistic.

"Impossible." Fast as a bolt of lightning, Ian's tone changed to the deadly slice of a knife. "She *laughed* at what she did to you. Every second she lives after that is too long."

I've had poetry written for me that didn't make me feel the same warmth.

"You get her, and I get Dagon," I said softly. "We're ending this even if we have to sit here all week."

He grinned, his expression changing from intense avenger back to his normal, cheerful arrogance. "Hope it's not that long. My bollocks are already freezing into ice cubes."

It *always* circled back to genitals with men. "They'll thaw," I said dryly, and began unpacking the rest of our bags.

Half an hour later, we were redressed in the tactical gear Ian had brought, with bone knives sheathed at our belts and other weapons strapped to our arms and legs. Then we crouched behind the remains of the fallen tree and waited.

I GAVE THE setting sun a hopeful look despite it being the third one I'd seen from my cramped perch behind the tree. Darkness meant another chance that Dagon would arrive—maybe. This would be a hell of a time for the demon to get modern and contact Ereshki by text instead of a personal visit.

We were running low on blood bags since we were both eating more to keep our energy at peak levels. We were also getting texts from Ian's people saying that Silver was acting "morose." I hadn't liked leaving him behind, but an outdoor stakeout was no place for a pet. I also couldn't risk Silver getting hurt when Dagon—hopefully—arrived and the fighting began.

"You're sure Ereshki's still in there?" I couldn't help but ask. This whole time, she hadn't once left to get food or water.

Ian gave me a baleful look. "For the third time since we started this stakeout, *yes.*"

He made no effort to hide his annoyance, but I was starting to wonder if Ereshki had tricked us. We'd never gotten close enough to the ski lodge to verify that Ereshki was inside since we hadn't wanted to risk being spotted. Could she have soaked an object in Dagon's power and left it there to throw us off her trail? She knew that Ian had the Dagon-power-sensing spell in him, so despite my vow not to kill her, she might have taken precautions to avoid being detected.

Several hours later, I was so convinced of this theory, I was about to summon my friend Leah. The ghost could enter the lodge to check if Ereshki was in there without being spotted. In fact, why hadn't I thought of this days ago? If Ereshki had tricked us, she could be continents away by now—

Ian suddenly tensed and his aura crackled with enough energy to make me feel as if I'd been stung by a swarm of bees. I gripped his arm, anticipation rocketing through me.

"Is it Dagon? Is he here?" I whispered.

"Yes," Ian replied with quiet savageness.

I threw the blanket off us. Then, with barely any noise, we both got to our feet. I palmed one of my demon-bone knives before I met Ian's eyes. The last time we'd ambushed Dagon, Ian had died. I wouldn't let that happen this time, no matter what.

He gave me a look I couldn't read as he handed me the sparkling blue diamond. Magic crawled up my arm, painful in its potency, but we needed every bit of it. I closed my fist over the diamond, and Ian took my clenched hand in his.

"This time, we win," he said as if reading my thoughts.

"This time, we win," I echoed. *No matter what.*

His hand tightened; then our surroundings blurred.

That blur stopped moments later, revealing an interior room on the first floor of the lodge. It was stripped except for a few benches, lockers, and counters where skiers must have once checked in. Now, graffiti covered the walls and trash covered most of the age-bowed wooden floors. The stench of old urine, feces, and garbage was almost overwhelming.

But beyond that, I smelled a hint of lilacs and lavender. Ereshki's scent. Ian was right, she *was* here, possibly on the second floor. Another sniff revealed the harsher scent of sulfur. She wasn't alone. Ian was right again. Dagon was here.

I went to the far side of the room, then looked at Ian. He checked the coordinates programmed into his smart watch and nodded, confirming that I was at the center of our pentagram.

I bent down, cleared the garbage away, and slammed the blue diamond onto the floor hard enough to puncture the wooden floorboards. Magic exploded with such a tangible rush that the garbage blasted out in all directions.

I felt that magic find the stones at the five tips of the pentagram's star and activate them. Then it found the five stones in the circle surrounding the pentagram and filled those, too. But the circle allowed the magic to go no further, so it boomeranged back toward the blue diamond with the force of a thousand speeding trains. Feeling it coming, I ducked and braced.

The boards covering the windows exploded inward. Wood shards and the window's remaining glass fragments pelted me before the magic caught me in a full-body blow that slammed me up and into the ceiling. Ian was thrown backward hard enough to tear a line of ski lockers off the wall. My head rang, my body ached, and I could barely see through the haze of garbage that swirled around like the world's ugliest confetti, but despite all that, I let out a hoarse cry.

"Got you!"

The magic that had blown us off our feet now prevented anyone from entering the pentagram that surrounded the entire lodge and some of its grounds—critical to keeping Dagon from bringing in demon reinforcements. But the circle around the pentagram was the real trap. It kept everyone inside its limits until the sun shone through the blue diamond that now lay like a discarded toy on the garbage-strewn floor. No way in, no way out. One way or the other, our war with Dagon ended tonight.

Ian untangled himself from the lockers, then threw the mangled mess aside to check on me. "I'm fine," I assured him, even though my arm felt like it was paralyzed from holding the diamond while all that magic funneled through it.

"Then let's get the sod." Blood practically dripped from Ian's tone. "The spell your father put on Dagon should have him on his knees from being this close to me—"

"I am not on my knees," a familiar voice hissed.

Both of us turned.

Dagon was at the top of the staircase connecting the second floor to this room. His blue eyes gleamed with malice and his pale blond hair swirled from the residual waves of magic, but as described, he wasn't on his knees. He did lean heavily on Ereshki, though, and she looked like she wasn't enjoying being his version of a pair of crutches. That could be because she looked exhausted. Whatever she'd been doing the past three days had taken a toll on her.

"What do you think you accomplished with that spell?" Dagon continued in the same snakelike tone.

"Consider the doors on this place locked," I replied with deep satisfaction.

Ian gave the demon a brilliant smile. "Used the blue diamond I stole from you to anchor the spell."

Dagon didn't look afraid at hearing he was locked in with us. I hoped that was overconfidence and not something more ominous.

Ereshki appeared rattled, though, which was cold comfort. "You broke your vow," she said. "Dagon told me you would."

"He was wrong," I replied. "I'm not going to kill you, Ereshki. Ian, however, has other intentions."

Ian's smile made ice roll over my skin despite it being aimed at Ereshki, not me. If death indulged in foreplay before getting to the final act, it would start with that smile.

"Shall we, poppet?" he purred at her.

Ereshki shuddered. Dagon spat. "We're all trapped in here for however long your spell lasts, so if you want me, here I am!"

He was taunting me to charge him. Doing anything that Dagon wanted me to do would backfire, so I stayed where I was. Ian must have thought it was a trap, too. He put a hand on my arm.

"Don't move," he said through newly gritted teeth. "I feel something building . . ."

I pulled the pin on my other nature, trusting that more than whatever the demon was about to do. Power flooded me, blacking out my vision while sending my other senses into overdrive. I sent that power toward Dagon, seeking every drop of liquid in his body. Then I tightened my power around them and yanked. He couldn't hurt us if he was too dehydrated to move.

Dagon's fluids hit the floor in a wide swath of red I felt rather than saw. The crash I heard was Dagon crumpling to the ground, Ereshki unable to bear the full brunt of his weight any longer. Then the multiple satisfying thumps must have been his body hitting the steps as Dagon fell down the stairs.

I had an instant to savor the sound before Dagon's magic slammed into me with such force, all of my senses blinked out.

$\mathcal{I}$ opened my eyes, revealing that I was now crumpled in the same spot where my vampire half had stood. I rose to my feet, noting with detached surprise that everything hurt. I couldn't see a wound, so there was no obvious source for the pain.

Ian was across the room, his outstretched arm almost touching Dagon, who was in a heap at the foot of the stairs. I grasped my bone knife and started toward the demon—only to have an invisible wall stop me. Agony shot through me as a wide circle around me flared into view. Then it vanished, showing only the warped wood floors and carpet of trash.

"'ull me . . .'way . . . from him," Dagon rasped.

Ereshki hurried down the stairs, giving Ian wary looks as she stepped around him. He still looked unconscious, but she was careful not to touch him as she grabbed Dagon's arms and hauled him away from Ian. She kept away from me, too, making a wide berth as she dragged the demon to the entrance of the ski lodge.

"Far enough?" she asked with a grunt of exertion.

"'or . . . now."

I tried to yank any remaining fluid out of Dagon, but felt my power smack against the walls of the circle that imprisoned me. The circle didn't merely trap me inside its invisible circumference; it also succeeded in trapping my abilities, too.

"Clever," I said. My vampire nature howled; her form of agreement, I supposed.

Dagon's smile split his severely cracked lips, but he didn't have enough blood left in his body for them to bleed. Then he said something too garbled for me to translate.

"Don't bother talking until you heal enough to speak intelligibly. It appears I have the time to wait."

Dagon held up his middle finger. No translation required there. Then light burst from his chest, briefly blinding me. A few blinks later, the flashes were gone and I could see again.

The demon's skin was now as hydrated and vibrant as a youth in full vigor. He tapped his lips as if admiring their plump smoothness, then smiled at me with boyish charm, as if that detracted from the new, ugly spark in his eyes.

"How do I sound now?"

In reply, I hurled my power at him. It hit the walls, lighting them up. In the same instant, another full-body ache made me wish I could rip my bones out because they felt as if they'd caught fire. My vampire half howled in pain, too. And rage.

This isn't helping! I felt/heard her snap.

Did she think she could do better? Very well, then! I wasn't the one who'd fallen victim to the demon's clever trap. Let her deal with its repercussions. At least she'd earned them.

This situation is all yours, I thought, and fell back into the cage she'd long ago forged for me.

I slammed back into the mental driver's seat with a gasp that made Dagon's grin widen. Hatred flooded me along with the pain that had made my celestial nature decide to take a vacation day. I bit back my next gasp, gritting out a curse instead.

"How the fuck did you heal so quickly?"

Dagon tilted his head in a friendly way. "Burned through my last extra soul, of course. I used the others to give Ereshki the raw magical material to formulate these traps. What do you think she's been doing for the past three days? The circles are linked to each other, and they were both set to activate as soon as my blood touched them. I knew you couldn't resist using your blood-ripping powers on me, and I wasn't wrong."

I wanted to scream with frustration, but that would only delight him. I had to think up a way out of this. Quickly, before Dagon tired of gloating and got down to murdering us.

"Your extra souls?" I clucked my tongue in a disapproving way. "Have you been collecting on your demon deals before their expiration date to get so many, so fast?"

"No, you stupid whore," he replied in that same cheery tone. "While you were busy scouring the globe looking for the other resurrected people, I was slicing open their new bodies and taking back the power they stole from me. Acquiring their souls again was equally easy. People will agree to anything to make very creative torture stop."

I closed my eyes. Those poor people. "You used a spell to trace your power in them from the very start."

His snort opened my eyes. "I didn't have to. They rose from their graves, and I already knew where those graves were because I'm the one who killed them. I only left you the ghoul in Mycenae as a trap. Who do you think uploaded that video of him screeching in ancient Greek?"

Dammit, dammit, dammit! Why had my father tasked me with tracking down the other resurrected people when all along, Dagon had had a virtual map to their locations? Hadn't my father known that? Or, in his usual, apathetic way, had he not cared that Dagon had a huge advantage while I'd had nothing except an endless supply of false Internet leads to comb through?

"Now, he's the only one left," Dagon said, with a glance at Ian that made me hurl the strongest spell I knew at the walls confining me. They glowed amber from top to bottom, the circle flaring into fire before I dropped to my knees from the agony that shot through me.

Third time wasn't the charm.

"Keep it up," Dagon said in an approving tone. "Every time you touch or use magic on those walls, you trigger their defense mechanism. I am older than the creation of the human race and I've had over a month to plan my revenge, so I assure you, I thought of everything. Don't feel like a failure," he added mockingly. "You came closer to killing me than anyone ever has. I actually felt afraid back at that theme park several weeks ago." Then his voice turned caressing. "Then, you and Ian lured me into a trap by leaving just enough traces of my tracking spell in the Simargl for me to follow. Now, I trapped you by using that delicious spell inside Ian to lure you both to Ereshki after she contacted you. Fitting, don't you think?"

I did not, but I did glance at Ereshki long enough to catch her taunting smile. "At last, you die, girl."

She'd called me Ariel in her last communication. Now, I was "girl"—the only name Dagon and my other captors had given me.

"Oh, she doesn't die yet," Dagon said with obvious relish. "A quick death is too easy. No, she took what I loved from me—my power—so I'm going to take what she loves from her, and all she'll be able to do is watch and scream."

Ereshki's clear brown eyes gleamed with malevolent glee as she glanced at Ian. "How will you kill him?"

Dagon leaned closer as if sharing a secret, but his gaze was all for me as he said, "You'll see."

Ian groaned, yanking my attention back to him. He rolled over, shielding his eyes as if seeing something too bright to look at. Then, he bolted to his feet, bone knife at the ready in one hand while his other flung a tactile spell at the circle entrapping him. It glowed, illuminating a circumference far wider than mine, before pain slammed into me and my own circle glowed in response. The sudden, merciless slice of pain once again dropped me to my knees, then my gasp became a choking sound as blood poured from my mouth.

Dagon's laugh rang in my ears, covering whatever Ian said. I only caught the tail end of ". . . rip your entrails out and give them away as party favors!" before another bellyful of blood spraying from my mouth claimed all my attention. It felt like Dagon had teleported a chainsaw inside of me.

"Did I forget to mention the other aspect of the circles?" Dagon said with glee. "Touch or magic triggers their defenses, but only to *your* circle, girl! It's possible Ian could free himself, if he casts a powerful-enough spell. But that will kill you, and your father isn't available to resurrect you anymore." Dagon wagged his finger at me. "Which will it be? Will you watch him die? Or will you watch as he murders you to free himself? Either way, you suffer before your end, so *I win*."

Ian's gaze swung to me, an incredulous form of rage in his expression. "Tell me this arsehole is lying, and you *didn't* forget to tell me you're no longer immortal!"

I spat the last mouthful of blood out before answering. "Knew there was something I left out," I said with a terrible imitation of a laugh. Then, agony of a different sort gripped me as I stared into Ian's eyes. "If you can save yourself, do it. He's not letting me live no matter what happens to you."

"Oh, that's true," Dagon replied cheerily. "And if Ian breaks free from that circle, he'll be lucky to have enough energy left to run from us, so forget about him avenging you."

Ian gave him a look of such hatred that my blood chilled. It was as if he'd channeled all the rage from everyone slain before their time and lasered it at Dagon. The demon's smirk actually fell beneath the silent, seething onslaught. Then, he caught himself, and his arrogant smile returned.

"Or, I'll watch you die now, boy. That'll be fun, too."

With that, two humps swelled beneath the garbage that layered the bottom of Ian's circle. Ian jumped back, pulling out more weapons. In the moments it took the forms to burst free from the trash covering them, Ian had already fired several rounds into both of the growing humps.

He'd hit his marks, but no blood spattered the creatures that rose up from the trash piles. They grew impossibly fast, going from the size of dogs to horses in the scant time it took Ian to holster his guns and hurl silver knives into their heads next. The metal pierced skulls that looked leonine, if lions also had horns, but then the knives fell out without any visible damage to the creatures. Feathers slithered over their torsos, skipping their hairless, lionlike heads and humanoid hands and arms. Then two wings unfurled from their backs.

I stared in disbelief. These creatures had been carved into stone murals when I was a child, but I hadn't known they were *real*. Dagon saw my reaction and laughed.

"You do recognize them! Anzus were considered demons to ancient Sumerians, but what else do you expect primitive humans to call lesser divinities? They're also rarer than Simargls, so you'll appreciate the effort it took me to bring them here. Cost me two souls a piece."

One of the Anzus reared up and swiped at Ian with its huge, claw-tipped, humanoid hand. Ian leapt back, hitting the walls of his circle. The circle's defense mechanism slammed into me with the force of a car crash. Breath exploded out of me and my bones instantly broke. I staggered, avoiding touching the sides of my own far smaller circle because I didn't want to be hit with another blast of defensive magic, as Dagon called it.

Ian gave a worried look in my direction. The other Anzu seized on the distraction and flew at him faster than he could avoid. Claws ripped through everything except Ian's bullet-proof vest. Ian's blood spattered the walls of his circle. I felt new inner slashes from even that slight contact. Then, Ian threw the creature aside. It slammed into the circle's barrier, setting off another chainsaw-rampage sensation inside of me.

All I saw was blood for a few agonizing moments. It spurted from my eyes, mouth, and nose, forced out from the internal damage I could neither defend against nor protect myself from. When it stopped, I was on the floor, dangerously close to the edge of my own circle. Ian screamed my name. I looked up to see him stab his demon bone trident through one of the Anzu's eyes with absolutely no effect.

"Destroy the head," I croaked, hoping the old myths were true.

Ian flew up to avoid the second Anzu's attack, leaving his trident in the first one. The Anzu ripped it free, then broke the trident under a massive back paw.

Ian torpedoed back down, landing on the Anzu's back hard enough to snap the spine of any other creature. The Anzu didn't even lose its balance. It began flying around the circle, bucking wildly, striking the walls and the other Anzu in its rage to get Ian off its back. Between bursts of agony from the repeated contact with the circle's walls, I saw Ian hold on . . . and slam his longest, widest knife through the Anzu's skull.

The breath I held exploded out of me when the Anzu ripped that knife out of its skull with one of those humanlike hands, then bent down and rammed Ian against the circle's barrier hard enough for me to hear his bones shatter. I didn't hear anything except my own screams after that. The circle's defensive ricochet from that tremendous impact ripped me apart on the inside.

When I could focus again, Dagon's laugh was the first thing I heard. Then the blood left my vision and I saw Ian, far bloodier than before, flying out of the Anzus' reach while trying to avoid the sides of the circle. He must have figured out touching them was the source of my debilitating damage.

"Did I forget to mention my favorite part about Anzus?" Dagon's voice rose with vicious satisfaction. "No weapon forged can harm them."

Chapter 41

I could stand to watch Dagon gloat, and I could stand to die. But I could *not* stand to see Ian die again.

"Use your magic to get out of there, Ian!"

My hoarse shout made Ereshki smile. I didn't care. If Ian managed to survive the Anzus, he had enough magic in him to free himself from the circle. Then all he had to do was stay alive until the first rays of dawn shone through the blue diamond, and he could teleport out of the lodge. Dagon couldn't attack Ian directly because the spell my father cast on him meant he couldn't get close enough, and I didn't think Ereshki had the energy. Not from the way she looked. Setting the groundwork for Dagon's trap appeared to have taken everything she had left.

"No," Ian snapped, getting a bloody swipe to his side from one of the Anzus for his reply. That's how fast they were. One moment's distraction was all they needed.

Dagon smirked. "See how long his loyalty lasts when the Anzus are feasting on his flesh."

Ereshki's smile widened. Despair and rage shook me.

She laughed at what she did to you, Ian had said earlier. *Every second she lives after that is too long.*

My jaw tightened until cartilage snapped. Ereshki *had* lived too long. So had Dagon. I should have killed her the moment I recognized her at Yonah's, and I should have killed Dagon as soon as I saw him at that theme park in Paris. I hadn't. Now, Dagon would continue his murdering, soul-damning ways, and Ereshki would continue helping him. Countless more people would suffer and die, starting with me. But Ian didn't have to be next.

"If I die, I'll find a way to come back to you," I swore in a desperate attempt to sway him. "My father said the power to resurrect resided in me. Use your magic and free yourself from that circle! If I die, I will return to you!"

A lie I wished with all my heart were true. Maybe, if I wished hard enough, it *would* be true. I had no way to know. There was no margin of error for whether or not I could self-resurrect. If it didn't work, that was it.

"Yes, free yourself by killing her!" Dagon urged, grinning so widely, his lips should have split. "I want the last thing she sees to be you sacrificing her to save yourself."

Blood painted Ian's face red, making the flash of white from his teeth a sharp contrast as he smiled. "No weapon forged can harm these creatures? Thanks for the tip."

Then he tore off his outer tactical gear as he flew out of the Anzus' reach. A thick belt filled with weapons bounced off one of the Anzus before it hit the floor, then the two automatic rifles strapped to Ian's back, then the extra silver knives he'd strapped to his forearms. Dagon watched, cocking his head in curiosity.

"Giving up so soon? How boring."

Ian tore his shirt off in response. The gleaming expanse of pale, muscled flesh actually made Dagon stare for a moment before he caught sight of the dark bands encircling Ian's upper arm. Then the demon's gaze narrowed.

"What is that?"

Ian gave him a brief, savage grin. "You'll soon find out."

Hope flared, bright yet fragile. Caught in the grip of every horrible way Dagon had thwarted us, I'd forgotten about the horn, which had been created by the gods. Not forged by man. Could the ancient relic be enough to take down the Anzus?

I sucked in a breath as Ian flew at the Anzu that was flapping its great wings to reach him at the top of the circle. Right before

Ian slammed into it, his arm shot out. The horn did, too, stabbing the creature through its open, fanged mouth. The impact rocketed them both to the ground, Ian's entire arm disappearing down the creature's throat. They hit the ground hard enough to make it shudder. My heart seized. Nothing was happening. Just like before, the Anzu wasn't hurt—

Ian ripped his arm forward. The dark tip of the horn sliced through the Anzu's back like a butcher cleaving off a tender piece of meat. It didn't stop even when it reached the Anzu's head. Another brutal rip, and two bony halves fell to the side, while an eruption of a thick blue fluid burst from the center. The Anzu shuddered once and then it lay completely still.

Dagon turned paler than his normal ivory visage. Then he screamed and flung himself at Ian's circle, beating on it. But the same spell that kept Ian and I trapped also locked the demon out. Ian's circle had the same defensive reaction to being touched on the outside as it did on the inside, though. I fell over, more blood blinding and choking me while my organs felt like they were exploding, then burning.

"Die, die, die!" Dagon screamed.

I felt like I would. That must be Dagon's goal. A person's body could only take so much, vampire healing abilities or not.

Then Ian's voice cut through the merciless pain. "Veritas!"

Dammit, one more costly distraction could be Ian's last! I forced myself into a sitting position, my abrupt wave saying *worry about yourself, not me!* I wasn't the one locked in a circle with an Anzu.

Dagon kept chanting "Die!" while beating on the circle. Every blow slammed into me. Once again, all I saw was red and all I tasted was blood. I didn't know it was possible for my body to contain this much blood, or produce this much pain. It maddened me, making me grasp at anything that could help.

I yanked my other nature out of her cage, crying out in relief at the brief respite of her being in the forefront instead of me. It lessened the pain, allowing me to see through her far more detached eyes as she rose up from my blood and the thicker, heavier things I'd retched to look at Ian.

It reminded me of Ashael's unique spying method. Everything was coated in red, making the struggle between Ian and the remaining Anzu look more like a blood-soaked nightmare than reality.

The Anzu tore into Ian's shoulder, fangs ripping out hunks of flesh as it slammed Ian into the circle's invisible wall. Agony exploded, so intense that it seared me even through my other half. When it lessened and I could see again, Ian's right shoulder was gone, his arm was hanging by only a few stubborn ligaments, and the Anzu was closing in for another gouging bite.

I screamed, hearing the echo of it leave my other half's lips. She no longer felt as separate from me, just as I could no longer use her as a shield. The pain had stitched us too tightly together. Or maybe we were both struck with horror at the sight of the Anzu savagely ripping into Ian. His huge mouth closed over Ian's shoulder once again, tearing at the gaping wound. Ian's right arm hit the floor, severed. Then his back bowed from the creature's weight as the Anzu bore down on him, wings flapping for maximum assault velocity.

Dagon howled in victory and stopped beating on the outside of Ian's circle. Ereshki ran forward, clapping with the delight of a child. Ian dropped to his knees beneath the Anzu's massive form. His blood splattered the circle's edge, sending more stabs into me that paled next to the anguish of seeing Ian on his knees.

The Anzu reared back for another flesh-rending bite—

Ian twisted, using the blood slicking the ground to slide past the Anzu's descending head. Then he stabbed the horn through the creature's mouth so violently, the tip went straight through the Anzu's head and into the wall of the circle.

Pain blasted me, but beneath it, I felt a *crack!* that stopped the pain for a blissful moment.

When I looked up, the horn's tip was still embedded in the wall surrounding the circle, and now, a spiderweb of fractures spread out to reveal that part of the invisible wall.

"No," Dagon whispered. "It's not possible!"

But it was. Brute force and multiple blasts of magic hadn't made a single fissure in the circle, but somehow, the horn could damage it. And if it could be damaged, it could fall.

Ian kicked the dead Anzu aside. Then, its blue blood mixing with the scarlet swaths that splattered him, he rose, eyeing the crack with single-minded focus.

"Use the horn to break the circle!" I shouted, a fierce thrill of hope acting as a shot of adrenaline. "It isn't the same as using magic. That crack you made stopped the pain!"

"No!" Dagon screamed, now beating against the walls with everything he had. Ereshki ran over to join him. Their double assault ripped into me with blinding ferocity, but amidst that, I felt another, stronger *crack!* that briefly stopped the pain.

"It's working!" I croaked when my throat cleared of blood enough for me to speak. "Don't stop!"

He didn't. I felt each hammer of Ian's fist against that wall in the snap of my bones becoming slower and the pulverizing of my insides becoming less crippling. Soon, I caught glimpses of Ian through the blood that took longer to block out my vision.

Ian had the horn wrapped around his hand like a pair of brass knuckles as he hammered at the wall with the determination of the damned. Fractures made the entire circle visible from floor to ceiling, resembling cracked glass. Dagon and Ereshki had switched to beating against my circle instead of Ian's, and the fury on Dagon's face was balm to my endless pain.

Dagon wouldn't be so furious unless Ian was winning.

"Don't stop!" I repeated before my vision and mouth flooded with blood again. I felt like I was drowning, but that was impossible. Vampires didn't need to breathe to survive.

Then I felt the magic, foul and putrid, pulsing through the pain. Dagon and Ereshki had stopped using physical force on my circle. Now, they were casting the darkest of magic at it. The circle reacted with all the defensive violence in it. Soon, even the relentless hammering of Ian's fist wasn't enough to counter it. I wasn't being drowned; I was being plunged toward death.

"Veritas!"

Ian's voice cut through the currents pulling me under. I tried to lift my head, but it was too heavy.

"Answer me, Veritas!"

The sharpness in Ian's voice was nothing compared to the detonations going off inside me. Dagon and Ereshki's magic was too strong. My body was giving out. I didn't know how much damage Ian had done to the circle, or if it would be enough, and I couldn't open my eyes to look. I didn't have the strength.

"If you don't answer, I will stop beating this circle and let them kill me!"

Fucking hell. Was it really too much to ask that he *not* get killed for me again? I, at least, had a chance at coming back from the dead once I died. Ian didn't, but was he letting that stop him from making his threat? Of course not.

"Veritas, I mean it!"

I still couldn't speak or see, but I marshaled all my energy in order to move one finger. It was my middle one, and I stuck it straight up in the direction his voice came from.

A harsh laugh preceded his reply. "Good. I'm almost through this wall, but it's taken quite a lot from me. When it goes down, I need you to be ready because Dagon *will* attack you. Do you hear? You can't stay slumped in a pool of your own blood."

Did he think I was lying in my own pureed guts because it was a hot new fashion trend? If I could've flipped him off with both hands, I would have.

"Whatever you did to terrify Tenoch all those years ago, I need you to do it again," Ian went on, shocking me. "That part of you is buried too deep to be beaten down by this spell. It's also been waiting a long time to come out. Now, you need to let it."

Tenoch's face flashed in my mind. Not one of the memories I cherished; the one I'd tried the hardest to forget. *The horror on his face when he stared at the bodies lying beside pools of darkness around me, and worse, the revulsion in his eyes when he looked up from them to stare at me . . .*

"No," I croaked, so appalled I managed to speak.

"Yes," he snapped. "I won't let Tenoch's fear cost you your life. And do you think Dagon will stop at you? Do you want me to break down these walls only to get slaughtered by that sod?"

With each word, he continued hammering at the circle. I felt it in every flash of relief in my broken body, but now I was worried, too. How much had it taken from Ian for him to keep beating on that magic-imbued barrier? Was it everything he had?

I reached down inside myself and felt around until I brushed the most forbidden aspects of my other half. Yes, that power was still there, but would it be enough? Worse, would it be too much? Ian was right; that part had been held back for so long that I had no idea what it would do if I let it out again.

"Can't . . . control it," I managed to say.

"You don't need to." A shout that coincided with a *boom!* that shook me to my core. "I trust you, *all* of you. You won't hurt me, and nothing you can do will ever horrify me. Let yourself free, Veritas! Every bit of you!"

I could feel the cracks on the walls widening. Soon, they would come down, and Dagon would come at us with everything he had. He didn't even need to get close to Ian to kill him, either. A shot through the heart with a silver bullet would be enough, and Ian had left automatic weapons filled with silver rounds at the bottom of his circle.

Ereshki might be magically and physically depleted from her part in Dagon's spells, but she could also take Ian out with one of those guns, and if Ian was in as bad shape as he implied, he might not be able to stop her, either.

But would summoning the darkest part of my power be worse? Tenoch had believed that so much, he'd created not one, but *two* assassins to take me out, if I brought it forth again. My other nature hadn't hurt Ian before, but if I let the worst of it out, would it stop at killing Dagon? Or would it kill Ian, too?

It didn't kill Tenoch.

The thought seared me, bringing another blast of hope. When I'd let the darkest aspect of my power free so long ago, I'd only killed the vampires who'd kidnapped me. Not the sire I loved. At the height of everything Tenoch had feared until his dying day, I'd still protected him.

Did that mean Ian was right? Was my power only as evil *as I allowed it to be?*

"Veritas, now!" Ian shouted.

How could I pick between over four thousand years of Tenoch's conditioning versus Ian's claim that he was wrong *this instant?* But not picking was its own choice. The walls were crashing down. Who should I believe? The sire who'd known me most of my life? Or the man I loved, yet had only known months?

Dammit, why should it be a choice between the two of them? Didn't *I* have control over me, even the most frightening parts of me? Even demons had free will! Why should I be any different?

My father had *chosen* to "stray where it was forbidden" by impregnating Ashael's mother and then, later, mine. He'd also *chosen* to lose his position as Warden of the Gateway to the Netherworld to bring Ian back after I begged him to. If the most fearsome otherworldly creature I'd met could choose despite the inclinations of his nature, then so could I!

And I chose *not* to let Ian get hurt by Dagon or Ereshki when I had the power to stop them. No matter what terrifying form that power took, or what I'd have to do to bring it forth, because there hadn't been two aspects to my nature back then. There'd been only one.

"Ian," I rasped. "When you get free, take Ereshki and get as far away from me as the pentagram allows."

"The hell you say?" he snapped, but then I felt a resounding *boom!* that overwhelmed even the pain. He'd broken through the wall. Dagon's howl of rage confirmed it.

"What I'm going to do could swallow everything in its immediate vicinity!" I said, the falling wall giving me strength to shout. "You can't be near it, so take Ereshki and go!"

Then I reached down, feeling for the cage that housed my other half. But this time, I didn't merely open the door or pull her out of it. No more partial measures.

I smashed the cage completely.

Chapter 42

*B*lackness rolled over my vision as I felt my other half rise, but for the first time in over four thousand years, I didn't draw away to keep her separate. I embraced her, feeling a shocking surge of ice and heat as both halves began to merge into one. More shocking was how, almost instantly, she wasn't "she" anymore. It was just me, with so much more to me than there had ever been before.

"Ian," I managed to say between blasts that made me feel as if I'd detonate at any moment, but not with pain. With the kind of power I'd never felt before. "If you love me, trust me and *go*."

I thought I heard him mutter, "Five minutes. That's all you get," but I wasn't sure. I did feel him leave in a whoosh, though, a cut-off scream indicating he'd grabbed Ereshki, too.

Vow not to kill Ereshki myself fulfilled.

As for Dagon . . .

I opened my eyes. Dagon's icy blue gaze met mine. Just as I'd guessed, the demon had one of Ian's guns, and he didn't hesitate. Silver rounds slammed into me, throwing me backward, but my heart was protected by the bulletproof vest.

I rolled behind the counter that had once serviced ski patrons, expecting another volley to blast through the wooden barrier at any moment. It didn't. Instead, I only heard the rapid patter of footsteps that quickly faded.

He was running away from me.

I dragged myself to my feet. The spell that had secured the circles meant I healed slower than I would have normally, but I *was* healing, so I forced that unfamiliar feeling of sluggishness aside and chased him. With the pentagram's boundaries still in place, Dagon couldn't get too far.

He didn't. I found him at the end of the star's tip on the top of the ridge, beating against the spell that didn't allow him to go any farther. He had his mobile phone in his other hand, of all things, and he screamed "Now, now, now!" at whoever was on the other end of it.

"Did you not pay attention when Ian and I said that no one can teleport into or leave the pentagram until dawn?"

He whirled, boyishly handsome features almost deformed from the hatred that twisted them. "Stay away from me."

"Stay away?" I repeated, closing the distance between us. "Stop? Don't? Please? How many times have you heard those words? I remember that they only amused you . . . and incited you to greater acts of cruelty."

"You cannot best me in your condition." A snarl that sounded more desperate than confident. "You can barely walk!"

He had a point. I wasn't nearly healed enough to fight him, and his distance from Ian meant that he was in far better shape than he'd been before. In a hand-to-hand battle, Dagon would win. That's why I wasn't using my hands.

"True," I replied. "But I am my father's daughter."

I let the power I'd only accessed once before rip through me. When it overflowed, I saw Dagon through eyes no vampire had.

Darkness poured from him in putrid waves, staining even the ground he stood upon. Not a glimmer of light broke through it. Unlike most people who committed terrible deeds, Dagon hadn't been warped by cruel circumstances or a distorted view of what was best for the world. No, Dagon knew exactly who he was and what he was doing, and he'd taken the darkest joy in both.

I had my own darkness, made up of the other side of eternity instead of the stain of too many foul deeds to count. I let it billow behind me like a cloud before it pooled at my feet, widening as it snaked toward Dagon. He saw it and leapt back, but the barrier of the pentagram left him nowhere to go.

"What are you doing?" His voice, always so confident, cruel or amused, now sounded plaintive. "Stop! Stop, please!"

I ignored that, just as Dagon had ignored similar pleas countless times before. At last, everyone who'd pled for mercy from him and received none would get their long-overdue justice.

"No," I said, my voice booming in a thunderous way I'd never heard before. It sounded, I realized, like my father's did when he was angry. "You've been sentenced."

I plunged every bit of that otherworldly power inside Dagon. It didn't curl around the water and blood that plumped his skin and made his features as ruddy as a youth's; it went deeper, wrapping around the foulest part of him.

His soul.

Dagon screamed as I grabbed that part and pulled. For an instant, there were two Dagons: the body that made up the demon and a translucent duplicate that struggled in my power's grasp. I pulled again and his soul broke the surface of his skin, blurring it. The darkness around me became liquid and plummeted to depths that went all the way to the netherworld.

This was what Tenoch had seen back when his enemies kidnapped me to coerce him into complying with their demands. Tenoch hadn't yet reached the point where he was so powerful that few dared to cross him, and as a new vampire, I hadn't been able to defend myself against Tenoch's older, stronger foes. But being at the mercy of the merciless again had triggered a frenzied PTSD attack that brought forth the darkest of my other abilities. Tenoch had arrived to see me ripping the souls out of my captors, forever causing him to fear me.

Now, it was Dagon's turn to fear. I tightened the grip my power had on his soul, about to rip it free—

"Veritas," a shocked voice gasped. "What are you doing?"

I would have expected that question from Ian. Telling me to do my worst and actually *seeing* it were two different things. But this wasn't Ian's voice. It was feminine, and it was speaking in Mandarin.

I turned around, confirming Xun Guan was indeed behind me, as close as the encircled pentagram would allow. She wasn't alone. No fewer than four council members were with her, with an additional two Law Guardians and six demons flanking them.

I let out a short laugh and turned back to Dagon. "That was the call you made? You had your demons teleport Law Guardians and some of the council here?"

Dagon's grin was back in all of its cruel glory. "Yes, and"—he raised his voice so those watching us could clearly hear him—"I know demons aren't usually the ones to do this with the vampire court, but I'd like to lodge a formal complaint."

$\mathcal{I}$ actually looked behind me again to make sure I wasn't hallucinating. How dare Dagon bring the police to a demon-and-death's-daughter fight! He truly was an asshole.

"Veritas!" Haldam's voice cracked the air like a gunshot. Of course, Dagon had made sure the council's official spokesperson was among those here. "What is the meaning of this?"

"Let me go, and you can make up any story you like," Dagon hissed, now too low for them to overhear. "Kill me, and they will all see you for the traitorous abomination that you are."

I'd often feared that one day, I would slip up and be caught. Turns out, my fears hadn't been ambitious enough. You didn't call pools of darkness pouring from me and wrapping around Dagon while magic crackled the air and my silver gaze cut through the ephemeral darkness a *slip*. It was more like a landslide.

Yet, oddly, I wasn't afraid. Maybe the ice-cold calmness from my newly blended nature was overpowering the more volatile emotions of my vampire side. Maybe it was the fact that deep down, I'd always known this day would eventually come, so now that it had, it was almost freeing.

Dagon's gaze gleamed with malevolence. "You can thank Ian for my finding out what your vampire identity was. If he hadn't sued the council when you left him, it might have taken me months to realize that the bitch I sought and the spouse-abandoning Law Guardian named Veritas were one and the same."

As if he'd summoned him, Ian appeared. This was the first I'd seen him since we'd been freed from the circles, and I was appalled.

"Taken quite a lot," he'd said of the effort it took to break down the wall. That didn't begin to describe the damage. His severed right arm was only a small stump protruding from his right shoulder while his left arm was stripped of all flesh, the horn still wrapped around his knuckles as if it had fused with his bones. His left shoulder only had some rough sinews attaching it to his collarbones, and his whole body looked shrunken, as if it had cannibalized itself for energy during his battle to take the wall down. Worse, he didn't appear to be healing.

Please let him just need lots of blood. Or time for the magic's ravaging effects to leave him. Please, let this not be the cost of him saving me!

Whatever his body looked like, Ian himself hadn't changed. "Who called the bloody cops?"

"Dagon," I replied, looking back at the demon.

His soul might be swimming right beneath his face, but it didn't lessen the venom in his smile. It enhanced it.

"Long ago, you stripped me of all my power and position," he said in a caressing voice. "Take my soul now, and you will know what that feels like, Veritas. And you will rue it."

He'd never called me by a name before. I'd only ever been "girl" to him. Now, my name left his lips as if it were a curse.

I glanced back at the council. If I tried very hard, I might be able to do what Dagon said and pull off a "this isn't what it looks like" defense. I could say my eyes and the darkness billowing behind me was the result of a spell Dagon had hexed me with, and point to the dead Anzus and all the damage done to Ian as proof of what the demon could do.

Or, I could think up a cleverer defense. I could literally say anything to persuade them to believe that what they saw wasn't caused by a forbidden hybrid lineage and illegal magic . . . if I let Dagon go instead of killing him.

That's why he'd had his acolytes teleport several members of the vampire council plus a handful of Law Guardians here. It was, to use an American term, his Hail Mary pass.

"Kill me, and you lose everything you've built during the many years of your life," Dagon repeated, as if I was too stupid to realize the implications myself.

"Veritas, explain this!" Haldam commanded.

Dagon's eyes gleamed with almost a feral light. "Yes, explain, or prove what you are beyond all doubt—"

I yanked his soul out. Dagon's body collapsed at the loss of the writhing, diaphanous form. Seeing it, the council members and Law Guardians recoiled in horror. Then they let out a gasp when I drew Dagon's silently shrieking soul right up to my face.

"You don't get away again," I said. "No matter what this costs me: You. Are. Done."

Then I threw his foul, reeking soul into the darkness that pooled at my feet, giving the new Warden of the Gateway to the Netherworld— whoever that was now that my father had been fired from or abdicated the position—another passenger to transport to the most feared section of the afterlife.

Shocked silence filled the air. I used it to concentrate as I pulled back my power. To my surprise, it went easily, without the struggle that had marked my former issues with my other nature. The darkness that had pooled around me vanished, too, revealing the dry, hardened earth of winter, and when I turned around, I could see that my gaze now glowed emerald, not silver.

The demons gave a horrified look at what I'd done before teleporting away. Guess they didn't care about Dagon enough to attempt avenging him, or they knew they'd need bigger numbers to try. Either way, word of what I'd done would travel. If I didn't have a bounty on my head in the demon world before, I would now.

That was fine. When they came for me, I'd be ready.

Haldam was the first to find his voice. It shook, but to his credit, his words weren't fearful. "Arrest her!"

What was left of Ian's muscles coiled; a panther about to pounce. Dawn peeked over the horizon. Soon, the pentagram's confining barrier would be down. Ian must not think he could teleport us away, so he was readying himself to fight.

"Ian, don't!"

He paused, anger and incredulousness washing over his expression. "You think I'll let them take you?"

At that, every one of the Law Guardians drew a weapon. His threat could not have been clearer. But in his current condition, a fight with them could prove deadly for Ian.

I could use my abilities to overcome them, but they didn't deserve to have their souls ripped out, and I wasn't sure I could stop myself from doing that versus only tearing out their blood and water. That power felt too close to the surface, too ready to be unleashed again. If I let it out again so soon, who knew what would happen?

"You *will* let them take me, Ian," I said, struck with an idea. "Then you'll call me later, when you're someplace safe."

His breath blew out in the harshest of laughs. Then he swung around to glare at the newest council member, who muttered, "You won't be alive later," under his breath.

"Ian!" My voice rose as the promise of death filled his gaze. I couldn't let him attack the council, for many reasons. "I said when you get someplace safe, *call me.*"

The killing rage left his gaze. I heaved a sigh of relief. Good, he understood. Then, I turned to the council.

"I demand a formal trial before any sentence is carried out. Considering my millenniums of service, it's the least I deserve."

"She is right," Hekima said, though her glance held no hope for the sentence to be anything except death. "We will reconvene in Athens, where all eleven of us will be present. Until then, Veritas, you are under arrest. One of you, restrain her."

"You'll have to wait a few minutes," I replied calmly. "The barrier around this area doesn't drop until dawn."

They tested that, of course. Then they stood on the other side of the barrier, exchanging awkward looks with each other.

Ian came over to me. I took his hand in mine and winced at how I only felt bones. *Please, let him heal,* I thought again.

He must have sensed my worry because his mouth curled. "I've come back from worse, or so I've been told."

This *was* the second time that fighting by my side had reduced him to a near-skeletal state. "Marriage is proving to be harmful to your health," I replied with a shaky laugh.

"That's saying something for a vampire," he quipped. Then his amusement faded and he said, "Ereshki is dead," with savage satisfaction.

How he'd managed to kill her in his state was remarkable. Then again, Ian had always surprised me—and anyone who dared to underestimate him.

"Good," was all I said.

The sun was coming up. In moments, it would shine through the smashed-out windows of the ski lodge and touch the blue diamond, breaking the boundary on the encircled pentagram.

"I love you," I whispered, reaching for his hand again.

He squeezed, the horn making a cracking sound as if it had turned into nothing more than a dried twig from all the power it had expelled taking down the walls of our trap.

"Love you, too, my little soon-to-be-former Guardian."

I felt the spell drop the next moment. A breeze came from the pentagram as the potent magic was extinguished like a candle being blown out. The council members and Law Guardians felt it, too. They shifted before one of them put a tentative foot over the invisible line that had been blocked off before.

Ian's bony hand tightened around mine. For an instant, the trees, lodge, and mountainous slope began to blur. Then that blur collapsed, and he gritted out a curse.

"Can't do it, luv."

I had no doubt that he couldn't teleport. I didn't even know how he was still standing.

"Don't let your guard down," Ian whispered, so low I could barely hear him even though he was right next to me. "Can't be sure, but I think I feel Yonah's spell activating."

I gave him a surprised look. One of the council members or Law

Guardians had traces of Dagon's power in them? No. None of them would consort with, let alone become branded by, a demon. It must be the spell in Ian short-circuiting because of the state he was in.

Or . . . could Dagon have ordered his people to bring part of the council and several Law Guardians here for more than the hope of saving himself? Could one of them really be his secret acolyte?

"The barrier is down," Haldam said, with an impatient swipe toward the Law Guardians. "Arrest her."

The Law Guardians glanced at each other, at me, and hesitated. After everything they'd seen, none appeared eager to be the first to try.

Xun Guan was the one who stepped over the spot that had been blocked by the pentagram's encircling barrier moments before. Her expression reflected her pain, but her steps didn't waver as she pulled out a pair of restraints and came toward me.

"Faithless to the end," Ian said with contempt, earning him a look that was so cutting, it should have made him bleed.

"This is your doing," Xun Guan snapped. "None of this would have happened if not for you."

"You're wrong, Xun Guan," I replied. "Ian didn't make me who I am. I was that person long before I met him. He only helped me accept it."

Once again, pain etched her lovely features. "Then, all this time, you were lying to me."

Maybe it was my newly merged nature that prevented me from feeling the shame Xun Guan obviously wanted me to feel. The other half of me had seemed incapable of emotions like that. Or maybe, that merging now gave me the clarity I'd lacked before to realize that I wasn't the one who should be ashamed.

"It should upset you more that I lived in a world that forced me to hide what I was," I replied. "I was born different, but that doesn't mean I was born wrong. *No one* is. What's wrong are the laws that make people like me hide what we are because others are too bigoted or too afraid to let us live in peace."

A slow, proud smile curled Ian's mouth, but Xun Guan stared at me in disbelief. Hekima closed her eyes, shaking her head in what could have been regret. She was one of the few council members who'd voted against sentencing Cat's daughter to death.

But Haldam snapped, "That's enough. You will have a chance to say your piece at your trial, unless you waive your demand for a full hearing and want your sentence carried out now?"

The sound Ian made had me gripping his hand until I heard the snap of fractures. "No," I said, dropping his hand to hold my wrists out to Xun Guan. "I demand a full, formal trial. I'll speak to you later, Ian. Now, please, go."

He gave me a frustrated look, then gave another, even more frustrated one down at himself, as if silently cursing the state he was in that prevented him from teleporting us out of here.

Then, for the second time in the past hour, Ian left when he didn't want to.

Chapter 44

I an didn't head toward the lodge to retrieve the priceless diamond we'd left lying on the floor. He walked deeper into the woods. I watched him until the thickening line of evergreens blocked him from my view. Then, I turned back to the council.

Haldam was staring in the direction Ian had gone while stroking his long beard. "Perhaps we shouldn't let him leave so easily. He should stand trial, too."

I gave the highest official in the council a look that made him take a step backward. "You *don't* want to do that."

"Veritas is the only one in violation of our laws," Hekima said, stepping in front of Haldam so she blocked the lethal glare I gave him. "We have no need to question her husband," she went on. "For all we know, he was here because he was trying to stop her."

I stifled my snort. I'd always liked Hekima, and she was helping as much as she could under the circumstances. I wouldn't disrespect that by pointing out that Ian had zero respect for the law, and even less for people who zealously followed it.

"Your wisdom is appreciated, Hekima," I replied.

"The prisoner will not speak again!" Haldam thundered at me. To everyone else, he said, "Does anyone have a mobile? We need to arrange transportation out of here, as well as contact the other council members and convene a full trial immediately."

He certainly seemed in a hurry to execute me. Could he be the person Ian sensed Dagon's power coming from?

Then again, Haldam and I had never been close. Now, he had all the reasons he needed to despise me. Out of all the council members, he'd been the most vocal opponent of mixed-species people and magic practitioners. It took a special kind of coldness to sentence a child to death, yet Haldam had done it to Cat's daughter without even feigning the same hesitation that other council members voting for her death had.

Maybe I'd let Haldam see what it was like to be on the receiving end of a summary execution decision. It would be so easy to reach inside him and yank out his soul . . .

I gave myself a quick shake, as if trying to physically dislodge the thought. This was the danger of merging the half of myself I'd long denied with the rest of me. That half might not be evil, but it contained the same borderline-sociopathic logic that allowed my father to transport people to the pits of the Netherworld without a hint of remorse. Now, it was fully a part of me, so to say that it could affect my sense of right and wrong was an understatement.

Haldam might indeed deserve to die because of his merciless actions, but that didn't mean I should appoint myself as his executioner. If I meted out death to everyone I and I alone deemed worthy of it, I would soon become more monstrous than the council at their very worst.

I'd also be proving the council's fears about people like me, even though I hardly represented all mixed-species people, let alone all people who practiced magic. And inevitably, I'd end up harming those who didn't deserve it. No one was above being wrong, least of all me.

"Put the web spell on her, Xun Guan," Haldam ordered, as if somehow sensing me struggle over my new desire to execute him. "She's far too . . . unconfined as she is."

Xun Guan's mouth turned down, but she pulled a magic-infused gem from her belt. Long ago, I'd told her never to be without one. She'd heeded the advice. Then, in the original language of the spell, she spoke the words that resulted in layer upon layer of sticky, unbreakable substance wrapping around me as if giant spiders were cocooning me in webs.

Despite everything, I was proud. I'd taught her that spell several centuries ago, when I was training her, as all Law Guardians needed to know defensive magic. Most of the other Law Guardians had been unable to master such a complex spell, but Xun Guan did. Now, she executed it perfectly. It was also ironic that the last time I'd been caught in this spell, it had resulted in Ian and I being forced to marry.

Had that only been two months ago? It felt so much longer.

"Finished," Xun Guan told Haldam.

He gave a short nod, but stayed as far away from me as he could without being obvious about it. He needn't worry. I wasn't going to kill him, even if more than a small part of me was still convinced that he deserved it. Instead, I settled into the web spell as if it were a warm blanket.

I had nothing to do now but wait, so I may as well be comfortable while I did.

VERMONT IN WINTER wasn't a hot spot for vampires, so it took over two hours for the first of the council's reinforcements to arrive. They consisted of three Enforcers and two more Law Guardians, who took up positions around the exterior of the ski lodge. I had been carried inside the lodge over an hour ago, then dumped next to one of the broken circle traps. Only scorch marks on the floor revealed where they'd been.

Well, that and the two dead Anzus inside Ian's former circle.

The Anzus had gotten a lot of attention, not that I could blame the council members. It wasn't every day you saw the remains of two creatures that had been thought to be only myth up close. The Anzus were poked, prodded, and examined, then ordered to be brought back to Athens for further study.

I stayed where I'd been dropped, pretending to doze. If not for Ian's suspicion that one of the people here had traces of Dagon's power in them, I might have napped for real. But he'd told me to keep my guard up, so my dozing act was to see if anyone tried to take advantage. There was a lot going on, with council members arranging for transportation, scheduling an emergency trial, and arranging for even heavier security to transport me than the Law Guardians who were already here. All that on top of the Law Guardians chronicling the magic traces left over, gathering up the stones at pivotal points in the pentagrams, and making sure any nosy humans didn't disturb us.

With all that, someone could attempt to sneak up behind me and slip a silver knife into my heart, if Dagon did indeed have a secret acolyte among them. If that happened, they'd discover I had a bulletproof vest beneath my black shirt, and I'd discover that the power-seeking spell inside Ian wasn't on the fritz.

But thus far, I was ignored by all except Xun Guan, who kept casting looks at me that ranged from angry, to sad, to betrayed.

I regretted hurting her, but my lies had been a matter of survival, not preference. Vampires often looked down upon humans for their many bigotries, but in reality, we were no better. We simply chose different reasons to oppress each other.

"The helicopter will be here within the hour," Hekima announced from the other side of the lodge. "It will take us to the airport, where a plane will be fueled and waiting."

"Good." Haldam's voice, disgust dripping from it. "This hovel stinks more than I can stand . . ."

His voice trailed off. I opened my eyes from their mostly closed slits to see what had distracted him. Then my eyes widened and I pulled myself into a sitting position.

The air had turned to gold. That's the only way I could describe the thick shimmer that now filled every crevice of the blood-spattered, garbage-strewn lodge. If my hands had been free, I would've swept them through the golden haze to see if that glorious shimmer would coat my skin instead of merely hanging in the air, but I couldn't move beyond stunted crawls.

Hekima did it for me. No, the bright shimmer that looked as if a cloud of gold dust had gently exploded didn't stick to her skin. It also didn't coat her hair or her clothes. It might be so thick that it made the room hazy, but somehow, it wasn't tangible enough to touch.

Haldam turned toward me. "Stop that this instant!"

"I'm not doing it," I replied with the absolute truth.

"Then who?" he demanded.

Who indeed? Was this some sort of spell from Ian? He was the only one who knew we were here, except for the demons who'd fled. But Ian hadn't been in any condition to do this kind of magic, and demons didn't flood a place with a strange, non-corporeal version of gold dust before they ambushed. Demon attacks were violent. Not sparkly.

Drops of light began falling into the thick golden haze. They hung in the air instead of dropping to the ground, looking like tiny stars against a golden sky.

Hekima gasped.

Xun Guan barked out an order for the remaining Law Guardians to protect the council. Soon, I couldn't see the council members behind the rush of vampires that hurried to obey. All the while, more starlike drops filled the golden haze.

If this was Ian's doing, it was his most impressive spell yet—

A beam shot down into the room, fast as a lightning bolt and twice as bright. I shut my eyes against the glare, then dipped my head when that still wasn't enough. When the glow penetrating my closed lids dimmed enough for me to tell that it was no longer blinding, I opened my eyes, making out the darker silhouette of something tall and big against the golden-starred sky.

Something that was moving directly toward me.

I yanked my power to the forefront, ready to hurl it at the figure if it wasn't Ian. I couldn't tell yet. Then that disorienting light faded enough to reveal a shirtless muscular man with large golden wings that touched the floor when he folded them behind his back. His skin was a rich honey shade, his hair was the blue black of a raven's wing, and his eyes were the color of newly minted gold coins.

His features were also so stunning, I understood for the first time what the word *blasphemous* meant. Nothing short of the Most High god should be allowed to possess this much beauty.

But he wasn't Ian, so I sent my power at him to rip all the fluids from his body if he made a threatening move toward me . . . only my power skipped right over him and moved to the vampires huddled around the council members behind him.

What?

I tried it again to the same futile effect. After I tried and failed a third time, I realized what the problem was. My power kept skipping over him because the man didn't have a drop of blood or water in his body.

That wasn't possible. All species except ghosts had either one or the other, and he was no ghost, as he proved when he reached out and plucked Xun Guan's unbreakable web spell from me as easily as if he were removing a speck of lint. Then he removed my wrist restraints with only a look.

"What are you?" I asked as I backed away from him.

"Phanes," he replied in an orchestra-worthy baritone.

I kept backing away. "What's a Phanes?"

Surprise flashed over his features. "Not what. *Who*. Phanes is my name. How do you not know me?"

"Easy," I replied while searching my memory. No, I would have remembered that face, not to mention the huge golden wings. "We've never met."

"We have not," he agreed. "The last time I felt your power, you were not at the spot it originated from by the time I arrived."

The last time . . .

"How long ago was that?" I asked warily.

His wave was dismissive. "Four or five thousand years."

Ice shot through my veins. He didn't mean my fluid-ripping power. He meant my soul-snatching one. If he could feel that, and he didn't have any blood or water in him, could he be . . . could he be like my father?

He didn't *look* like my father. My father didn't have wings or gold-colored eyes, and the Warden to the Gateway to the Netherworld had certainly never had golden clouds precede his presence. Phanes also spoke Greek the way it had been spoken thousands of years ago versus the more modern dialect.

Wasn't there Greek mythology about a lesser deity named Phanes? If so, his name meant "to shine," which would explain the star-studded, gold dust fog-machine effect that heralded his arrival. What it didn't explain was why Phanes was here at all.

"Why should I know you, if you admit that we've never met?"

Phanes smiled. A flock of doves soaring into the sky on sunlit wings would've been less lovely. "Because your power proclaims you to be the child of the eternal river bridging this world and the next. Since long before you were born, you were promised to be my bride."

The. Fuck?

I opened my mouth to tell him what I thought of that, but a tremendous inner yank claimed all my attention. In the next instant, the gold-shimmered room with the council members cowering behind visibly shaken Law Guardians vanished, and I was inescapably pulled toward somewhere else.

Ian had placed his call.

Chapter 45

The next thing I saw was the large stone fireplace and white wood-framed windows of Mencheres's Hamptons cottage. Ian was on the floor in front of that fireplace, the symbols that made up my name for the summoning ritual written in my blood in front of him.

"Ian!"

He leapt up in a lithe motion that belied his still frighteningly injured body. Then he pulled me to him. I gripped him back as hard as I dared, once again hoping that rest, time, and lots of blood would repair the horrific damage he'd inflicted on himself to free us from Dagon's trap.

"Can I come out yet?" a familiar, impatient voice asked.

"No," Ian replied while I pulled away in surprise.

"Ashael's here?"

Ian flashed a tight smile. "Couldn't risk bringing you to me until I was far enough away for the council not to find us. Also couldn't hijack a car and drive that distance since someone in that group might be associated with Dagon, and I didn't trust leaving you in their care for long. So, I chanced walking to the nearest bar and toasting Ashael in it to see if he'd answer."

Despite his dislike of Ian, my brother had answered. Ashael must have teleported Ian here, which would have been risky for him with the bright sunlight and nearby ocean. It must hurt Ashael to even be inside this cottage. Being indoors might protect him from the sun, but I could taste the salt from the surf in the air. It must feel like knives grating his skin.

"Thank you," I said, a catch in my voice.

I heard Ashael let out a soft, wry grunt. "Anything for my baby sister."

Ian let me go to dump several bottles of hydrogen peroxide onto the symbols he'd drawn. The liquid bubbled on contact, dissolving my blood more thoroughly than bleach. Trust a vampire to know how best to get rid of blood. Then, despite not a hint of the symbols remaining, Ian dragged the thick area rug over the spot to cover it.

I was touched. I'd trusted Ian with the secret of how to summon me, and he was making damn sure he kept that secret.

Finally, Ian drew the drapes, blocking the sunshine from streaming into the room. "If she permits it, you can come in now," Ian said, arching a brow at me.

"Yes," I replied.

What I had to ask took precedence over my lingering anger at Ashael for sending Ian after that horn. If not for Ashael's doing that, we'd still be trapped inside Dagon's circles. Or dead. Ashael's duplicitous trick had helped save our lives.

Ashael entered, wearing deep blue silk pajamas, of all things. He even had on matching blue slippers. No question what he'd been doing when Ian's toast reached him. "Sorry to have woken you," I said to Ashael. To Ian, I said, "We're in more trouble than you realize."

Ian snorted. "I've been in trouble since the day my father set me up for my brother's murder so I'd be the one imprisoned instead of his legitimate heir. Being a fugitive might be new to you, luv, but not to me. Don't fret." He gave me a quick, sly grin. "I know all the best places to evade the law. Be like a vacation for you. You'll love it."

"Being a fugitive is suddenly the least of my concerns," I said, marveling at the irony.

I'd taken such care to avoid being discovered for what I was.

Now, the vampire council, Enforcers, and Law Guardians' wrath seemed trivial things to worry about.

Ian's brows rose. "You mean Dagon's potential allies at the highest levels of vampire law? Assuming I haven't lost my teleporting abilities for good, I'll pop in and verify if what I felt was truly a mark of Dagon's power on any of them or not."

"Not that either," I replied.

Now I had his full attention. "Then what?"

I turned to my brother. "You're twice my age, and you know a lot more about our father than I do, so . . . did you hear anything about me being betrothed prebirth to a gold-winged, possibly ancient Greek deity named Phanes?"

"The fuck you say?" Ian burst out.

"My thoughts exactly," I said without a touch of irony this time. "Well?" I prodded Ashael, who had paled.

"How did he find you?" Ashael asked in a stricken voice. "Our father cloaked you so that none of the other deities or demigods could feel you!"

"Another piece of news I've never heard before, but not the most relevant at the moment," I said through gritted teeth. "It's true? This Phanes, whatever he is, thinks I'm promised to be his bride?"

"Over my dead body," Ian snapped.

"That's exactly the terms Phanes will demand, once he hears that Veritas married you," Ashael replied darkly.

Oh *hell* no. "That's not going to happen because no one gets to decree who I marry, let alone do it before I even existed!"

Ashael gave me a look of calculated alarm. "Independence may be prized in this world, but it isn't in the celestial realms. That is why our father sought to protect us from them."

I couldn't claim you, my father told me long ago. I'd assumed it was because impregnating a mortal was a no-no for his kind, so he was protecting himself by staying away from me. Or that he lacked the emotional depths to care enough to claim me. If Ashael was right, there was a more compelling reason.

I took Ian's hand. Once again, everything I thought I knew had turned out to be wrong or very, very incomplete. Still, I'd survived Dagon, finally gotten justice for everyone he and Ereshki had harmed, and now had the man I loved at my side. That was infinitely more than I could've said a month ago.

In fact, it had taken me my entire life to get to this point, so somehow, I'd find a way to survive these new challenges, be they a demon-acolyte council member, being hunted by both the vampire and demon world, or some gold-fogged lesser deity who thought I was his mandated fiancée.

Wasn't I the optimistic one all of a sudden? Love did strange, wonderful things to people indeed.

I tightened my grip on Ian's hand. He squeezed back, a silent promise that we'd face this together. Then, I let out a sigh.

"You need to tell me everything I don't know about our father's world, Ashael, and you need to do it now. I don't know how long we have before Phanes finds me again, but whenever he does, we have to make sure we're ready."

Ian and Veritas will return in
WICKED ALL NIGHT,
the next Night Rebel novel!